Praise for

Down from the Mountain

"The action and the psychological realism combine to make an intriguing story, with believable characters and events. An absorbing treatment of a fascinating subject."—*Kirkus Reviews*

"Fixmer (*Saint Training*) draws on her experience counseling former religious cult members to create believable and detailed accounts of Eva's encounters with the "heathen" world...Fixmer's references to C.S. Lewis's Narnia books persuasively contrast the image of a loving god against the harshness of Reverend Ezekiel in this absorbing and smartly paced novel."—*Publishers Weekly*

"Fixmer, a therapist who has counseled former religious cult members, has written a taut psychological drama with believable and sympathetic characters. The first-person narrative sustains a tense mood throughout...Readers will be caught up in this realistic story of a brave girl rebelling against a fundamentalist society."
—*School Library Journal*

"It's impossible not to root for Eva as she learns to trust her instincts and her own feelings. Teen readers fascinated by religious cults will be drawn in by Eva's story."—*Booklist*

"Fixmer presents a fascinating inside look at daily life in a religious cult in this suspenseful coming-of-age story. Readers learn of the psychology that compels continued membership despite the demanding lifestyle."—*VOYA*

Down from the Mountain

Elizabeth Fixmer

Albert Whitman & Company
Chicago, Illinois

Library of Congress Cataloging-in-Publication Data

Fixmer, Elizabeth,
Down from the mountain / Elizabeth Fixmer.
pages cm
Summary: "Fourteen year-old Eva tries to be a good disciple
of Righteous Path, a polygamy cult in Colorado, but her forays into the 'heathen world'
cause her to question all she knows"—Provided by publisher.
[1. Cults—Fiction. 2. Polygamy—Fiction. 3. Fanaticism—Fiction.
4. Christian life—Fiction. 5. Mothers and daughters—Fiction.] I. Title.
PZ7.F5927Dow 2015
[Fic]—dc23
2014027714

Printed in the United States of America
10 9 8 7 6 5 4 3 2 1 BP 20 19 18 17 16 15

Cover design by Jordan Kost
Cover image © Cat Lane Photographer/Getty Images

For more information about Albert Whitman & Company,
visit our web site at www.albertwhitman.com.

For my father, Robert Kenneth Fixmer,
who had a deep faith, a great mind, and with whom I enjoyed
wonderful philosophical discussions over the years.
He would have had a lot to say about Righteous Path.
I miss him every day.

October

One

My hands automatically form fists so no one will see my trembling fingers as I walk to the front of our little chapel. I try not to stare at the discipline paddle that hangs on the wall near the bare table we use as an altar. Fourteen swats if I mess up the Bible passage. One swat for every year of age.

I try to avoid looking at the pulpit because I know Reverend Ezekiel is standing behind the podium watching me. I don't want to see his stern face and his dark, piercing eyes because they make me cringe.

Oh Lord, please help me recite my verse perfectly for Ezekiel. Thou art my shepherd; I shall not want. Thy rod and thy staff they comfort me. I know that the prayer refers to God's rod and God's staff, but sometimes I think that Ezekiel *is* God. Especially since God talks to Ezekiel and has given him the job of shepherding us to keep us pure. He commands us to follow God's will and doles out rewards and punishments to keep us on the righteous path.

I slide into the first pew next to Jacob and Annie, who sit in front to support me. Jacob, right in front, just for me. He usually sneaks into the pew farthest back and keeps his head down to avoid being noticed, but not today. He flashes me a rare smile, letting the empty space show where his two front teeth used to be before the fight. And he quickly gives my hand a little squeeze. I control the tears that want to flow.

"You memorize real good," Jacob reminded me when we were doing chores earlier. "You're good at all that school stuff."

Annie's smile is nervous. She blew her verse the last time and got paddled.

Behind us is whisper, chatter, whisper. The mothers are probably talking about the rumor that Ezekiel plans to make a special announcement tonight. I heard Mother Cecelia say that someone might be with child. That would be great news! God promised Ezekiel a son years ago. But, though a few of the mothers have become pregnant, they always lose the baby in the first trimester. It's because we haven't been worthy. We haven't prayed enough, repented enough, made enough sacrifices. But now we might have another chance. I hope it's Rachel because she wants a baby so badly.

Ezekiel thumps his fist on the podium and the chapel is immediately silent. He begins the evening prayer. I'm tempted to turn my head and look for Mother Martha. Her face would light up and she'd nod her reassurance. But I don't dare. She's my birth mother, and we've been in trouble so many times for having a "special relationship." You'd think that after ten years in Righteous Path, Mother and I would have accepted the rule. It's hard because she *is* special to me. My rock. But I have to remember that *all* the women are my mothers.

"Eva, it's time," Ezekiel says.

I walk the few steps to the podium, grateful that my knees don't buckle. The only sound I hear is my own ragged breathing—until I accidentally step on the one squeaky floorboard I thought had been fixed. The squeak just showed up last week. Ezekiel was furious because everything in God's house has to be perfect to honor God.

We built this chapel with our own hands three years ago when we first moved here, using the pine trees from the compound. The chapel is small and modest, but we poured our hearts into building it. It's built in the shape of a triangle—one wall each for the Father, Son, and Holy Ghost.

We built it even before we bought trailers to sleep in or a kitchen or a proper dining room. God must always come first.

Thankfully, Ezekiel doesn't respond to the squeak. He still stands at the podium, so close that I can still smell the sulfur from the wooden matches he always chews. His eyes are knives cutting into me. I stand taller to fight my fear.

"I hope you're ready, Eva," Ezekiel says.

I pull up confidence from some hidden place inside. "Yes, Reverend Ezekiel, I am."

I look out at the people. Seventeen pairs of eyes look back at me. I clear my throat and begin.

"Saint…Saint Matthew, Chapter 13:3-9." The words are coming back to me, but my throat is so dry it hurts to swallow.

"'And he spake many things unto them in parables, saying, 'Behold, a sower went forth to sow; and when he sowed, some seeds fell by the wayside, and the fowls came and devoured them up.

Some fell upon stony places, where they had not much earth: and forthwith they sprung up, because they had no deepness of earth.'"

For some reason I can't remember the next part and just stand there frozen. I wipe sweat off my forehead. I look for Mother's face. When I catch her eye, she changes her expression from concerned to confident and sends me one of her sunshine smiles. As if by magic, the words come back to me. "'And when the sun was up, they were scorched; and because they had no root, they withered away. And some fell among thorns; and the thorns sprung up and choked them. But others fell into good ground and brought forth fruit, some a hundredfold, some sixtyfold, some thirtyfold. Who hath ears to hear, let him hear.'"

My breath is easy now, and when Reverend Ezekiel walks up to me, all smiles, relief floods my body.

"Very good, Eva. Now can you tell us what the parable means?" he asks.

This is the easy part. I know what the parable means because Reverend Ezekiel has told us before. "The seed is really the word of God, and people are the soil. Everywhere outside of Righteous Path, God's word falls in stony places or on soil that isn't deep enough because heathens don't have ears to hear. But Reverend Ezekiel has ears to hear and so we are growing in good soil."

"That's right! Exactly right." He walks over and lifts my chin so that we are looking eye to eye. "We are blessed to be chosen, Eva, to be the soil where the truth of God grows the strongest."

I can feel the smiles of the whole congregation. It's like a warm embrace on my insides, like hot chocolate on a cold day. I'm relieved to be done with my verse, but also grateful that I'm here at Righteous Path, where I have salvation. Ezekiel says that God is choosing only 444 people to survive Armageddon and live in the Kingdom of Heaven when we die. For some reason, I am one of them. It makes me glow inside when I think of it.

Ezekiel motions me to take my seat with a respectful nod instead of the flip of the wrist he uses when he wants one of us to disappear from his sight. I'm all lit up inside but I keep my smile dim so no one can say I have too much pride. I sneak a peek at Mother Martha. Her eyes sparkle and her cheeks glow, and that makes me especially happy. For weeks now she's been looking puny.

When Ezekiel starts his sermon, I pray that it's a short one. Now that I'm done with the recitation I'm suddenly exhausted. He's in a great mood tonight, not angry or warning, which might mean that we'll get a shorter sermon. Sometimes they go till midnight though, and that's tough. Especially if you have to go to the bathroom and don't dare leave.

Tonight he flits around the stage, on fire with God's word. Finally he stops talking. He looks at something in the back corner. "Mother Martha, please stand."

We all look to where she's pulling herself up from the pew.

"It's time to share the news God has blessed us with," he says.

All eyes are on Mother Martha, searching her face, eagerly awaiting the news. I notice Mother Rachel who sits next to her. Her eyes get big and she bites her bottom lip. She's nodding slightly as if she's just figured out the mystery. The color has once again drained from Mother Martha's face, and though she smiles, she looks sick like before.

"The Lord is fulfilling his promise to us. Is he not, Mother Martha?" Ezekiel says.

Mother Martha nods and smiles, but the sunshine is gone from her eyes.

Reverend Ezekiel seems unaware of this. He continues. "She carries my seed in her womb. She will bear a child in spring."

I can't believe what I've just heard. Electricity shoots through me as if I touched the fence that protects the compound from outsiders.

Mother Martha can't have more children. She almost died when she had me, and the doctor told her she could never have another. That's why she and Dad called me their miracle child. No one understands this. Everyone is clapping and making joyful sounds. But as the group moves toward Mother Martha to hug and congratulate her, Reverend Ezekiel holds out his hand to silence us.

"There will be time for congratulations later. But now let us give thanks to God through prayer." Everyone stops wherever they're standing, and we all bow heads. "Let us give Him our praise. Lord, we pray that you bless Mother Martha and the child she carries within her womb. Please do not punish us or test us by having her lose the baby." A noisy sob escapes Rachel's lips. "I vow that we will pray more, fast more, and keep our hearts pure during this pregnancy."

He begins the end prayer. "We trust in you, oh God, and give You praise," he says. He holds out an open hand signaling for us to repeat his words.

"We trust in You, oh God, and give you praise," we repeat.

All my excitement drains out of me. I can't focus on prayers when my brain is full of questions and concerns. Maybe God is giving us a miracle and everything will be okay. But what if Mother dies having this baby? I couldn't bear it. If the baby lives, will I still be important to Mother? Will she continue to find special time for me, or will I shrink into the background?

It's wrong to want her to be special just because she gave birth to me. I know this. I ask God to take away these selfish feelings, but they keep coming. I even feel jealous of the attention Ezekiel will give Mother and the new baby. He'll love the baby more than us other kids because it's his only real child. Mother will love the baby more because he'll make Ezekiel happy. The baby might even be holy like Ezekiel.

"You, Lord, are our salvation," Reverend Ezekiel says.

No, no, no. Stop this! I silently command myself.

But I had Mother Martha first, for four whole years before we joined Righteous Path. And we look just alike. Even the heathens think that. Once when we still lived in Arizona and kids were allowed to go into town with the mothers for marketing, one of the clerks looked surprised when I referred to Mother Miriam as Mother. She looked at me and Mother Martha and said, "Oh, I thought *that* was your mother. You look so much alike with your wavy auburn hair and blue eyes. You even have the same smile."

"We will follow you every day of our lives, in all that we say and do. Amen," Ezekiel says.

I long for a private talk with Mother Martha right now.

I am selfish, selfish, selfish. *Dear God, help me to stop being so selfish.*

Mother Esther announces the ending song choice, "Nearer My God to Thee," and uses her pitch pipe to get us on the right note. Usually singing's my favorite part of Evening Service, but my voice is small tonight. As soon as it's over, I make my way to Mother Martha to take my turn giving her a congratulatory hug. When she catches my eye, I try to look happy.

As I walk home, a cold wind suddenly whips up dirt and flings it in my face. Dirt hits my eyes and gets into my mouth. Some even settles in my hair. I hold my sweater out as a shield, rub my eyes, and spit several times. I sure hope this isn't a sign that we're headed for a rough winter.

Two

Annie hugs and hugs me when we get back to our room. She's so happy for me that I remembered my passage. And she's thrilled, like everyone else, about the baby news. She didn't see what I saw on Mother Martha's face. Maybe no one except me saw it.

That's just the way it's always been between Mother and me. We seem to see things in each other before others see them. But somehow I missed the pregnancy. Maybe because she's been sort of hiding out lately.

When I wake up to go to the bathroom sometime late in the night, I can't get back to sleep. I keep seeing Mother's face and try to imagine what she's thinking. Is she scared that God will let her die in childbirth? Is she afraid there won't be enough food for us all like last winter?

Last winter was the first time Righteous Path was really and truly out of money. Before that, our money came from members. Like everyone else, Mother turned everything over to Ezekiel when she was chosen to be a member, though I was too young to understand. Soon after we'd moved into the Arizona compound, I remember begging Mother to take me home.

She held my face in her hands and shook her head. "Honey, this is our home. Our forever home. God needed us to sell our Chicago home so we could help Ezekiel collect souls. Saving souls is more important than having a nice house, don't you think?"

By then I knew the term *collecting souls*. It was what Ezekiel did when he went into town. He would preach and help people let go of their worldly possessions. We were always told that he needed to collect 444 souls, the number God promised to save before the end days. But he hasn't been fishing for quite some time. I think he only went once in the three years we've been in Colorado. That was shortly after our move here. He was gone for three months, and when he returned, he brought us Rachel but wouldn't tell us what happened that kept him away so long. Whatever happened changed him. He seemed angry and skittish about anyone leaving the compound.

For the last two summers, many of us have worked as laborers for the ranch west of ours. It's owned by a Greek family and they mostly do lambing. We tended the lambs, picked vegetables, removed stones from the field, and harvested hay. We each got paid two dollars an hour. The money went straight to Ezekiel, of course, and didn't last through winter.

Dawn is here, and I watch Annie sleep. A couple of times she stirs. I long to wake her up, to talk to her about this, but it's too dangerous. Annie seems to get asthma attacks whenever she's worried or anxious, and lately they've been getting so bad that I find myself being really careful with what I say to her. I don't dare talk to anyone else because if they thought Mother was anything but happy about the baby, or that I was having doubts, they'd report us at a Community Concerns Meeting and we'd be punished for not accepting God's will.

From the edge of my bed, I enjoy the dancing aspen leaves that have scattered over the common area and as far as I can see down our driveway. The trees have been bare for weeks, of course, but thanks to a mild fall so far, they continue to blanket the compound. A strong breeze gives them new life. If I watch just a little longer, I'll get to see them shimmer all golden and beautiful in the early morning sunlight.

Brother Paul's grandparents planted the aspens fifty years ago. Otherwise we'd be looking at nothing but pine trees, pine trees, and more pine trees. They're so thick that they hide us from the outside world, so thick you could actually get lost among them between here and the highway.

The door to the old house opens and I see Brother Paul hurry toward the barn to do the milking. That means it must be almost six a.m. He must be real quiet when he dresses in the morning because my friend, Jacob, his roommate, has trouble getting up for a seven a.m. breakfast.

Jacob and Paul are the only ones of our group to live in an actual house. It's small and kind of dilapidated, especially the outside where the white paint has worn away and the wood is practically bare. The rest of us live in trailers—three for the women and children and a fancy one for Ezekiel.

I scan the trailers that surround our common area, looking for signs of life. Nothing, not even in the trailer Mother Martha shares with Mothers Cecelia, Rebecca, Helen, and MaryAnne. I wonder how Mother Martha slept last night and whether or not she's awake yet. If only I could walk over there right now and check on her. But that's not allowed, of course.

There's no stirring in the trailer on the other side of Ezekiel's house either. That's where Mother Alice, Mother Miriam, Mother Esther, and Mother Rachel live. Mother Rose is the dorm mother in the kids' trailer where the twins, David and Daniel, live and, of course, Annie and me as well.

Ezekiel's is the biggest one—a double wide—even though he's the only one who officially lives in it. Each night he chooses a woman to bed with him since they are all his wives. I don't know how he decides who and how often, but I do know that his decisions cause tension and pain among the women. It's not like the subject is ever discussed, but I've heard Mother Rebecca slam her trailer door, and somebody—I think Mother Helen—sobbed in her trailer once when Rachel was chosen for the fourth night in a row. You can also tell by facial expressions and moods. Several mothers have had to confess the sin of jealousy at Community Concerns.

A shadowy movement and then another from Ezekiel's trailer make it clear that he and whichever wife is staying with him are up. It's probably Rachel. She's been his favorite for some time.

It's getting much lighter out. The sky is several shades of gray and pink. The breeze turns into a sudden wind that blows the aspen leaves out into the fields, destroying the colorful blanket they had formed in the common area and driveway.

I hurry to get dressed. I figure that if I get to the dining room early, I'll have a chance to talk to Mother Martha. She's on kitchen duty this week, and it may be the perfect time to squeeze in a word with her before everyone else arrives.

Brother Paul rings the wake-up bell just as I lean over Annie to get her up. I'm dressed but I need her to button the back of my blouse. She sits up but takes her time with each button. Patience, I need to be patient. I wave good-bye to Annie, who's stretching awake in bed, and run through the common area to the old house where the kitchen and dining room take up most of the first floor.

The dining room is empty except for Mother MaryAnne, who is placing a water pitcher on each table. We exchange "good mornings," and I peek inside the kitchen. Mother Alice is the only other person working. When she sees me, she looks relieved.

"Oh, Eva, I'm glad you're here early. Mother MaryAnne and I could sure use your help."

I grab an apron from a hook on the wall and accept the spoon she hands me. She motions to a pot of oatmeal on the stove, and I take over the stirring while she begins to slice bread.

"Anything wrong?" I ask, not wanting to mention Mother Martha's name.

"Mother Martha is sick this morning," MaryAnne says.

I stop stirring the kettle. "Too sick to help?" Mother always works no matter what. Everybody always works. It's the Righteous Path way.

"It's nothing to worry about, dear," Mother Maryanne says. "Women get morning sickness during pregnancy all the time." She points the bread knife at the stove. "You can turn off the heat now."

People are already bowing their heads for Morning Prayer when Jacob races in and plops down across from me. Annie and I exchange looks. Brother Paul shakes his head as if to say "typical." Which it is. Jacob is always late. But he usually manages to avoid punishment by pulling stuff off at the last minute. Ten seconds later, and he wouldn't be allowed to eat. Before the end of the prayer, I raise my eyes to see his scraggly blond hair. He must feel my gaze because he gives me a mischievous look.

At breakfast, the women are all talking about last night's news.

"I hope it's a boy, for Reverend Ezekiel's sake," Mother Rose says.

"I hope it's a boy for the child's sake," Mother Cecelia adds.

It hadn't occurred to me that the baby could be a girl. Of course it will be a boy. God promised Ezekiel a son.

"And to think she conceived when she's over forty," Mother Rachel says. The slight edge in her voice draws everyone's attention. She blushes and quickly adds, "Praise God that she can still have a baby!"

It was only a year ago when Rachel lost the baby girl in her third month of pregnancy. She took it hard, harder even than Reverend Ezekiel. He thought that God was punishing us for some transgression. He stayed in his trailer for days, and we had to fast for weeks.

"Please pass the bread," I say to break the sad silence. Mother Helen reaches for the basket. She lifts the cloth and shakes her head. "Last piece," she says and passes it to me. "Would anyone like to share this with me?" I ask to be polite. A chorus of voices responds:

"No, you eat it."

"No thanks."

"I've had plenty."

"Plenty" is a good word. It's a word that sits comfortably in my stomach and takes away my anxiety over not enough. Our new relationship with the flea market may make "plenty" a more common word.

"Are you going to sell jewelry at the flea market tomorrow?" I ask Rachel.

She sighs. "Yes, if we have enough stuff made to sell. But with Mother Martha sick, we haven't made nearly enough necklaces and earrings. Plus I need more stock. We might have to skip this week—maybe go to the bead store instead."

We've only been making and selling jewelry for the last two months, but it's definitely helped bring in money. Rachel came up with the idea after she and Mother Rose went into town to get groceries and saw that Boulder had a flea market. We cannot defile ourselves by wearing jewelry, but Ezekiel said that it was okay to make and sell the stuff for outsiders since they were already lost to God. God wants us, his chosen people, to have enough money.

"It's too bad you don't have more time for making jewelry, Eva. You're good at it."

The compliment warms my insides and I smile. I love making jewelry. I especially love working with all the different colors, shapes, and sizes, and getting to create stuff. I secretly wish I could wear earrings and bracelets and necklaces. It's shameful to feel that way, but I do so like pretty things.

When I see Mother Rebecca standing to begin morning announcements, I hurry to finish my oatmeal.

Lord, I need a chance to talk to Mother Martha. If it be your will, let her be well enough for chores and please let me work with her this week.

But it must not be God's will because when Rebecca reads off the chore list, we're nowhere near each other. Martha is assigned to the sewing room, and I have animal care and garden cleanup along with Jacob and Annie, as usual.

In the barn, Jacob calls dibs on feeding the cows.

"Fine," Annie says, "but Eva and I get to take care of the horses."

"Yeah, and don't think you're going to get out of shoveling manure or helping to collect eggs," I add.

Annie and I don't wait for a response. We head for the hayloft and throw several bales down the chute. It takes both of us to carry one bale to the horses. Annie, just ten, is so much smaller than me that the bale goes up to her chin when I carry it above my waist. I hear a sudden sneeze and she drops her side of the bale, making me drop the other. I laugh as another sneeze seizes her whole little frame.

"Sorry," I say. "I meant to hold it lower."

"Sure you did." She frowns, but I know she's not really mad. As long as Annie's outside with the animals, she's always happy and usually dirty.

I pick a piece of straw out of her braid and lift my side of the bale, this time holding it low. She smiles and we resume walking.

"Is something wrong today?" Annie asks. "You seem about a million miles away."

"No, I'm fine."

"I bet it's about the baby."

I drop the bale into Aspen's stall. He immediately starts eating. Berthoud neighs in the next stall.

"We'll get yours next, boy," I assure him.

"You can share anything with me," Annie says.

"I'm worried about Mother Martha," I say, sighing. "She may not be able to carry another child."

Annie looks puzzled. "Why would you worry about that? It's all up to God. If she's supposed to be okay carrying the baby, she will be. If God wants her home in heaven, she'll return to heaven."

"Right," I say. Because she *is* right. If I had the appropriate distance from Mother, it would be easier, but I don't. I love her so much. I think about her all the time.

It's midafternoon before we finish garden cleanup and head to the classroom. Jacob is in a great mood.

"We won't have to do much schoolwork today," he says.

I don't respond, so he starts in with his typical teasing.

"Don't cry, Eva. You'll still get some learnin' in."

"You're just jealous because I'm better at math than you are," I say.

"I'd say you're crazy when it comes to math. Who does all the problems in a whole textbook when they don't have to?"

I laugh. "Me, that's who. It was fun."

"Book learning doesn't matter to salvation," Jacob reminds me. "Look at Ezekiel. He only went to school through the ninth grade, and God chose him to lead us."

"I know, but it's fun to learn new things."

Jacob shakes his head. "For *you*." He kicks a pebble into a pile of leaves. "What was that book you cried over so hard when Ezekiel burned it?"

I feel my body stiffen. Jacob can't know how painful that memory is for me. I say nothing.

"It was *The Lion, the Witch, and the Wardrobe*," Annie says.

"By C. S. Lewis," I add. "Mother Grace only had that one, but she said there were six books about Narnia altogether."

"I have to admit," Jacob says, "I sure liked that teacher."

My mind flashes back to the months when Mother Grace was our teacher, right before the Big Test. She brought books with her—even novels—when she joined Righteous Path. I read every single one of them. But we only had her for three months before Ezekiel decided to get rid of any heathen lies we were being taught. Now the only books we have besides the Bible are textbooks. And they have a lot of things blacked out or ripped out so we only learn God's truth.

When we get to the classroom, Mother Cecelia looks at her watch nervously. "We have less than two hours to cover four subjects," she says. "We're getting behind."

The classroom is more like a closet than a real room. Located on the second floor of the old house, it has just enough room for the four desks, one each for Mother Cecelia, Jacob, Annie, and me, along with a single bookshelf that holds the same twelve textbooks we've had forever. Who knows where the twins will fit when they start school next year.

When class starts, we're allowed ten minutes to study the blackboard where Mother Cecelia has placed a map of the world. Then she covers the blackboard with an old sheet and has us draw from memory. We are to show the continents and fill in as many countries as we can remember.

I quickly make the shapes of the seven continents and focus on Asia. The country I pay most attention to is China. I put in the major rivers and mountains and place Beijing, Hong Kong, and Shanghai where I think they belong. Those were the cities I used to hear Daddy talking about when he left me to do research there. Mother says he took off two years from teaching so he could study in China. But I'm sure he's back now, teaching Chinese at the university.

I shouldn't care. Not only is it wrong to think or talk about people from the past, but he divorced Mother and didn't keep his promise to write me every week and call me, even though it's long distance. He went away and I never saw him again.

When Mother Cecelia asks why I'm so interested in China, I don't know what I'll say, but I'm going to have to lie if I don't want to get in trouble.

A sharp knock at the door brings everyone to a halt. Mother Cecelia opens it, and for a second I hear whispers in the hall. I am drawing as fast as I can. I spent too much time on China and have to hurry to get more down before the time is up. Mother Cecelia taps my shoulder, bringing me out of my reverie. She motions me to come with her.

Once we get to the hallway, she says, "Ezekiel wants to see you, dear." Her face looks concerned. So does Mother Rachel's.

"But I'm not done with the test," I say. Then it clicks. *Ezekiel* wants to see me. Ezekiel wants to see *me*. He's never asked to see me before.

Three

As I follow Rachel, my legs feel like jelly. She takes my hand and squeezes it. "You'll be okay, Eva. You'll make it through this."

My shoes squeak as I stop dead.

"Through *what*?"

She pulls on my long-sleeved shirt. "Just come along. You can't keep Ezekiel waiting."

My feet obediently move forward, but my brain is stuck. What could he possibly want from me? Just before we get to his trailer, a terrifying thought crosses my mind and I stop cold. Surely he isn't going to tell me that God wants him to marry me. Not when I'm only fourteen.

I follow Rachel right into the trailer. I've never been in Ezekiel's trailer before. His wives have, of course, but there's never been a reason to let us children disturb his sanctuary. I'm surprised— awed really—by how beautiful everything is, how my feet sink into the soft carpeting, and how I'm suddenly bathed in the rich colors of the painted walls, so different from the dull off-white of the rest of the compound. I'm tempted to sit on the fancy couch or one of the matching overstuffed chairs just to see what it feels like, but Rachel pulls me down a hallway to an open door that must be Ezekiel's office.

I take in a sharp breath when I step inside. Ezekiel is pointing a gun right at our heads.

He gets a big kick out of our shock, laughs, and uses the gun to motion us in. "Relax, girls. It's not loaded."

"But why do you have a gu..." I begin. Ezekiel's sharp look stops me in a flash. I drop my eyes, realizing that, once again, I've been a poor disciple. I have no business asking questions. It's inappropriate for any of us to ask questions of Ezekiel, but it's doubly wrong because I'm a girl. I need to learn to be more feminine: silent, speaking only when spoken to, obedient, and patient.

"Forgive me, Reverend Ezekiel," I say, hoping to avoid a lecture. But I wish he could see that I pray about these faults, and I do try. I stop my questioning brain a dozen times a day. It's just that my efforts don't always show.

Ezekiel focuses his attention on Rachel. "Thank you, Mother Rachel. You're excused," he says.

When Rachel turns to leave, I have an impulse to grab on to her skirt and hide behind it. But I keep still and silent.

Ezekiel motions for me to sit. I have a choice between two overstuffed chairs, one in dark green leather and the other in a plaid that has that same green in it. I choose the cloth chair.

"So what do you think of my trailer?"

"It's beautiful! I love all the colors and how soft these chairs are. I had no idea..."

He laughs. "Okay, Eva, and now that you're becoming an adult, you'll soon be in my home more often."

Something closes up inside me. The mothers only come in to clean or bring him food when he chooses to eat alone, but mostly they come for their marital nights with Ezekiel.

He leans back in his swivel desk chair, wearing a puzzled look. "You do realize that you're almost an adult now, don't you?"

I hide my hands inside my folded arms so he won't see that I'm shaking.

"Look at me, please." He must sense my panic because his voice is softer now. But I learned a long time ago that when he says "please," it's really a command.

I look at him.

Wearing a half smile, as if indulging a small child, he takes the matchstick out of his mouth and sticks it behind his ear. I don't dare look away.

"You're almost fifteen."

"Well, yes," I say, feeling a rush of heat flood my cheeks. "But not until May 23, and that's"—I pause to count on my fingers— "seven months from now. So I'm really fourteen and a half."

"That's really just around the corner." He flaps his wrist dismissively.

I nod. Maybe he's tricking me. We don't celebrate birthdays at Righteous Path. Maybe he'll think I'm vain for knowing mine. Just in case, I add: "The date of my birthday isn't important, though. Celebrations belong to God."

Oh God, please don't let marriage be on his mind. He's married all the adult women and Rachel when she was only sixteen. Isn't that enough? Plus, he's old, God. Please have mercy on me.

"What's the matter, Eva?" His voice sounds irritated.

Here I go again, shaking. This time he'd have to be blind not to notice. "I don't know," I say. But it's not true. He has complete power over me and my life. And I'm terrified. Suddenly I'm teeth-shatteringly cold.

"I called you in here for a reason, Eva." He leans back in his chair, swiveling it just a little. "Now that you are almost an adult, God has called you to do a very important job. He has given you a gift, and that gift will help us through these lean times."

I'm puzzled. What's he talking about?

"It's your jewelry. The pieces you made for the last flea market did quite well. In fact, they sold better than everyone else's combined. Even when Mother Rachel doubled the prices, they still sold. You are to continue making jewelry—not just in your spare time, but as the main jewelry maker."

"Oh," I say. Because it's such a surprise and relief that I can't think of anything else. It sounds so responsible, so grown up.

"We need to make as much money from the flea market as possible. Until God sees fit to bring more of the 444 people he's promised to save, it will be our primary source of income. This is God's will, Eva."

"Okay," I say again. And it is okay—it just sounds like everything is on my shoulders, and that's scary. "So I'll be making jewelry instead of doing other chores."

"No, you'll be able to do chores too. You'll make jewelry during school hours and, if necessary, during free time."

It takes me a minute to realize what he's really saying.

"No more school?"

Ezekiel looks at me as if daring me to argue. But I'm not going to argue. I'm not even sure how I feel. As much as I love learning, I've gone through the textbooks at least three times each. What I need are different books, more information to answer all the questions I have.

"You've had plenty of schooling."

He sounds like I'm arguing with him, and I'm not.

"When the end times come, schooling won't make a difference. But even if the world wasn't coming to an end, you're a girl, and the only thing girls need to know is how to read so they can read the Bible."

My mouth opens, all on its own. But I manage to stop myself from saying anything. I'm thinking, though. Thinking about how God has changed his mind about when the end times are coming. It may be tomorrow or a hundred years from now. So it doesn't make sense to live like life is ending soon.

I scare myself with my own thoughts. *Thank you, God, for helping me not speak so boldly. Ezekiel is your voice on earth, and I have no right.*

He continues looking at me for a minute, then pushes himself out of his chair, stands, and motions me to leave. "Mother Rachel is waiting for you. You can get started right away."

I'm almost out the door when he stops me again.

"Eva, do you remember the rules for being in the presence of heathens?"

"Ye...yes," I say.

He drums his fingers on his desk. "Repeat them."

It's been so long, I have to search my memory. Mercifully it comes back. "No speaking to the heathens except when absolutely necessary."

He nods.

"Stay with your partner at all times."

He nods again.

"Keep custody of your eyes."

This time his lips move into a partial smile when he nods. I begin to gain confidence.

"Do not give personal information or any information about Righteous Path to anyone under any circumstances. Get your business done as quickly as possible, and don't let anyone touch you."

Now his smile is full-on.

"Stay pure in thought and action."

"Yes," he says, a stern look on his face. "You will be working with worldly goods and the heathens who buy them. I'll be watching you to make sure you stay pure and sweet."

I feel the heat rise in my face, and I know I've turned red.

"You never know what God has in store for your future."

He smiles in a strange way I've never seen before. It makes me feel like running.

"Can you tell me *now*?" Annie asks for the third time tonight. We are on our way to our trailer where the two of us have shared a room for the last three years. She wants to know about the meeting with Ezekiel and why I didn't return to class. But I can't tell her now. Mother Rose is behind us, gaining speed. She probably already knows. Word spreads like the measles among us, and I need a little bit of time to adjust before I talk to anyone. I also have to make sure to have a good attitude about it or someone will report me at the Community Concerns Meeting.

"Later," I return.

Annie and I sit on the bench outside to pull off our muddy boots. It takes us a minute because they lace up to mid-calf. Annie is always faster than me. We place the boots on the landing and walk inside in our stocking feet. We both wear the same clothes— long-sleeved shirt and long skirt, all in gray. We have to help each other undress because the sixteen buttons on our blouses are in the back. Ezekiel says this is to help us remember that "no man is an island" and that "interdependency brings about harmony."

When we get to our little room at the back of the trailer, I unbutton Annie first. With her back facing me, I can unbutton while whispering in her ear. "I can't go to school anymore."

Annie swings around. "But why? You love school!"

She is much too loud, so I place my index finger over her lips. I let her hug me briefly, hiding the hurt and anger Ezekiel's decision ignited in me. I turn her around and finish her buttons.

"I have to earn money for the compound."

"How can you do that?"

"By making and selling jewelry."

"Can't you have school too?"

I turn my back to her so Annie can begin on my buttons.

"Ezekiel says no. He says I'm an adult now, and I have to start contributing. He told me that the only reading I should be doing is the Bible."

"But why does it have to be you?"

I shrug my shoulders. "It just is me."

"I'll miss you so much at school. You know how much I hate change."

I nod. "I know you do."

Unbuttoned now, I reach for my nightgown. I can hear Annie wheezing. Selfishly I pray that she doesn't have a full-blown asthma attack because then I'll be taking care of her all night. I try to be cheerful to help her calm down.

"I love making jewelry," I say brightly. "And I have to admit that I am good at it." I lower my voice to a whisper again. "Remember that wooden bead bracelet I let you try on?"

Annie beams. "The blue and green one. It was so pretty! I wish I could have kept it."

I cringe at the idea of someone hearing her say this. "Shhhh! You can't talk like that. You know you could get paddled."

"That's why I only tell you." Annie smiles impishly.

Creeping to the door, I peer down the hall to make sure that Mother Rose is nowhere near. She's not. I hear the twins reciting their evening prayers and know that she'll be tied up with them a little longer.

"I wish I could make pretty jewelry for the heathens and get out of school," Annie says.

"Don't say that, Annie. You should appreciate school as long as Ezekiel will let you." I sigh.

"I don't know why school's so important to you anyway. We have the same old books we've always had and the stories Mother Cecelia comes up with," she says.

"You're right. I do learn from Mother Cecelia's stories, though." When Mother Cecelia teaches, she brings up things from the outside world that pique my curiosity. I don't want to live with the heathens, but I'm curious to know about how they think and how they live. I don't say this to Annie, though.

"Anyway, I hope I make us a lot of money," I say.

"Me too. Then we'll have enough to eat this winter."

She slips into her sleeping gown and unravels her braids for the nightly brushing of her waist-length hair. Hers is black, shiny, flyaway. Mine looks about the same length as hers, but it's auburn, thick, and wavy, and if you stretch it out, it's actually much longer than hers. It's usually snarled too, because I insist on wearing it down.

We can hear Mother Rose's squeaky voice before we see her in the doorway. She can't help it. She always sounds like she has laryngitis. "You girls have ten minutes till lights out. You better hurry and get washed up."

Annie and I grab our towels from the hooks next to our beds and head to the bathroom. To my relief, Annie's wheezing has stopped. But by the time we've said good night to Mother Rose, finished our prayers, and climbed into bed, I hear her struggling to breathe again.

"Are you okay, Annie?" I ask. I hate to see her suffer so often.

"Yeah," she answers. "But I've been thinking."

Right. That's what usually brings these attacks on.

"If Ezekiel sees you as an adult, all the mothers will too. And that means they might want to move you to one of the adult trailers." Her voice gets whiny. "I'm gonna be left behind."

"Oh no they won't. The mothers love being the elders—even Rachel—and they won't want to share that with me. They'll still see me as a kid."

I decide to change the subject. "Guess what I get to do tomorrow? Rachel plans to take me to Boulder to the bead store!"

Annie sits up in bed. "Where is this store?" she asks. "Is it far from here?"

"Well, it's farther than Grand Hill," I say.

"Oh, it's far then," Annie says.

Neither of us has been outside the compound since we moved to Colorado three years ago. The town closest to us—like three miles away—is Grand Hill.

"I think the bead store is in Boulder," I say.

"Wow," Annie says wistfully. "Be careful that you don't get polluted with wrong thinking, but I do want you to tell me everything you see and do."

I laugh. "Everything."

Annie laughs too.

We're silent, but I can tell that Annie is thinking about something serious.

"Wait," she says. "How come you're allowed to go into Boulder? Ezekiel said that it's dangerous for us to be seen in public because one of the betrayers might see us and follow us back. Or nosy people might want to find out more about us, and we'd end up with Social Services nosing around."

It's true. When Ezekiel announced that God wanted all the women to be his wives, Righteous Path went through a big test from God that ended in a great exodus. But while all this was happening, God gave us a wonderful gift. It turned out that Brother Paul's parents had died and left the Colorado ranch to him. As soon as Paul got the paperwork, he signed it over to Ezekiel. God clearly wanted us to keep saving souls.

Ezekiel shepherded those of us who remained off the Arizona compound. We moved with whatever we could fit in the three vans and took off in the middle of the night for Colorado. This way, no one would know where we were. Those of us who remained are considered especially holy because we passed the hardest test God ever gave us.

I was eleven. It's not like I had a real choice about staying or leaving. And Mother Martha was thrilled to marry Ezekiel. She saw it as such an honor that she could be that close to someone who was so special to God.

"I don't worry about Rachel," Annie says. "Her parents are dead and her aunt doesn't care about her, so she's safe from being kidnapped. Mother Esther is safe for the same reason, but you have a father out there somewhere. What if he tries to find you? You could be kidnapped," Annie says.

"Oh, Annie, my father hasn't cared about me since I was four years old. If he wanted to look for me, don't you think he would have done it by now?"

Annie lies back and closes her eyes. I continue to watch her breathing and notice that it's getting ragged again.

I pray that the attack will subside, but God doesn't help. Maybe because he knows my prayer is partially selfish. I've told God that I'm tired and need to get some sleep. But it does hurt my heart that Annie has to struggle so often just to breathe.

There's no point telling Mother Rose because she won't even comfort Annie. In fact, she usually reminds Annie that God is punishing her for her sins and that she needs to pray for forgiveness.

Mother Rose is Annie's real mother, but she doesn't show it in any way. She's not the least bit affectionate with Annie, which makes her an obedient disciple. If Annie craves special attention, she's never admitted it to me. But I would rather get in trouble for having a special relationship with Mother Martha than to have no special family at all.

"Eva…will you…tell me…a stor…y?"

"Sure," I say, noticing how bad her breathing has become. I sit on the edge of her bed so she can hear my whispers and begin *The story*—the one that makes both of us feel better. It's a story that takes Annie and me to a very different world. And when I tell it, she's often sleeping peacefully before I'm halfway through.

"Once there was a little girl named Lucy. She was playing hide-and-seek with her brothers and sister, Edmund, Peter, and Susan, when she suddenly discovered that the wardrobe she'd hidden in went right outside to a strange world called Narnia. She couldn't believe how beautiful this world was. But there was an evil ice queen who wanted to do her harm and a wonderful lion, Aslan, who helped her and made everything spring again."

When the rhythm of Annie's breathing tells me she's asleep, I return to my bed and think about how much I love that story. I loved the story before I knew it was an allegory. I loved Aslan the lion who was powerful and strict and just, and kind and humble. The witch put a spell on Narnia, making it always winter and never Christmas and never spring. But Aslan prophesied that when four human children found their way into Narnia, he would return, and Narnia and everything would return to normal.

Ezekiel burned our books after God admonished him for

letting us have too much contact with the heathens and with the heathen media. I was ten at the time. I can still hear Mother Grace, our teacher, making a case for keeping each book. When he picked up *The Lion, the Witch, and the Wardrobe*, she got especially upset.

"This book is nothing but lies!" he'd said, holding it over the flames of the bonfire.

"It's not lies," Grace had said. "It's fiction, fantasy. It isn't supposed to be about facts. It's an allegory about Jesus." She explained that an allegory is like a parable. It's a story that has meanings on more than one level.

"Jesus is never mentioned, but the story tells about Jesus and the crucifixion, and good and evil.

Ezekiel still looked puzzled.

He said that fantasy was the work of the devil and threw the book in the fire. I started to sob and clung to Mother Grace, who was crying too. She left after that.

Once, she even took us to a library. It was amazing. There were so many books that you couldn't count them all. You can learn about everything in libraries. They don't black out sentences or rip out pages. I have smidgeons of memory from before I was in Righteous Path. My parents loved to read me stories that I picked out when we went to the library. They read to me every single day.

Now I'm too wound up to be sleepy. I think about my strange meeting with Ezekiel. If I could just talk to Mother. She's the only safe person I can talk to about what Ezekiel said and didn't say. I want to tell her that he seemed to almost gloat when he told me I could no longer go to school, and that I got the impression he actually wanted me to argue with him. And that look he gave me. Like he was trying to tell me something.

I don't know what she'd say about the way he looked at me, but she'd probably say that the school thing was Ezekiel testing me to see if I was getting better at unquestioning obedience.

When I remember the look I saw in Mother's eyes last night, and how sick she's been lately, I feel guilty for wanting to burden her with my problems. She wasn't at dinner tonight or at the evening prayer service. When I do get to talk to her, I won't burden her with my problems. I'll just talk to her about the baby and how she really feels about it.

Just as I'm finally drifting off to sleep, I remember Ezekiel pointing a gun at me and Rachel. I thought it was wrong to shoot people. *Please God, please help me understand why you want Ezekiel to have guns.*

Four

The whole time Annie and Jacob and I are doing chores, I think about how Mother was not at breakfast again this morning. Going to town with Rachel is great, but mostly I wish I could talk to Mother, or at least get a glimpse of her to see if she's okay.

I hear someone call my name. It sounds like it's coming from right outside the barn. Mother Esther? I put down the scoop of chicken feed I'm holding and run to the door.

"How long until you get done with your chores?" Mother Esther asks. "We need to get going so we don't have to take those treacherous roads after dark."

My heart sinks. I had no idea that Esther would be coming with us. I turn toward Annie and Jacob, who've followed and are peering at me. Jacob's look is unreadable. He hasn't said a word about my new position, and I suspect he's a little jealous that I get to go into town.

"I—I don't know. A while, I think."

"No," Annie says. "You go ahead. Jacob and I can finish the chores."

Jacob nods silently.

"Thank you, children," Mother Esther says and pulls my arm forward.

I turn again to Annie and Jacob, raise my shoulders, and put a what-can-I-do? look on my face.

"Are you ready to venture into town?" Esther asks as we walk.

"Yes," I say. I don't dare admit that I'm excited. She'll think I don't realize all the dangers. I do, but I'm curious about seeing new things. And my faith is strong. I'm not about to let anyone or anything pollute me.

She leads me to the kitchen where Rachel has bread and peanut butter on the counter.

"Lunches," Rachel says. She motions to me with a bread knife. "Why don't you get three apples from the pantry?"

"I bet this is the first time you've been off the compound since we moved here," Esther says.

"Yes, it is," I say, careful to keep my words even.

"Wow," Rachel says. "I guess I'm lucky to be one of the drivers because I'd go stir-crazy if I never got off the compound."

"Hmph, it's probably good you feel that way," Esther says. "With Mother Martha pregnant, you may be the only driver, not counting Reverend Ezekiel, of course. But, as for me, I don't need to leave the compound." She turns her head from side to side. "I have no use for the heathens and their materialistic ways. Besides, I hate to be in public when we could still be in danger from the traitors who left."

"I truly don't understand all this fear," Rachel says. "But then I wasn't here during the Big Test."

"No you weren't, and I can assure you, you'd feel differently if you had been," Esther says.

"I was there," I add. "Ezekiel said it was a test of faith, and anyone who left failed the test."

"I can imagine," Rachel says. "It must have been so weird seeing people defy Ezekiel."

I think about hearing a couple of the men sob at night. We didn't have trailers in Arizona. We had lots of little cabins. Suddenly the women had to sleep in the cabins without their husbands, and the men slept in tents next to the children's cabins. Ezekiel had told them that they were no longer married to their wives. One by one, the women became married to Ezekiel, according to God's will.

"I think what hurt the men so much was that most of their wives had little trouble accepting God's plan," Esther says. She laughs. "Except me. I was Ezekiel's only wife for thirty years before this, you know. And I suddenly had to share him." She throws up her hands. "But God's will is God's will. I understood, though, why his new wives felt honored and important. You can't help feeling like you're more important when you're married to someone who hears God's voice."

"Ezekiel makes you feel that way too," Rachel says. "He *told* me that I'd have a higher place in heaven by marrying him."

"Let your faith be strengthened by this test," Ezekiel had said in Arizona. We were in the chapel when he told us. But instead of strengthening faith, it broke the faith of many.

"I am humbled by God's will," he told us that hot night. But the next time we were in chapel, Jacob's dad told Ezekiel that he didn't think Ezekiel was a bit humbled. Mother Sarah rushed us kids out of there and back to our cabins right away. But even though our cabins were the farthest ones from the chapel, we could still hear the yelling. So Mother Sarah had us sing songs.

Then a few days later, Annie and I were crouched in the garden picking tomatoes while Brother Ralph and Jacob's father were slowly walking the path nearby. "I can't believe in this anymore," Jacob's father said. "I'm out of here!"

Brother Ralph began sobbing. "I know."

Mother Esther pulls the wax paper out of a drawer and begins wrapping the sandwiches as Rachel finishes them. She lets out a long sigh. "I still have images of Brother Ralph dragging Mother MaryAnne by the hair when he insisted they leave Righteous Path. She screamed and begged for him to let go. 'You're forcing me to disobey. You're damning my soul!' she cried. 'Please don't make me come with you!' But eventually she caved in and left with him."

Rachel stops in the middle of cutting a sandwich. "But MaryAnne is still here."

"Yup," I say. "She managed to get away from him three days later. She came back to the compound." I remember her showing up at the gates, dirty, hungry, and exhausted. "And then there was Brother Jay, Jacob's father. Did you know that he knocked out Jacob's two front teeth?"

"I heard about that," Rachel says.

That was my hardest memory of the Big Test. "I was on my way to the barn for chores when Jacob's father practically ran me over to get to Mother Helen. The next thing I knew, he'd hit her in the face. Then he dragged her by the hair.

"Then Jacob got involved. He couldn't stand seeing his mom treated that way, so he tried to protect her. He got between them and grabbed his father's arm. But Brother Jay was stronger. He threw Jacob to the ground and hit him three times in the face. Jacob swallowed one tooth and spit out the other."

I can feel my voice shaking. It's still hard to talk about this. "The worst was what Brother Jay said to Jacob. He stuck his finger in Jacob's bleeding face and said, 'I wash my hands of you. I don't ever want to see you again.'"

Rachel takes the bag I hand her and wipes away a tear. "Oh Lord! What a terrible thing to say to a son. I'm glad Mother Helen stayed." She grabs a tissue from the counter and blows her nose. "I knew it turned into a big exodus, but I didn't know the specifics. But that was in Arizona. The traitors don't know that you moved to Colorado, do they?"

"I don't think so," Mother Esther says.

We left the Arizona compound without telling a soul where we were going or even that we were leaving.

"We had thirty-five members before, but in three short months, only sixteen of us were left. Seventeen since you came. Now it's all women and children except for Brother Paul.

"When the dust was beginning to settle and it looked like everybody who wanted to leave had left, Brother Paul gave Ezekiel a timely gift. Two weeks earlier, he had learned that his father died. He'd lost his mother several years earlier. They left him the Colorado ranch, along with two horses, three cows, and forty-seven chickens. Ezekiel saw it as a clear gift from God. Brother Paul signed the property over to Ezekiel and we moved right away."

We head to the van. Rachel carries a small box of jewelry that will serve as samples so we can get more of the same beads and findings.

I sit in the back and start getting sleepy before we even get off our property. I've always done that. Mother says that they used to put me in a car when I was colicky as a baby because the car's motion always put me to sleep. Plus I've had precious little sleep the last couple of nights. But I force myself to stay awake. I want to see everything.

The road is unpaved and narrow. When a tractor-trailer passes us, we have to hug the side of a cliff and barely miss hitting him. All I can see, at first, are pine trees, but here and there, I see a small clearing, usually punctuated by a mailbox. Once in a while I can peer down the clearing far enough to see a house. But they're few and far between.

My stomach leaps because of the hairpin curve Rachel takes. "Wow, Rachel, I'm impressed. I could never drive a road like this!" I say, looking down a steep incline on this narrow mountain road.

Rachel laughs. "Sure you could. I'm a great teacher, and I may need you if Mother Martha can't help."

"No. Eva can't drive," Mother Esther says. "She's too young. We don't want to ask for trouble with the law."

"Ezekiel didn't worry about the law when he married me at sixteen," Rachel says.

Esther takes in a sharp breath. Rachel's comment borders on heresy.

"That's different!" Esther says. "We'll always follow God's will before the laws made by man. Your marriage, like all the marriages to Reverend Ezekiel, came from a direct command from God. But God hasn't given an edict about driving, so we follow the law with licenses and insurance to avoid trouble. Any mistake Eva made could get her in trouble with the police and draw attention to Righteous Path. Then the heathens would end up at our gate, nosing around."

We're all silent but the tension is thick. After a few minutes Esther continues.

"Also, we don't have to worry about trouble with a so-called 'underage marriage' because outsiders won't know unless someone from the compound tells them. And who would do that?"

Esther gives Rachel a significant look. I can feel the threat of a Community Concerns Meeting in the air. Ezekiel wouldn't just be angry about the conversation; he'd be disappointed that Rachel questioned their marriage.

"You make a good point," Rachel adds almost too hastily. "What happens in Righteous Path stays in Righteous Path. God's holy will be done."

I begin to breathe easier. But I can't help wondering how Rachel feels about her marriage.

Outside, the landscape is suddenly changing. We must be in Boulder because the road has become a street with a neat row of houses lining one side and rows of small buildings on the other side. I feel almost dizzy from turning my head back and forth and trying to take it all in. So much is happening at the same time. Cars and people are everywhere—backing out of driveways, speeding through inter-sections, suddenly stopping at red lights. I can't imagine how Rachel can navigate through all of this, but she seems confident and relaxed.

"See over there," she points to the buildings on our right. "That's Pearl Street Mall. It's an outside mall. Keep your eyes open for a parking spot."

The cars make me nervous backing up, squeezing into little places that seemed too small for them to fit. But it's the place Rachel referred to as an outside mall that grabs my attention. There's so much to look at that I make myself dizzy trying to take it all in.

Two giant black dogs practically drag their walker—a man wearing an orange cap and mittens that say "Broncos" on them. He waves to someone on the mall, and the dogs escape with their leashes and run straight at her. She backs up against a storefront as they leap and lick her. Watching people like this is like seeing lots of little stories unfold. A four- or five-year-old girl steals her little brother's ice cream cone. An elderly woman nudges several people with her cane when they don't move out of her way fast enough.

Rachel backs into a parking space. "Here we go," she says. "You two gawkers have been no help at all." She chuckles. "We've got about two blocks to walk. Can you handle it with your arthritis, Mother Esther?"

"I'm fine," she says dismissively.

It takes Mother Esther forever to get out of the van, but I'm so mesmerized by everything around me that I don't even think to offer her help. Two girls around eighteen or nineteen, Rachel's age, look the three of us up and down as they pass by. One whispers something to the other. They both laugh. I look at the three of us, dressed identically in drab gray skirts and blouses, no makeup or jewelry, and I want to hide.

All around me is an explosion of color. I can't believe what these heathens wear. A tall girl wears a red skirt so short that it barely covers her bottom. Under that, she's dressed in something that's a cross between tights and pants. Whatever it is, it only goes to her knees. She wears a sparkly red jacket that barely touches her waist. Both girls wear pointy high-heeled shoes and lots of face paint. I know that I should turn away but I can't—especially when I see the most remarkable thing of all. One of the girls has a diamond in her belly button!

Ezekiel told us about harlots, but I never thought I'd get to see one, much less two.

Mother Esther does not seem to notice the women who are now moving on. Rachel has her arm, but Esther is so stiff that she moves slowly. I ease in behind them so they don't watch me watching everyone and everything around me.

I notice that it's not just the harlots who wear jewelry in odd places on their bodies. And not just women, but men! One guy has seven stones in his earlobe; another has four earrings in his nose.

A woman wearing fingerless mittens and a multicolored skirt leans against a tree playing her guitar and singing in a lilting voice, high and pure. She sounds the way I imagine an angel would sound. Her voice is beautiful, and without realizing it, I pause to listen. Other people stop too. Someone throws a few coins in her guitar case.

The singer sees me watching and faces me, her smile as angelic as her voice. Is it possible that a woman who sings like an angel could be damned for all eternity because she doesn't follow Ezekiel? "Vermin," Ezekiel would say. "They're nothing more than vermin, and God will destroy them all so that we, the pure, may begin a new civilization."

The singer opens her mouth to hit a big note and I see it: a stone inside her mouth. In her *tongue*?

This is too much. Still, her voice is beautiful.

"Hey, keep up," Rachel calls from ahead of me. I can see by her smile that she's amused by how I'm reacting to all this.

I hurry to catch up. "Did you hear that woman sing?" I blurt out.

Mother Esther stops and turns on her heels. "She may sound beautiful to you, but that woman could be the devil in disguise wanting to tear you off the path." I nod. I hadn't thought of that.

I almost trip when a guy scooting on a little board with wheels darts in front of me. "Sorry," he yells out. I watch him fly down the hill we just climbed. He pushes off with the foot he has on the ground, and he's off. It looks like more fun than anything I've ever done in my whole life!

Rachel backs up and loops her arm around mine. "Don't get any ideas. I don't want to scrape you up off the sidewalk. Besides, we're here." She points to a sign on the next building: Beads Galore. Then she swings open the door, setting off a sweet jingle sound.

Five

The store is wall-to-wall beads. Not just the plastic and ceramic beads I'm used to working with, but every kind and size you can imagine! There are itsy-bitsy beads called seed beads and others as big as a fist. I quickly see that they're divided into sections depending on the substance. There are wooden beads, glass and clay beads, beads made from shells—even gemstones and crystals. And if that weren't enough, there are drawers and drawers of gold and silver clasps, and even more drawers of spacers that you can put in between the beads to create something unique.

I'm most drawn to the gemstones and pearls that hang in strands on the back wall and fill bunches of bins. Almost immediately I forget about Rachel and Esther altogether and head for the crystals and gems. They're so pretty, they make me want to sing.

I can't help myself. I have to touch everything. All these stone beads in different sizes and colors. I run my hands over one of every kind, loving how the different textures feel on my fingers. Little signs tell me their names: jade, the color of our evergreen trees when the sun hits them just so. Rose quartz—some smooth with only a hint of color, others cut into shapes of hexagons and octagons, some even square. I like the ones shaped like teardrops. When I fan them out, they look like newly blossomed wildflowers in the spring. I begin to picture them in various combinations and lose myself in new ideas.

The pearls tug at my heart for some reason. They come in several sizes. Some are labeled "natural" pearls and others say "freshwater." I begin to weave a strand of freshwater pearls with similar-sized rose quartz. They're beautiful together.

"Have you looked at the prices of these precious stones?" Esther hisses in my ear when she discovers me. "We don't have that kind of money, so put those back." She lumbers off to another room of the expansive store.

I look around for Rachel. She's leaning over a drawer filled with clasps, spacers, and wire. When I get her attention, I motion for her to come over.

"Can I help you?" someone asks from behind me. She's a short teen wearing a white apron and a name tag that says *Marcy*. I pull in a sharp breath at the swath of purple hair that's only on one side of her head because the other side is shaved.

"Oh, no, um…I'm just looking." A sudden chill pinpricks my body. A heathen is talking to me. *God protect me from any evil influence.* She starts to turn away.

"Wait!" I say to the clerk a little too loudly. "I noticed that a lot of shoppers have those little boxes with fabric lining the bottom."

"Yes," she says. "Those are the best tools to lay out jewelry ideas. I can get you one or two of those as well as a basket." She returns smiling. "I'm Marcy, by the way." She holds out a hand for me to shake, and I reluctantly take it. "You can get really creative in here. Have fun!" She looks my clothes up and down. "Ah retro," she says, nodding her head approvingly. "Nice."

I have no idea what she's talking about, but I like the word so I repeat it in my head: *retro*. At least she said it with a smile, like it was something good.

"If you're interested," she says, "you could take a look at our jewelry display right over there." Marcy points to three glass cases above the cash register. "It may give you some ideas if you need any. Also we have classes so you could learn to make some of these if you wanted."

I follow her to the cases. The bead combinations are beautiful—mostly of stones I've never seen before. One combines clear crystals and deep blue stones that the sign refers to as lapis. Another combines a stone bead called hematite with rose quartz and lots of silver beads in between.

"Can you tell me what these numbers mean?" I ask Marcy, who has returned with a sheet showing the class schedule the store offers. I'm referring to the two sets of numbers under each piece of jewelry.

"Sure. The top number is the suggested retail price, and the bottom number is what it costs to make."

"What?" I know it makes me sound dumb, but I want to understand.

She looks mildly surprised but explains anyway. "Retail is how much you'd charge for it, while cost is how much it costs to make it using our supplies. The difference is your profit."

I go from one jewelry piece to the next with this new little formula. Retail minus cost equals profit.

I look up to see Rachel approaching. She's picked up several magazines with jewelry designs. "Rachel, have you seen these?" I ask.

"Sure," she says. "But most of them are more than we can afford, and people don't want to spend that much at farmers' markets and flea markets."

"Who told you that?" Marcy asks.

Rachel swings around to face Marcy.

"I don't mean to be rude," Marcy continues. "But people in this town love nicer jewelry and think of the flea markets as an opportunity to get higher-end stuff for less. I think that if you can make this stuff and make it well, you'll be able to sell it at high-end prices. You may even find that people commission certain pieces at the flea market and farmers' markets."

"Really?"

Rachel seems truly surprised. But the supplies are so much more expensive.

Encouraged, I start going down the line. "This one sells for eighty dollars and the materials cost thirty-eight dollars, so that's over a fifty percent profit. We only make a few dollars' profit on the cheaper ones."

"That's true. But we'd need a lot of money to make such a big change," Rachel says.

"You could always space these with less expensive beads," Marcy says. "Look at how many pieces of jewelry combine different types of beads." She glances at the line that's formed by the cash register and excuses herself to assist those customers.

"Couldn't we give it a try?" I must sound like a begging child. And I'm not sure why this is so important to me, but I actually *long* to work with the gemstones, especially the pearls and rose quartz that I just now realize I'm still holding. "It wouldn't take us any longer to make a necklace out of gemstones than it takes to make them out of wood or plastic or ceramic beads, and if we make more money..."

"Mother Esther would never go for it," Rachel says.

"No, I would not," Esther says as she approaches us. She holds a basket filled with plastic and wooden beads, cord, fish wire, and clasps. "I'm going to sit over there while you two finish up." She points to a comfortable-looking chair on the opposite side of the room. "Put the gemstones back, Eva. I told you that. We can talk about all this later."

I avoid the gem shelf and find myself clutching the stones harder than before. I can't put them back. It makes no sense, but somehow they speak to me, and I want them badly.

Get on with it, I command myself, but it's Ezekiel's voice that I hear in my head.

I reach to hang up the rose quartz in obedience, but everything gets fuzzy because my eyes are watery. I miss the hook and they smash to the ground. When I scramble to recover the rose quartz, the pearl strand slips and beads fly everywhere. They hit the shelf behind me; they roll into the aisle and under displays. I slump to my knees and scramble to pick them up, but my actions seem to be in slow motion.

A chorus of voices swells behind me. Several people, including customers and store clerks, help with the pickup. So many people are scrambling to recover the beads.

"Oh no, Eva," from Rachel.

"Look what you did!" from Esther.

"Let me help you," from Marcy.

"You know we'll have to pay for these," Esther hisses.

"I'm afraid so" from Marcy. She points to a big sign above the displays that says "You break, you buy."

I'm crying, and all the words seem to be going through a long tunnel before they reach me. I can barely see the beads on the floor.

"It's okay," Rachel says, hugging me. She lifts my face to meet her eyes. "Eva, my goodness, you're pale and shaking. It's not the end of the world."

I am barely aware of leaving the store and walking back to the van. My dad's face floods my brain, and I suddenly remember what these beads mean to me.

The last time I saw my father was on my fourth birthday. I remember driving Mother crazy because he was coming to the house and I couldn't stop jumping around in excitement. I was a daddy's girl, but all of my begging never made a difference.

Some things about that day are so clear in my mind that they could have happened this morning. Other things are fuzzy, and I'm sure there's lots I've forgotten.

I do remember the fancy dress Daddy got me because it was so beautiful. It was white with purple puffy dots. I don't know the name of the fabric, but it was soft and wispy and layered. If you picked up just one layer, you could see through it. Mommy did something special with my hair. She pulled back hair from both sides, braided it, and attached a bow where the braids came together on the back of my head. It matched my dress and made me feel beautiful. I couldn't wait for Daddy to see me.

Daddy only lived three blocks away, but it was so hard for Mother to be around him that our visits weren't anywhere near as often as I wanted.

Even now I can feel his prickly mustache against my cheeks and the beard that tickled me when he kissed my face. I would pretend to hate his beard and yank on it a little. He would pretend that I was hurting him. Then we'd both giggle.

Mommy started yelling at Daddy about something. I think it was because he let me dive right into opening my presents instead of making me slow down and open the card first.

I know he gave me several presents and that made Mommy mad. "You're spoiling her," she said. Daddy would yell back that he only had one daughter and he could spoil me if he wanted to. But only two of the gifts stand out in my mind. One was a red-and-white tube with ribbon on both ends. The other was a little box with a bow on it.

I tore open the first but Daddy had to explain what it was. "It's a calendar for two years. That's how long I'll be in China. Every time you wake up in the morning, you put an X on another day and each X brings us closer to the time we can see each other again."

I probably shrugged the calendar off because I hadn't grasped how those little boxes related to time passing. And I didn't want to think about him going far away to teach. I was much more interested in the little box. I'm sure I ripped it open eagerly.

Inside was a pink and white necklace that I thought was beautiful. "Your name is hidden in this necklace," he said. I loved puzzles, but no matter how hard I studied it, practically cross-ing my eyes, I couldn't find the puzzle. Finally he laughed and told me the secret. "The pearls are lily white. That's for the Lily part of your name."

I laughed.

"And the pink stones are…"

"Rose!" I shouted.

"That's right, rose quartz for my favorite girl—Lily Rose!"

He told me he had filled each bead with love and that when I wore them, they would remind me how much he loved me. He folded me inside a bear hug for a long time after that and reassured me that he would send me letters every week and call me whenever he could. I was to wear the necklace always, and when I needed Daddy's love, it would be there.

I wish that had turned out to be true.

Every day after that, I hid behind the living room curtain, beg-ging in my heart for him to drive up in his blue car. I missed him so much that I would have gone to China with him. Or maybe he'd come back just to be with me. I watched for the mailman every day, but whenever he came, Mommy would say there was no mail for me. The phone didn't bring Daddy back either.

Last year, in one of the secret conversations we'd hold while gardening or in the hayfield, Mother told me that we had lived in Hyde Park because it was near the University of Chicago, where Daddy taught Chinese. When the divorce got messy, he took two years off to go to China.

When I was little, it made me so mad that he broke his promise that I ripped the calendar into little pieces. There was no way I could put it back together again and I was sure I could never get him back now, because I had destroyed his gift. But at least I still had the necklace. I would wear it as long as I could.

I press my cheek against the cold window until it feels numb. If only I could numb these memories. *Stop it!* I yell at myself inside. He left me. He's a heathen. And it's a sin to think about him. I force my attention back in the van just as Rachel skillfully navigates a hairpin turn on the mountain road.

It wasn't long after Daddy left that Mother brought Reverend Ezekiel home for dinner one night. He was a traveling preacher and she wanted him to have a good meal while he was in Chicago gathering souls. He invited his wife to join him, and together they stayed another two weeks. By that time Mom believed in him fully and we went with him back to Arizona.

I watch Rachel maneuver the van around sharp curves and barely make it around a pile of rocks that had dropped from the mountain since we were here this morning. We collectively let out a sigh of relief when we're safely back on the road again.

"I've been thinking about all your ideas for jewelry," Rachel says now. "Since we already have the gemstone beads, let's be as creative as possible and see how we do at the next flea market. As long as we make a good profit, I don't think we need to report you to Community Concerns. What do you think, Mother Esther?"

"Well, I don't know. I told her to put them down and she disobeyed. That sounds like an offense against the community to me."

I hate that she's talking about me as if I'm not here. "I'm very sorry that I didn't put them down the minute you told me to, Mother Esther. But it truly wasn't my intention to disobey. I simply got distracted and didn't realize I was still holding them."

"Your disobedience cost us more than money, dear. It cost us so much time, having to select the findings and clasps and—everything—that we could combine with your gemstones."

"You're right," I say, feeling humble and physically weak. I don't dare beg for her not to report me because then she'd have the begging to report.

"I'm not saying that Eva shouldn't be punished," Rachel says. "But you know that the punishment will depend on how great the loss is to the community, and we won't know that until after the next flea market. If we had to buy expensive beads and can't sell the jewelry made from them, it will be a different matter than if we sell them easily and instead of losing money actually make money."

Esther is silent for a moment."I guess we could wait and see," she says. "It will give me time to pray about it."

Rachel and I exchange smiles as Mother Esther gets out of the front seat. Rachel's never done anything like this before—protected me from consequences. I sure appreciate it.

It's only four p.m., so we have time to do some beading before dinner. But I want to see if Mother Martha ever made it to her chore assignment. So I tell Rachel that I have an idea and will be right back. Mothers Cecilia and Rebecca sit mending socks when I burst into the sewing room. Mother is not there. I say that I need three feet of their heaviest thread for a jewelry project. As they're getting the thread for me, a chill ripples through me. When did it become so easy for me to lie like this?

November

Six

Annie and Jacob peek through the window of the bead room and make faces at me. I suppress a giggle because I don't want Rachel or Mother Esther to see their antics. They manage to duck down just as Mother Esther finishes looking over my creations.

"My dear," Esther says after a few minutes, "I don't think you need to worry about me reporting you to the Community Concerns Committee for your disobedience last week at the bead store. You've made some lovely pieces, and if they sell the way Rachel claims they will, I'll consider your actions nothing more than an inconvenience, and one that ultimately will benefit the community."

"Thank you, Mother Esther. Thank you so much!" I'm so relieved I could cry.

"But know this. If you disobey again or if your pieces don't sell, I will still report you next week."

"Yes, Mother," I say, bowing my head. When I look up, I see her hobbling out the door.

Rachel grins. When Mother Esther is out of earshot, she reassures me. "You don't have a thing to worry about. We've never had such a beautiful array of jewelry. If we sell half of these tomorrow, we'll have more profit than ever before."

"I hope you're right," I say.

"You hope who's right?" Ezekiel says from the doorway.

The necklace I'm working on slides through my fingers, but I catch it before it falls to the floor. It always throws me off balance when Reverend Ezekiel shows up unexpectedly.

"Good afternoon," Rachel and I both say at the same time.

"I was just telling Eva that this was some of the nicest jewelry we've ever made," Rachel said.

He points to a pair of earrings. "Who made these?" he asks.

"Eva did," Rachel says.

He points to a necklace. "Eva," Rachel says. He points to a bracelet. "Eva again," Rachel says. He picks up another pair of earrings. "That would be Eva." Rachel laughs. "She's so good, I'm beginning to get a complex."

Ezekiel nods, thinly masking how pleased he is. "So how much will you sell these for, and how much profit will that bring?" I'm not sure if he's talking to Rachel or me. He paces back and forth in the small space, continuing to examine everything—even a few of the old plastic beaded necklaces, which he tosses to the side. He picks up the earrings and bracelet set I made this morning.

Finally Rachel answers his question. "We're just going to have to see how much we can get for them—but I think they'll sell for much more than any we've made previously."

"They'd better," he says. "The materials look to be far more expensive than we've had before. If the new style sells well, it could make all the difference this winter."

I know his eyes are on my face, even though I'm focused on the necklace I'm making. I slowly look up to see him beaming down at me. "I'm proud of you, Eva," he says.

"Thank you," I say weakly.

He starts toward the door, and then as if remembering something, he turns back. "God is good!" he says.

"God is good!" we repeat.

Rachel and I exchange surprised looks. It is so rare for him to say the coveted words "I'm proud of you." I don't know if he's in a sunny mood to match the beautiful weather outside, or if he really thinks my work is that promising.

"It feels good to be on the right side of him, doesn't it?" Rachel says.

"Yes. Oh yes," I say, relief washing over me.

I look down at the necklace I was working on when Ezekiel came in. Without realizing it, I've been making a necklace much like the one Daddy gave me all those years ago—two pearls, a silver spacer, a rose quartz heart, silver spacer, and the pattern goes on.

It was the first or maybe the second day after Mother and I arrived at the Arizona compound that I lost my necklace. I don't remember the trip from Chicago, but I remember a laughing, singing Mother instead of the crying and angry person she had been before Ezekiel.

We sat in the chapel listening to a forever sermon. I had to go to the bathroom, but each time I tried to tell Mother this, she would press hard on my leg with her hand—a motion I knew meant "be quiet."

It got more interesting when Ezekiel started calling members up to the altar one by one. He thanked several for all that they had given Righteous Path. Everyone clapped. Then he called up persons he thought were holding back. He thought they could give more, and each one did.

He called, "Eva." I thought he was talking about someone else at first, but when Mother pushed me forward, I remembered that Eva was the new name he gave me right when we got here. But I liked my real name, Lily. I hid my face in Mother's dress, but she pushed me away from her. "You must obey," she said.

I was afraid, but when Ezekiel smiled so big at me, it was easier to go to him.

"Eva, do you understand that you are chosen?" he asked when I got to the altar. "And because of that, you will live with God in heaven when you die."

I nodded, even though I wasn't sure what he meant.

"And God wants you to give up your toys and clothes to follow Him."

I could see that he was staring at my necklace—the one Daddy gave me with the little pearls and rose quartz hearts. I expected him to tell me that it was pretty but he didn't.

"All of these are things people have given to Jesus," he said, pointing to the big basket that held rings and watches, necklaces and bracelets, even a few fancy pens. "Now it's your turn."

I covered my necklace protectively. "I *can't*," I whined. "My *daddy* gave this to me."

All of a sudden, Ezekiel's face got dark and his voice turned angry. "You must forget your daddy," he said. "Your daddy was not chosen by God for salvation, and he won't be welcome in the Kingdom of Heaven."

This was too much. I plugged my ears and my stomach suddenly hurt. "Daddy's not bad. Daddy's not bad," I kept saying. But Ezekiel firmly pulled my hands down.

I searched for Mommy's face in the crowd. When I found her, I reached out my arms so she would come and take me away from this man, but she just shook her head no and lowered her head.

In a flash I realized something important. She was no longer in charge. This man was the boss of me now, and Mommy's boss too. He was the boss of everybody.

"Now you will obey me and give me that necklace," Ezekiel demanded.

He paddled me hard until I gave it to him. That's when I wet myself in front of everybody.

I could cry all over again thinking about it. It was a powerful lesson, one that I needed to learn—that God comes before any material possessions.

The craft room that seemed so sunny just a few minutes ago is now oppressively heavy. Somebody sucked out all the air.

Rachel must feel it too because she stands up and opens a window. "Do you know that it's almost seventy degrees out there?

In November too!" she says. "Annie and Jacob are out collecting wood for a bonfire tonight. Why don't you go help them—get a little air? You won't see another day like this until spring."

I love the idea. "Okay, as soon as I finish attaching this clasp." In my hurry I prick my finger on a needle. The darned thing bleeds like it's a knife wound or something.

"Out!" Rachel says. "You'll get blood all over our jewelry."

I race to the kitchen where the Band-Aids are kept. In the dining room, a solitary figure sits at a table. Miracle of miracles, it's Mother nursing a glass of milk. Alone, finally.

When she sees me, she holds out her arms. I practically leap to get the hug I've wanted for so long. I hope no one comes around because I hug her for a long time, drinking in her love.

"You're bleeding!" she says. I stick my finger in my mouth and plop down on the chair next to her.

"It's nothing. A pinprick. The important thing is how are *you*? I never see you anymore—not even at mealtime."

"Hurry and take care of that finger, then we'll talk, God permitting."

I stay put. "Tell me."

"I'm supposed to be on bed rest."

"Why?"

"To keep the baby healthy, Mother Martha says."

She's hiding something. It makes me so mad. "I'm not a little girl anymore. I'll be fifteen in May. Please tell me what's going on."

"Okay, honey." She sighs. "I started bleeding several days ago. It could mean that I am having a miscarriage. But with bed rest, I have a better chance of keeping it."

"So, why aren't you in bed?"

In answer she holds up the glass of milk. "I can't get enough of it."

"But, Mother, even before you started bleeding, you didn't seem happy about the baby. I know the doctor said you couldn't get pregnant again, so this is a miracle, right?" I notice the dark circles under her eyes, and it seems that her face, even her fingers, are puffy.

"No, Eva, the doctor didn't say I *couldn't* get pregnant again. He said I *shouldn't* because my body can't handle it. It's dangerous for me."

"But Reverend Ezekiel said it's a miracle," I say.

"Yes," she says. "It's a miracle because with all these wives, no one has been able to bring a baby to term. And God told Ezekiel that I will have this baby." After a few seconds she puts a smile on and gives my shoulder a quick squeeze. "We'll just have to trust that if God wants me to have this baby, he'll keep me safe, won't we?"

I nod. *Please God, please keep her safe.*

"I heard that Ezekiel pulled you out of school. It makes me sad."

The way she avoids my eyes doesn't look like sadness, though. It looks and feels like guilt—as if there is something she should be able to do to change Ezekiel's mind.

"I know, but I get to go to Boulder and make pretty things."

She looks around to make sure no one is listening. "Eva, don't ever let anyone know that you like going to Boulder. You know better. It's like saying, 'I like being around heathens and temptations toward evil.'"

"I *know!*"

"I wish..." she begins.

We both hear it at the same time—footsteps in the hall. I grab Mother's empty milk glass and head to the sink so that we're not together when the person comes in or passes by. I pull the Band-Aids from the top shelf above the sink, though my finger stopped bleeding a while ago.

The intruder is Mother MaryAnne, here to begin the evening meal. We each greet her casually, and she doesn't seem at all concerned that we're together, especially after Mother explains her need for milk and I wave the finger I've just bandaged in front of her.

"You can have as much milk as you want," Mother MaryAnne says, winking at Mother Martha.

When MaryAnne begins to take out pots and pans, I sneak a quick kiss on Mother's forehead. I try to make my face say that everything is going to be all right. But I'm not convinced of it myself, and I know she's not either.

When I get outside, I find that Annie and Jacob have gathered enough wood for three fires. But we keep gathering anyway because it's fun to be out on this sunny day and special for me to have time with them again. I try to forget my conversation with Mother Martha and enjoy the moment. But I keep coming back to the sentence she started and didn't finish. "I wish..." How would she have finished that sentence? *I wish...I wasn't having a baby. I wish...you could get more education. I wish we could leave here.*

My own thought stops me cold. No! That's blasphemy. She would never say that.

One thing I remember is how happy Mother was when she decided to join Righteous Path. It was like night and day. Before she was angry with Daddy all the time, but after she met Reverend Ezekiel, she would sing songs of praise with so much joy.

I force myself to stop thinking of Mother and put all my attention into getting ready for the bonfire.

After dinner, the campfire seems to lift everyone's mood. Annie sits on one side of me and Jacob on the other.

"We could make four campfires," Jacob says. Annie and I can't stop laughing when we hear this because Jacob's voice keeps cracking and he shifts between a familiar high voice and an emerging low voice in the same sentence. At first it looks like he's insulted, but then he laughs too.

Mother Rose tries to reassure him with *her* squeaky voice, which makes Annie and me laugh so hard my belly hurts. It feels good to laugh, though. It really does. Everyone around the circle is smiling with us. Except Reverend Ezekiel.

He looks at Jacob as if he's seeing him for the first time. As he watches Jacob, an awful coldness fills his eyes. I'm puzzled by his reaction to Jacob. When Jacob sees this, he seems to fold in on himself like he wants to disappear.

Jacob catches my eye. His look is a question. I give him a warm smile and shrug my shoulders as if to say, "Who knows what's going on with him?"

Everyone is quiet now, waiting for whatever will happen next.

Mother Helen hands Ezekiel his guitar, and as he starts to tune it, I begin to relax.

This may be the kind of bonfire night we used to have before the big split. We would praise God through song for hours, and sometimes Ezekiel would even encourage us to sing solos. Sometimes we even got to roast marshmallows on a stick.

"Who wants to hear a parable?" Ezekiel asks, his mood improving already.

"I do," we all say.

It's one of Ezekiel's gifts. He can take any parable and set it to song, complete with a good melody and refrain.

"What parable would you like to hear?" he asks. I look around for Mother but she's not here.

"The projigle son," Daniel says.

"Yeah, the projigle son," David agrees.

"It's *prodigal*," Reverend Ezekiel corrects. "So what does that mean, boys?"

The twins look at each other to decide in their silent language who will do the talking.

"It's about brothers. One is good and one is bad," Daniel says.

David chimes in. "Yeah and God loves both of them."

"Hmmm, I wonder why you two want that story," Ezekiel says.

Everyone laughs. The six-year-old boys are so cute with their matching blond cowlicks, light skin, and freckles. Mother Miriam has her hands full with them all day, especially with that left arm of hers. It hangs limp at her side. She can't bend or extend it since she broke it during the move.

Ezekiel begins singing the parable. His voice is strong and deep and holds such authority that you can't help but listen and follow. When I was little and new here, I obeyed him out of fear. But it was his singing—deep, clear, certain—and his radiant smile that finally won me over all those years ago. I wanted to please him. I craved hearing his voice directed at me when it was gentle and loving, and especially in song. I quickly learned that we all wanted that, wanted his approval and acceptance. In my mind Ezekiel's voice was the voice of God, and his smile was God smiling. Of course I wanted him to smile at me.

When we've finished that parable, Annie requests the song we made up that we sing to the tune of "Michael Rowed the Boat Ashore." But we sing it like this: "Mother Rose is heaven bound, alleluia. Mother Rose is heaven bound, alleluia. Mother Rose is the best around, allelu-u-ia." We sing it using one name at a time until we've gone through everyone's.

Annie leans in to me, and I lean in to Jacob. I peek at the twins' faces. Their attention never wavers.

God, thank you for bringing me to Ezekiel. Thank you that Esther has the heart not to report me for dropping the beads. Please help me to accept your word through him and to follow your will.

Seven

"That's it!" Rachel says, beaming. "We're sold out."

The two of us are at the Boulder flea market where we've hardly been able to take a breath since we opened at eight.

"And it's only eleven," I add, shaking my head. "Now I really don't have to worry about Mother Esther reporting me."

"Of course not," Rachel says. "We made more money than ever before, but we could have sold so much more."

Rachel locks the cash box while I begin folding the chairs and table. It's been just the two of us today because Esther managed to convince Ezekiel that a third person isn't necessary on these trips to Boulder. Like most of the women in Righteous Path, she hates going out in public. When she gets back from town, she takes at least two showers to remove the heathen poison from her body.

My eyes pan as many booths as I can take in—food booths that sell hot dogs and Cokes, one that sells cotton candy. That one always has a line of excited kids and harried parents. In the line down from me are booths with pies and homemade canned goods, sausage and honey, aprons and pot holders, and all sorts of crafts. It all feels so rich. My mouth waters at the thought of tasting some of each. But I get nervous around so many people. Why they want to cram together, practically touching each other, seems strange to me. I have to take deep breaths and look up at the sky every few minutes so I don't feel suffocated.

When it's not so crowded, I love to watch all of them. I especially love listening to their conversations because their words reveal how they think.

"Excuse me." The face of a vibrant, pretty woman interrupts my scanning and imagining. She looks to be in her early twenties and is wearing one of the necklaces I made.

"Can I help you?" I ask.

"Thank you," she says. "I'm looking for the jewelry booth. From the directions, it should be right about here."

"This is it," Rachel chimes in. "Is there a problem?"

"Oh no," she says. "My roommate got me this necklace, and I just love the design. I was hoping to see others, but it looks like you're closing up."

"Thank you. But, yes, we're sold out," Rachel says.

The girl nods. "I'm not surprised. This is beautiful." She fondles the necklace she's wearing. "I make jewelry too—just for myself. I was wondering where you get your supplies."

"Beads Galore," I say.

The girl looks surprised. "Really? They're too expensive for me!"

Rachel and I exchange glances. If there are cheaper places to get supplies, we sure don't know about them.

"Are there other bead stores around here?" Rachel asks.

"No. You'd have to go to Denver and they're not a lot cheaper, but have you gone online to shop?" she asks. "You have to buy in quantity but you can get everything cheaper. Sometimes you pay less than half the price."

Disappointment is written all over my face. "We don't use computers," I say. There I go again, blurting something out that no outsider needs to know.

The girl looks puzzled. She eyes us up and down. A new understanding dawns on her face. "Oh, you must be from a cult." Her face turns red and she slaps her forehead. "Um, I mean religious group, right?"

We both nod silently.

"Well, thanks for the beautiful necklace," she says. "I'll have to check back another time. I'm told every piece you make is unique."

I stay with our stuff while Rachel gets the van. The whole time I think about what it would mean to Ezekiel and Righteous Path if we could get cheaper supplies and make twice the money selling jewelry. Our work on the neighbor's ranch last summer meant we didn't get very much canning done the way we usually do. Not that the corn and beans we freeze and the canned fruits and vegetables go all that far, anyway.

Last winter I overheard Rachel comment to Mother Martha that she hadn't had her monthly for three months but didn't think she was pregnant.

"It could be because we fast so much," Martha had said. "You're not the only one with that problem." She had sighed then and made the comment that if we had more money for food, we probably would fast less often.

I was shocked. It had never occurred to me that we fasted for any reason other than that God told Ezekiel we must sacrifice by fasting. But this had made me wonder. Did God tell Ezekiel we needed to sacrifice by fasting, or was Ezekiel himself deciding we should fast for the practical reason that there wasn't enough food?

When we get into the van, Rachel hits the lock button and begins counting the money. "Four hundred thirty-five, thirty-six, and thirty-seven. My word! When we subtract the twenty-five we started with, we still brought in four hundred twelve dollars. That's the best we've ever done!"

"And that doesn't count all the tips," I say. I reach into my apron pocket and pull out a handful of bills.

Rachel looks shocked. "You kept your tips?"

"I didn't keep them for myself. I just kept them separate so we'd know how much we made from jewelry and how much from tips."

"Good idea," Rachel says, looking jealously at the bills I'm pulling out of my pocket. "I threw mine into the main pot, but I don't think I got anywhere near the number you did."

My stomach grumbles—loudly. I excuse myself but Rachel laughs.

"Me too," she says.

My search for the peanut butter sandwiches in the backseat comes up empty. "I was sure I packed them." I sound whiny, even to myself.

"Oh, Eva, I'm so darned hungry," Rachel says. She looks straight ahead and drums her fingers on the steering wheel in silence. After a minute she gives me one of her shiny-eyed I've-got-a-great-idea looks. "You know what? I'm sick to death of peanut butter, and we've got forty-eight dollars in tips. Plus we're done so early. Let's celebrate and eat in a real restaurant!"

Now it's my turn to look straight ahead. I understand why Rachel is tempted by the material world of restaurants and such. She lived as a heathen until she ran away at thirteen. It's my responsibility to tell her that this desire comes from the devil himself. I should tell her we need to go home hungry, even though that means we won't have anything to eat until dinner.

But I don't want to tell her this. She shouldn't have to suffer because I forgot our lunch. Besides, I haven't gotten to eat in a real restaurant since our move here from Arizona. We ate at McDonald's twice and a wonderful place I'll never forget—the International House of Pancakes. Just remembering makes my mouth water.

"We do have the tip money," I say. But I know Ezekiel would never approve. All money, no matter how it's obtained, belongs to Righteous Path. And the rule of thumb has always been that if you wouldn't do it in front of Ezekiel, you shouldn't do it at all. I open my mouth to protest but she holds her hand out to stop me.

"I'm the elder here, and I'm responsible. If I say we go out to eat, we do." She smiles, showing those deep dimples she has on each cheek.

I stifle a laugh. Rachel may be the elder between the two of us but she's only eighteen. As Ezekiel's youngest wife, she doesn't always get the same level of respect the other women do. It must make her feel important to be my boss.

We hop out of the van and practically skip to Pearl Street Mall. Rachel and I have two precious commodities we almost never have—time and money. I toss aside my concern and forget that I'm wearing "prairie-girl clothes," as one rude customer called them. I pretend that I fit into this strange world and that going out to lunch is something I do all the time. Besides, as Rachel pointed out, Boulder is filled with so many kinds of "different" people that we do almost fit in.

On the Pearl Street Mall, every third building seems to be a restaurant. We pause at each one so that Rachel can read the menu posted on the door or window. As hungry as I am, I'm far more interested in watching people than reading about food. I love watching families sitting at tables together, laughing, talking, sharing food. At one table, a boy and girl about four and six blow paper at each other from their drinking straws. Instead of getting angry, the parents laugh right along with the kids. A real family. I imagine the family consisting of me as the little kid with Mom and Ezekiel.

No! I push Ezekiel out of the scene and try to picture Mother, Daddy, and me. A terrible longing fills me too full. But it's guilt that makes me push the thought away. Daddy was not chosen; he's not saved. Thoughts of him put my own soul in jeopardy. I will him away just as I have so many times before.

"Perfect," Rachel says. We're standing outside a small café. "Not too expensive, yummy-sounding food, and it looks quiet too."

Inside the café are fifteen or so small tables. Every table is busy except one near the back. At first I notice that most of the tables have orange-and-white-checked tablecloths with a small pot of daisies in the center. Even though the flowers are plastic, they look springlike and cheerful on such a gloomy day.

Then it seems to register with both Rachel and me at the same time: These tables have computers too.

"Welcome to Wi-Fi Café," the menu lady says, smiling. She assures us that our waiter will be with us shortly and hands us a single-page menu written in such fancy cursive that I can hardly read it.

A guy about Rachel's age and carrying a pad of paper and pen approaches the table. "My name is Trevor," he says. "I'll be your waiter today." He looks like a lot of the guys I've seen today. A swath of his hair is painted pink, and he has piercings in his ear and nose. His face is friendly, though, with a light-up-the-room smile.

He motions toward a blackboard on the wall. "The specials of the day are listed there. Our soup is minestrone, and we have a bunch more lunch items on the menu. The ahi salad is awesome, and the prime-rib sandwich rocks. Did you want to use the Internet?"

Rachel's eyes get big and I want to yell, "Yes!"

"No," Rachel says firmly.

Trevor looks from her to me and then back to Rachel. I guess he can tell that we have differing opinions. "Well, in case you change your mind, the prices for using the Internet are on this card. Have you used our computers before?"

He doesn't seem to notice our shocked faces because he's too busy lifting a latch I hadn't noticed before in the center of the table. Up pops a computer screen that now rests in the middle of the table. "The keyboard slides out from underneath, like this."

I smile at him wordlessly, but I'm itching to try it out. Rachel says a polite thank-you, while he pushes the screen back inside the table, like magic.

Rachel and I both keep our faces blank, as we've been taught. This seems to embarrass the waiter because his face turns red.

"Sorry, I made an assumption. Can I get you two something to drink while you're deciding?"

"Tea, please," Rachel says. But I'm more daring. "I'd like a Coca-Cola, please."

When he leaves, Rachel shakes her head and I giggle. "Of all things—a computer!" I whisper, still laughing. "We're breaking rules we didn't even know we were breaking."

"Mercy," she whispers, holding her hand dramatically over her heart. "If Ezekiel came in right now, he'd…" She shakes her head. "I don't even want to think of what he'd do."

The thought of Ezekiel seeing this sends another ripple of anxiety through me and threatens to ruin my new adventure. So I push the thought away.

"Are you tempted?" I ask Rachel when I notice her fingering the latch that would release the computer. She shrugs her shoulders.

She's tempted. Otherwise she wouldn't have studied the price card or let the waiter show us how it lifts from inside the table and the keyboard.

I'm tempted too, really tempted. Beads at half the cost? Ordering beads online could make the difference between barely having enough to eat this winter and having the means to get all the food we need. And with Mother pregnant—well, I wonder if God is placing this opportunity before us so we can help the community.

My face feels hot because of the boldness of my own thoughts. This is prideful thinking. God would not show *me* how to keep Righteous Path from going hungry. He would show Ezekiel, holy Ezekiel. And Ezekiel would say that if God wanted us to have enough food, he'd provide it. If God wants us to go hungry, Ezekiel would say that God wanted to teach us something or that God wanted us to suffer for our sins.

The waiter brings a pot of tea, a cup and saucer, and my Coke. I don't recall ever hearing that having a Coke is a sin, but we don't buy stuff like that. Rachel orders a salad of baby greens and a chicken and avocado sandwich. Since I still haven't looked at the menu, I order the same.

When Trevor leaves the table, I take my first sip of my drink and laugh in surprise as it bubbles its way down my throat. It's sweet, and I'm not sure if I like it or not.

"I should have warned you about the fizziness," Rachel says. "I used to love that stuff."

I'm quiet, savoring the strange bubbly taste and taking in all the color in the room. When I think about how we suddenly have access to a computer, it seems more like a gift than a coincidence. I want to figure out how to look up bead prices something awful. I lean in to the table, ready to make my argument.

"Rachel, why is it that Reverend Ezekiel has a computer?"

"You know the answer to that. He has to keep up with what's happening in the outside world so that he can guide and protect us. He keeps us pure from all the heathen stuff out there by forbidding us to get on the computer."

"Right," I say. "But I think we could use the computer in a pure way to get jewelry supplies a lot cheaper and that would benefit Righteous Path too."

"Hold on!" she says. "So you think we should disobey Ezekiel and look up beads on this computer?" She leans back in her chair and covers her head with her hands. "Imagine the punishment, Eva."

I study my hands. I don't want to imagine the punishment. Instead I imagine a winter in which we have plenty of food, a winter free from an aching stomach and the sounds of the twins crying for more when watery soup is all we have. I'm suddenly ashamed to be eating out. Not that anyone at Righteous Path is hungry now, but we should be saving this money and figuring out how to make more.

"I am not going to use a computer. It's too risky, even for a worthy cause," Rachel says. "And you can't do it. You don't even know how to turn a computer on."

"Here you go," the waiter says. "Two baby green salads." He places one in front of each of us. "And I'll be right back with the sandwiches."

I don't say a word more to Rachel. I don't even look at her. I just dig into my salad, savoring every bite. I haven't had a green salad since the last of our lettuce died with the first frost. The lettuce is crisp, the cucumbers and tomatoes as fresh as if they came out of the garden this morning. And the dressing—with its lemony scent, it has a sweet and sour taste. I'm in heaven.

"Delicious," Rachel says to the waiter when he returns with our sandwiches.

"Good," he says. "Did I hear you say you don't know how to use a computer?"

I nod.

"Okay, things have gotten slow here in the restaurant. If it continues like this, I'll have time to show you when you've finished your sandwiches."

Neither of us says a word. He smiles and is off again.

I'm afraid that Rachel will devour her sandwich and bolt out the door, but I'm wrong. She eats slowly, relishing every bite.

Before we're finished, Trevor asks if he can join us, and when I say yes, he plunks himself down, straddling a chair backward. "Okay, I've got some time now. So let me show you how to use this thing."

Eight

The whole time Trevor shows me the basics of operating a computer and helps me pull up bead websites, Rachel sits across the table pretending to be uninterested. But when Trevor prints out price sheets, she's the first to study them.

"What a difference!" she says. "But it's no good. See here, to order these, you have to have a credit card, which we don't have, and they have to have a mailing address. We sure can't have beads sent to the compound. Imagine the reaction we'd get!"

She catches herself, probably because of the horrified look on my face. "We live way out in the country and can't get mail," she explains to Trevor, desperately trying to cover her mistake.

Trevor looks puzzled. "You can always arrange to pick up mail at the post office."

I can't think of a thing to say to help Rachel out. She even used the word "compound" to describe where we live. Instead I pick up the papers Trevor printed for me. Rachel gathers her stuff too, and after a hasty thank-you and good-bye, I give Trevor one of my more radiant smiles and we head to the door. I want Trevor to know how very grateful I am for what he taught me.

We leave around three, the time we'd usually finish selling jewelry. As we're driving out of Boulder, I clutch the pricing information that Trevor gave me and wonder where I can hide it at the compound. On the way home, Rachel is quiet and distant. I have no idea what she's thinking and I'm not about to ask.

I have a strange sense that no matter what happens on the outside—if Rachel is mad, if Ezekiel finds out about the computer—what is happening on the inside of me is more important. I don't have words for what that is, for what exactly is changing inside me. But for some reason I can't put my finger on, I am certain that the events of today are important.

"Remember," Ezekiel said to me many years ago. "You're named Eva after the very first woman God created for Adam. What do you know about her?"

What I knew was not good. But I had to answer. "She was kicked out of the Garden of Eden because she ate the forbidden fruit."

"Yes. She ate from the tree of knowledge. And she enticed Adam to do the same."

I'd felt it then. All the shame Eve brought upon mankind and womankind weighed on my shoulders.

Now the papers I hold bring that shame back. Have I eaten from the tree of knowledge?

We're headed up the mountain when I hear the click, click of the turn signal. Rachel turns into the lookout space and parks alongside another vehicle. Six people stand behind a fence peering down the canyon. But we remain in the van.

Rachel turns off the engine. And I wait for an explanation. After what seems like forever, she speaks.

"What we just did was really stupid," she says, "and the consequences could be dire. It's my fault. I'm the elder. I'm the one who's been entrusted with keeping you from bad influences when we're in the corrupt world. I should have told Trevor no when he offered to look up what we wanted. But I was curious like you."

I nod my head tentatively.

"To get back on track, we have to accept that we were tempted by Satan and we gave in to that temptation."

"Satan? Really?" I know I shouldn't challenge Rachel—she's just drawing me back to the everyday beliefs of Righteous Path. But I have to tell her what I think…

"I was thinking just the opposite, Rachel—that maybe God brought that lady to our booth so she could help us save money and help Righteous Path. Maybe God brought us to Trevor for the same reason. Maybe God doesn't want us to suffer so much this winter. I can't imagine that he wants us to go hungry."

My voice is getting louder now, more excited. "Rachel, I think God is giving us a chance to learn how to use computers for the good of our community. You know, use computers for our benefit the way we use the heathens when we sell them jewelry they shouldn't wear. You saw how much we'd save."

Then I see Rachel's face. She looks at me as if I am evil incarnate. She presses her back against the van window, in what looks like an effort to get as far away from me as she can. When she speaks, her voice is controlled and careful. "No, Eva. No. You are not seeing clearly." She takes a deep breath. "We have both been polluted—corrupted—by the material world. The lady who told us to look online and that waiter, Trevor, are from the devil, tempting us to disobey. They are not from God." She shakes her head. "Oh, Eva, we've got to repent."

But it wasn't like that. When Trevor offered to help, I could tell that he was sincere. His smile seemed real, and his laugh—it just bubbled out of him like he couldn't help being a happy guy who wanted to help. He had no idea how badly we needed to make money from the bead sales. Still, he gave us so much time and instruction.

When I hear Rachel's words, I keep my eyes lowered and will my arguments away. But the effort makes me want to cry.

My stomach hurts. I wish Rachel would at least consider what I'm saying. It's not that I question Ezekiel's holiness or his direct communication with God. But lately I've begun to wonder about how he *interprets* what God tells him.

Finally she speaks again. "What would Ezekiel say if he heard this?"

I can see his face, his anger and disappointment in me, and all my new thoughts slip away. The feeling is one of sinking, of shrinking into that unquestioning place of obedience where I am safe from punishment but itching for more. Safety is most important.

"Dear God," I say out loud. "Forgive me for questioning and for my disobedience. Forgive me for the arrogance of thinking I know what's best for me and for Righteous Path."

Rachel joins in. "Lord, I too ask your forgiveness. I led Eva into temptation by taking her to a restaurant. Please forgive me."

She reaches out to hug me. Peace feels better than jeopardy. But I'm confused about what I believe. I pick up the price sheets and rip them in several pieces.

"Good," Rachel says. She points to a trash can on the far side of the lookout.

I deposit the papers in the garbage can. I'm not sure if the relief I feel stems from knowing I won't get punished or if I'm actually penitent.

It takes forty-five minutes to get to Grand Hill even though it's less than twenty miles from Boulder. When we slow to twenty-five miles per hour going through the tiny town, the owner of the general store suddenly appears outside and waves to us to stop.

"What could he want?" I whisper.

"Be calm. He's friendly," Rachel says. She rolls down the window.

He has long, gray hair pulled back into a ponytail. He saunters across the street to the driver's side.

"Good afternoon, sir," Rachel says.

He smiles at her and acknowledges me with a nod. "The only 'sirs' around here are the fancy folk who visit from the big cities. But they don't bother us too often. I'm Ed, Ed Burns, but just call me Ed."

Rachel offers a dimpled smile. "Good afternoon, Ed. Is anything wrong?"

"I hope not," he says. "I wanted to let you know that some city guy was nosing around last week asking about you guys. He wanted to know if there was a religious group around here. I told him there wasn't anybody here who didn't belong here."

"Thank you," Rachel says. She keeps her face expressionless, and I try to hide my alarm the best I can.

"I'm pretty sure he was a reporter," Ed continues. "I've seen 'im before. This guy hung around the store, chatting me up about nothing for a while, and made it sound like an afterthought when he asked about you all. I made it clear that we like to keep things real peaceful around here. I thought you might want to tell your leader."

"We will," Rachel says. "Thank you for letting us know."

Ed nods. "I mean that. We like to keep things quiet and peaceful around here."

Nine

I hold my breath as Rachel tells Ezekiel about Ed Burns and the intruder. He grills us for more than an hour. He wants to know about Ed's facial expressions. Did Ed give a description of the man? Did the man carry a camera, a notebook, a tape recorder? When Ezekiel asks if Ed Burns was angry with us for being the cause of this intruder, I find myself reassuring him even though I have my own doubts.

Ezekiel instantly imagines the worst. He's sure it's Jacob's father come to claim him, or Brother Ralph, who will kill Ezekiel for marrying Mother MaryAnne. Or maybe it's my father who's finally tracked us down after all these years. That idea sends tingles up my spine. But I know better; my father abandoned me.

Desperate to reassure him, I take a risk. "He's probably just a reporter like Ed said." But my efforts ignite a fire.

He rails and paces up and down the narrow hallway of his trailer. "If he's a reporter, he'll write lies about us." He returns to his study, where Rachel and I are seated, to make his next proclamation.

"They could burn us alive like they did at Waco." Then he paces the hall to think some more.

I hate when he talks about Waco. We've heard the story so many times—how the government massacred more than one hundred religious followers several years ago. Ezekiel says that they were burned alive, just because they had stocked illegal weapons and wouldn't turn them over to the government. He's reminded us over and over that this is why we have to be careful to stay away from governmental agencies. They could storm Righteous Path without warning and kill all of us.

His reaction is way too big considering someone simply asked a few questions. That could be harmless. Still, I'm a little nervous. If only we could have kept it from him, but we didn't dare. This whole thing could be harmless—just a person who finds us interesting. Finally I say something, hoping to help.

"Ezekiel, it may not be that bad, really. It could just be…"

But he towers over me and spits his response inches from my face.

"*You* don't know anything, you stupid girl. What do you know? You make a few nice necklaces, and now you think you can advise *me?*" He looks up and down my body and dismisses me with a sweep of his arm. "That's what you are, just a *girl*, just a stupid *girl*." He says "girl" as if the word means "scum." "Now keep your mouth shut unless I ask your opinion." He begins to walk away from me, then darts in front of me again. "Go! Get out of here, and leave us alone."

I leave. It's amazing how my legs can move when he's slain me with his words.

I feel so many kinds of bad that it takes me a while to sort them out—clumsy, awkward, stupid, ugly, and scared of what he might do. I skip the lukewarm stew left over from dinner and hurry to my sleeping trailer where I bury my head in my pillow and wish I could sleep. I can't. Instead I force myself into the bathroom where I look at myself in the mirror—really look for the first time in ages. The sight makes me sick to my stomach.

Two little bumps protrude from my chest. Not breasts really, just sad little nubs. I force myself to look at the ugly mass of hair that protrudes under my arms, the same auburn color as the hair on my head. Ugly. I pray that no one ever sees it. I don't force myself to look at the hair below. It's bad enough that I can feel it every time I go to the bathroom. But I do notice the changes to the shape of my body—hips and a waist that make my clothes fit differently. No wonder Ezekiel has such contempt for me. I'm not a girl or a woman, just a sorry, strange mixture of both.

As I dress again, I wonder about what's happened to Ezekiel over the years. When did he become so mean? He's always been strict to lead us to purity, but he used to be joyful—so joyful and appreciative of us that he carried us with him into seeing God as good and great and loving. Where's all that love he used to show?

The sound of the chapel bell tells me what I already assumed. We're going to have an emergency meeting about the intruder, and nothing will be the same again.

Ezekiel continues to pace up and down, but this time at the pulpit. "We've had an intruder. Someone is lurking around Grand Hill, nosing into our business and threatening our sacred way of life."

The congregation gasps. Once somebody reported to Social Services that we weren't getting adequate schooling, and Ezekiel thought we kids would end up in foster homes. He warned that the government had stolen children from other religious groups and brainwashed them into believing the group was bad. Between that incident and all the reminders about Waco, everyone is pretty scared.

"Until we know who this heathen is and can be confident that we're safe, we will be on twenty-four-hour guard. That means one person will be stationed in the silo at all times for eight-hour shifts. Brother Paul is on lookout right now. I'll spend the night there."

I hadn't noticed that Brother Paul was missing.

"Anyone who tries to come onto this property will be given a verbal warning. If that is ignored, he will be shot."

I can literally see the shock waves radiating in the room. They look like heat waves but sound like blasts. Guns? Shooting for self-protection? Killing? This has never been a part of Righteous Path. I think back to the horror I felt when he pointed that gun at me in his office. A chill crawls up my spine. He could actually kill someone with that gun.

"How will we know how to shoot?" Mother Alice asks.

"We don't have guns," Mother Rebecca says.

"Are the heathens going to shoot us?" little David asks.

Ezekiel holds his hand out to silence everyone. "My children," he says. "God has spoken to me in prophecy. He tells me not to be afraid of the evils outside of here. He promises to give us the strength within the community to protect ourselves and to handle whatever Satan puts before us."

Maybe it's his fatherly voice or the fact that he walks among us and rests a hand on several shoulders, but everyone seems visibly calmer. His anger is gone and it's as if he's given us, his flock, a hug with his sudden warmth.

"When Brother Paul has finished his shift at three, I will take his place while Brother Paul begins lessons in handling, cleaning, and shooting a gun. You will all learn to shoot. Even the children must learn. In addition, we'll take turns patrolling the property on horseback and using the silo as a lookout.

"We must all pray extra hard. Tomorrow we have a Community Concerns Meeting. Make it count. Examine your conscience. Honesty brings about grace and forgiveness. Grace and forgiveness brings about purity, and purity allows clarity from God."

After a respectful moment of silence, a low rumble begins in the room and gets louder as the mothers whisper.

At the beginning of this meeting, Mother Martha looked okay but a little pale. I peek at her now and she looks awful, like she might throw up right here. I wonder how much of her misery is about morning sickness, and how much is a result of the gun shock Ezekiel just laid on us.

I could throw up myself.

What started as whispering among the mothers is getting louder by the minute. Daniel and David jump up and down. "We get to shoot a gun. We get to shoot a gun."

Ezekiel grins at the boys. "Yes, you do get to shoot. And every person will get his very own gun."

December

Ten

The tension in our chapel is electric. The Community Concerns Meeting is about to begin. I'm even more nervous than I was when I thought Esther might turn me in for disobedience. Ezekiel's mood makes him unpredictable. He's angry and suspicious all the time. And this new obsession with guns makes me think anything can happen.

Mother Martha takes the seat directly behind me. It's as close as we dare get to each other. She knows when something's wrong with me. She always knows. But I'm not about to tell her about Ezekiel's cruel words to me when we told him about the stranger. I've tried to shake it off, really tried. I tell myself he doesn't want me to get conceited about my jewelry-making skills, and that's why he put me down. But the contempt I saw in his eyes makes my heart hurt. And I feel so ugly.

Annie takes the seat on the other side of me. She smiles, trying to get me to smile back. I try, but I know she's confused about why I'm so down. I've been too ashamed to tell her.

It was even harder to face Rachel after that. She heard every-thing he said, of course.

"Nothing like shooting the messenger," she'd said after break-fast this morning.

I must have looked puzzled. "Sorry. I forget sometimes and use heathen expressions. It means that you shouldn't take out bad news on the person who gives you the information."

"Oh. I get it. But you were the messenger too. Why didn't he take it out on you?"

Rachel had put her arm on my shoulder. "Because I'm not the one who makes exceptional jewelry." She lets out a breath. "But I'm sorry he made that disgusted face when he looked at your body."

Her caring attitude brings tears to my eyes.

"Ezekiel's coming," she whispers. "Gotta get a seat."

Rachel hurries to take a seat because Ezekiel is approaching the altar.

"Let us pray," he says. We all kneel for the typical prayer. "Lord, make us clean and holy. Let us be like Jesus who, in his righteous anger, overturned the tables of the money sellers and banished them from his temple. Let us weed out any sin among us in this, your new temple. Guide our actions so that we do what it takes to make this a stronger faith community for your sake. Help us to punish the sinners, and help them change or banish them if they fail to change. We do this in your name. Amen."

It looks like we're about to get another lecture about our fail-ings. Ezekiel has told us again and again that when an intruder interrupts our lives it's because we haven't been strong enough in our faith. He talks about the intruder constantly, even though we haven't seen or heard anything of him.

Jacob suddenly appears at the chapel door—so late I'm embarrassed for him. The women start chattering, tsking, and rolling their eyes. He plunks down in the first empty seat he can find. The twins giggle. I dare to look at Ezekiel and draw an involuntary breath. He is darkness. This could be really bad.

"Confessions," Ezekiel calls out, staring dull eyed and hard chinned at Jacob. This first part of our bimonthly meetings gives each of us a chance to come forward with our faults. Confessions are way better than someone turning you in. The punishment is lighter because it shows that you're trying to perfect yourself. After confessions come the reports. It's not a perfect process. If someone's mad at you or jealous, she may look for an infraction to turn you in.

Jacob stands. "I accuse myself of arriving late for this meeting. I apologize to God, to Ezekiel, and to all of you."

I notice that Jacob's voice remains deep throughout. I'm not sure that's good or bad since an adult voice may mean an adult-sized punishment.

"Thank you, Jacob," everyone says.

Jacob continues to stand. He looks tall and stoic. Too stoic, I think. I wish he looked more penitent.

"How many times have you confessed this infraction, Jacob, hmm?" Ezekiel asks. His voice is calm and the room is completely still, like right before a tornado.

"Many times, sir."

"And what punishments have you received?"

"Many different punishments, sir."

"Name them."

"I have been assigned extra cleaning chores. I've had to write prayers over and over. I've had to apologize to each individual community member. I've lost meals when I was late for them. I've sat alone in a dark room for hours contemplating my sin."

Though Jacob looks like he's still thinking, Ezekiel breaks in with the inevitable question. "What punishment would finally help you change?"

"I truly don't know, sir."

I'm shocked. His tone is far from apologetic. It actually sounds arrogant. *Oh, Jacob, what are you doing?*

"Well, think of something, Jacob. Think of something *now*," Ezekiel thunders.

This seems to anger Jacob. "A paddling, I guess." He has the audacity to shrug his shoulders and look straight into Ezekiel's face—challenging him. The community holds one collective breath. It's the stupidest thing I've ever seen Jacob do, and I have no idea why he's doing it. I brace myself for what will come next.

"Come up here," Ezekiel says.

Jacob tries to hide how scared he is as he walks to the front of the room, but his hand is shaking when he hands Ezekiel the paddle and bends over the front table. Ezekiel seems to whack harder than ever before. I bow my head and pray for Jacob, hoping he can take his punishment in silence. But by the third whack Jacob is crying out, and by the fifth he is screaming in pain. I pray that he can bear all thirteen whacks—one for each year of age.

Someone sobs loudly. I turn to see Jacob's mother holding a hand over her mouth. My eyes burn from unshed tears.

I have never seen anyone get hit that hard. I've never seen Ezekiel use so much power that he was out of breath when it was over. Jacob takes several minutes to raise himself from the table he's bent over. He struggles to return to his seat.

Finally Ezekiel composes himself enough to continue the meeting. "We have allowed Jacob's behavior to go on for far too long. Anytime that Jacob is late from now on, he will be paddled right then. We will not wait for a Community Concerns Meeting to administer punishment." He pauses and takes in a deep breath. "We do this out of love for Jacob."

But I don't believe him. For the first time ever, I just flat-out don't believe him.

The way he looked at Jacob before and during the beating was not as a caring disciplinarian sadly administering a punishment to a child who needs to learn a lesson. The look was sheer hatred.

"Other confessions?" Ezekiel asks.

The room is silent except for the muffled sobs of Jacob in the back row.

"Concerns, then."

After a pause, Mother MaryAnne stands up. My thoughts return to the kitchen that day when I was talking to Mother Martha and she came in. She hadn't seemed upset about us talking privately, but maybe she was waiting for this meeting. I wonder if Mother Martha is thinking the same thing.

"Forgive me, Ezekiel, I meant to stand up during confessions."

He nods. "Go ahead, Mother MaryAnne."

"I accuse myself of having been wasteful. I misplaced a bag of potatoes and, thinking they were gone, allowed them to rot in the basement."

"How did that happen?" Ezekiel asks.

"It's dark downstairs, Reverend, with only one overhead light." Her lips quiver and her voice sounds like a plea. "I must have placed the bag against the wall where the light doesn't shine. Then I just forgot them."

"Who thinks we should give Mother MaryAnne a pass for this transgression? After all, it's dark in the basement and she didn't mean it."

To me his voice sounds sarcastic, but apparently Annie doesn't catch that, and she raises her hand. Behind me, the twins have also apparently raised their hands, which I learn when Ezekiel addresses them.

My heart sinks. I can see how the twins fell into this trap, but not Annie. Surely she must see that Ezekiel is out for blood today.

"So Daniel and David, why do you two think Mother MaryAnne shouldn't do penance when she wasted a bag—how big was it, Mother MaryAnne?"

"Ten pounds," she replies.

"She wasted ten pounds of potatoes!"

Annie's breath becomes raspy as she realizes her mistake.

"So, Daniel, why shouldn't she be punished?"

"She cooks good food," Daniel says, eliciting a brief smile from several people.

"She didn't mean to," David says.

"And you, Annie? Now don't pull that breathing crap on me. Tell me why she shouldn't be punished."

"She, she…" Annie gasps. "She made a mistake."

I squeeze Annie's hand to show support, but let go immediately. I don't dare get caught comforting her.

"My family," Ezekiel continues, "we face a long winter ahead. God is testing us with the meager resources we have. We must account for every ounce of food and waste none. We cannot be allowed to make mistakes. For this offense, Mother MaryAnne, you should go without dinner for ten days, one for each pound of potatoes. But because you confessed before God and your community, I will reduce your dinner penance to five days."

He turns to Daniel and David. "You must also learn that waste, intentional or not, is a crime against the community that cannot be tolerated. Because of your ages, Daniel and David will only lose dinner tonight. But Annie, who is older and knows better, will lose three dinners."

We are a sad, somber group. Mother Helen, Jacob's mother, has been crying since he was paddled. Now the twins are crying and Annie still struggles to breathe.

"Any other community concerns?" Ezekiel asks. If he feels bad at all for the punishments he's doled out, he certainly doesn't show it.

I'm thankful when the meeting ends. I'm eager to minister to Annie and to check on Jacob. But Annie wants to be alone with her bruised feelings, and by the time I get back to where Jacob was sitting, he's gone.

Eleven

The steps on the side of the old hayloft are rusty. I hope they will hold me. They're also slippery because of all the snow. I climb them anyway.

"You're early!" Jacob hollers from the top. "I have another thirty minutes."

"I know. I want us to have some time to talk." I'm focused on climbing the stairs so I don't see his face, but he makes a disgruntled sound, letting me know he doesn't like the idea. I've wanted to talk to him since he got paddled, but he hasn't been willing to talk to anybody. I'm not surprised. He's been silent and withdrawn from everyone since the paddling ten days ago. At the top of a silo, with no one else around, maybe I can find out what's going on with him.

The smell of wet hay makes me sneeze. I can hear the scratching and occasional squeaks of mice—I pray it's only mice—inside the hayloft The sound makes me cringe a little.

Jacob reluctantly scooches over to make room for me. At first I don't look down because the height scares me. But slowly I begin to enjoy how well I can see the whole compound from this perspective. To our left is the original farmhouse where we had to knock down the walls dividing the living room, dining room, and kitchen to make one big dining hall. The house has three additional rooms on the first floor: a laundry with two washers and two dryers, and two small bedrooms that became the craft and sewing rooms when we moved in. Jacob and Paul sleep in a bedroom upstairs. Next to that is the tiny classroom.

To our right is an outhouse that was here before plumbing. Thank God we don't need to use it to go to the bathroom, though several of us have been isolated inside as punishment. Then there are all the trailers—two women's trailers, the kids' trailer, and Ezekiel's trailer in a half-moon shape next to the long driveway. In the summer you can distinguish the garden from the cornfields, but right now all you can see is white, white, white.

It seems especially quiet because of the heavy snow that continues to fall silently, keeping everyone inside except us. The plume of smoke rising from the chimney of the farmhouse is the only indication of life.

"Have you seen anything suspicious?" I ask.

"Nothing," Jacob says. "But don't you worry. If I did see something out of the ordinary, I have this to protect us." He holds up a whistle and rolls his eyes.

I burst out laughing. "Wooh! I wouldn't want to fight you when you're armed like that."

Jacob laughs too, a kind of deep, guttural laugh that I'm not used to from him. "Brother Paul has the only gun, and he's using it out back somewhere to give lessons."

"I hear you're a pretty good shot," I say.

Jacob glows. "Yup, Brother Paul was impressed. When Ezekiel gets back from his trip, Brother Paul wants him to see firsthand what a good shot I am. But I doubt there's some kind of dangerous intruder."

"Shhhh. You're in enough trouble. And you know how dangerous it is to disagree with Ezekiel." I can't imagine why he's doing it.

I change the subject. "I'm glad to see you're walking better," I say to him. "You're practically your old self."

He nods, looks straight ahead, and casually chews on a piece of straw. "You're gonna freeze up here."

I notice then how raw red his nose and cheeks are. He's wearing paper-thin gloves with a hole in the left one. His cap barely covers the tips of his earlobes. "You can go a little early," I say.

He throws a clump of hay in my face. "Don't baby me. I can take it."

I take a clump and stick it down his back before he figures out what I'm doing. I laugh as he wriggles around trying to get the itchy stuff off his skin. "I wouldn't baby you. You're practically grown." I fall back onto a bale so that he can't shove hay down my back. We're both giggling like old times.

"Sit up and take it like a woman," he says. He's holding a huge wad of hay. I don't sit up. I dart from side to side to avoid his revenge. Finally he mushes the hay in my face. It goes up my nostrils, fills my mouth, even jabs my eyes. I gasp and choke trying to get it all out. Hay is stuck in my throat. I can't cough it out, and I can't swallow it.

"I'm sorry," he says. He hits my back, and some hay comes flying out of my mouth. He gently wipes it out of my eyes. He tries to pull some out of my hair but I push him away. I'm so angry that I could hurl him to the ground, but the twenty-foot drop would injure him or worse. Instead I punch his arm a few times until he grabs mine to stop me.

He reaches for his thermos. "Here, it's not hot anymore but it will help," he says.

I guzzle the cold tea. "Why did you do that?"

He shrugs his shoulders and looks away.

"I don't understand, Jacob. You've been so bitter since you got paddled—no—since before you got paddled, and let's face it, you practically dared Ezekiel to do it. It broke my heart to see you get hit like that."

"I know."

"Jacob…"

Suddenly he pushes me back into the hay and plasters a hard kiss on my lips.

"Stop," I say. He's hurting my mouth and squeezing me so I can't breathe. "Stop!" But now his kiss turns gentle. His lips barely graze my forehead. He kisses the tip of my nose, each cheek, my hands. "Stop," I say again. But my voice has no fight in it and I'm confused by the new feelings rising inside me.

He pulls me up into a sitting position. I watch his face turn from soft to hard again. "That's what's going on," he says.

"Oh," I say. I want him to say more, to put words to his feelings. Instead he changes the subject.

"Remember Matthew?" Jacob asks. He breathes into his hands to warm them.

"Of course I do—it hasn't been that long since your brother

left." I'm struggling to sort out what just happened and what it all means, and he brings up Matthew who has been gone since just after we moved here.

"Do you remember how Ezekiel acted when he said he was leaving?"

I nod. We were all grieving. No one wanted to see Matthew lose his soul by leaving, but Ezekiel did nothing to stop him. He actually seemed happy when Matthew was gone.

"Eva, he was my age when he left. Do you remember how he used to follow Rachel around?"

"I guess. Rachel was brand-new, and I don't think she was married to Ezekiel yet. So why...?"

"That's not the point. Ezekiel wanted Matthew to leave because Matthew had feelings for Rachel. Ezekiel wanted her for himself. I think he hates me because I'm getting older. I think he knew what I was feeling for you before I did. As soon as my voice began to change, he started yelling at me for every little thing. And all of a sudden it was like he hated me. Don't you see? He wants all the women for himself."

My head is spinning. "God determined what wives Ezekiel has. Why would he need to be jealous? Or don't you believe that?" There's a strange ringing in my ears, and it's like somebody stole all the air.

"Calm down, Eva! I'm not saying that at all. Yes. Ezekiel communes with God but he's also human and capable of mistakes."

It sounds like heresy to me. Yet something about it sounds right. I think about how mean Ezekiel was to me when Rachel and I told him about the stranger. I think about how he's gathering guns for everyone because one person inquired about Righteous Path, and it doesn't seem so preposterous.

"Look, what I want more than anything is for Ezekiel to care about me. It's okay by me that he's human."

I focus on a rabbit hopping through the snow. He stops, sniffs, and continues to hop. Falling snow quickly covers the paw prints, leaving no evidence of the rabbit's recent visit.

"Oh, Jacob, I'm so sorry how he's hurt you—not just the paddling but the rejection."

His eyes meet mine. "Thanks, Eva. Have you ever seen anyone get hit that hard? It wasn't a paddling. It was a beating. I had welts and open sores. If Mother Miriam hadn't filled bucket after bucket with hot water and Epsom salts for me to sit and soak, I probably would have had a terrible infection. Vaseline is the only thing that kept my clothes from sticking to me when the sores oozed like that."

I'm speechless. Because what comes to mind for me to say is what I've been taught—that the paddling was for Jacob's own good, that the pain inflicted on his body was for the sake of his soul. But I can't say that. Because the beating was not to save Jacob's soul. Ezekiel beat him because he was threatened by Jacob growing up.

Jacob interrupts my thoughts. "You probably think I deserved it because I was, well, a jerk, I guess."

"Of course I don't think you deserved a beating, Jacob. I couldn't understand why you were so flippant or why you seemed to bait him, but nobody deserves to be hit that hard."

Jacob lets out a sound. It's laughter, but bitter, hard laughter that comes from pain. "When I came late to that meeting I knew he'd be furious. I thought that if I gave him something to be angry about, maybe he'd get it out of his system once and for all."

"How awful, Jacob," I say. I try not to cry.

We talk through our eyes for a while because neither of us knows what to say.

Finally I break the ice. "Jacob, this is scary. We can't talk like this. We can't be alone like this anymore."

He looks like a wounded puppy. "I know," he finally says.

I shake my head emphatically. "Ezekiel would kick you out so fast—and probably me too."

His laugh is harsh. "He wouldn't kick you out, Eva. He'd marry you."

I gulp a mouthful of air. The idea of marrying him makes me shiver.

"He's got so many wives. I thought he was done marrying now. He's getting so old."

"I don't think so." He looks sad.

"Eva, I keep thinking that I should run. But I'd be lost out there. I have nowhere to go and no one to be with. And then there's the whole thing about hell. If Ezekiel's got it right and I run, I'll go to hell."

"I think you need to figure out a way to get along with him. It's the only way."

Jacob says nothing. So I nudge him. "You have to go now." I say it softly. "Your shift has been over for a while."

He pulls himself around to the top stair but pauses before he descends.

"Pray for me," he says. "I sure need it."

Twelve

Lookout in the hayloft is the most excruciatingly boring thing ever. Especially since absolutely nothing is going on. The only thing that keeps me awake is fear that I'll fall. I'm tempted to blow the whistle just for a little excitement.

At least I have a lot to think about.

It's weird how everything is changing between Jacob and me just because our bodies are changing. I wonder if he really wanted to kiss *me*, or if he wanted to kiss a girl and I'm the only one on the compound near his age. And I ended up kissing him back. Does that mean I have those kinds of feelings for him or just wanted to see what it felt like?

It felt good.

The only other time I thought about kissing was when I was around that waiter, Trevor. But he's gotta be eighteen or so—way too old for me. And maybe he thinks I'm ugly like Ezekiel does.

Then it hits me. Ezekiel was so mean to me, the way he practically sneered when he looked at my body. If he's being mean to Jacob because he doesn't want Jacob to like me in that way, maybe he was being mean to me for the same reason. He wants me to be ashamed of my body so I don't take an interest in Jacob or anyone else.

It worked.

How long have I been up here? I'm bored and thirsty. I reposition myself and stick a piece of straw in my mouth to chew like I do in the summer when it's growing fresh in the fields. I spit it out immediately because of the moldy, almost rancid taste. No wonder we don't use this old hayloft anymore. It would poison the animals.

I don't realize I'm hungry until I see Rachel trudging through knee-high snow with a lunch bag and thermos in hand. I'm so excited to see someone that I shout "hello" a little too enthusiastically. She understands and simply laughs at me. She brings me a peanut butter sandwich she's made using the two end pieces, just the way I like it, and some fresh tea. This little kindness feels huge. I hug her.

"Do you have any idea when Ezekiel will be back?" I ask.

She shakes her head. "I pray he comes back today so we can go to the flea market Saturday. But with this snow, he might have trouble getting up here."

I nod, my mouth too full of peanut butter to answer in words. I've been praying for him to come back for several days. He gave strict instructions that no one could leave the compound while he and Mother Esther were gone, and we've come to a halt with beading because we're practically out of supplies. Plus it's fairly obvious that we're running low on groceries from the strange meals we get lately: buttered noodles and applesauce, oatmeal for dinner, "vegetable" soup that's little more than broth. This morning I heard we were almost out of yeast. That means bread will soon be a thing of the past unless we shop.

I take a swallow of tea to get the thick peanut butter down and finally respond. "Pray that Ezekiel hasn't spent all our money on guns so that we can afford food and beading supplies."

Rachel nods. "I do pray for that," she says. The sun glistens off something shiny, and I do a double take when I realize that I'm seeing the reflection of Ezekiel's Beemer, as he calls his BMW. The car makes its way slowly down the snow-covered road slipping here and there. Rachel dashes down the stairs and I begin to follow her without thinking.

"You can't come down, silly. You're still on duty."

I sigh dramatically, but to deaf ears. "Wait, Rachel. How much time do I have up here?

She looks at her watch. "Just about two more hours. You can do it!"

Brother Paul and several of the mothers scurry to greet Ezekiel and Mother Esther. Even from here, I can tell that Ezekiel is in a bad mood because of how he bolts from the car, gives them a cursory wave, and dashes into his trailer. Mother Esther appears to be giving the women orders. She points to the trunk and back-seat. The mothers begin unloading suitcases and all sorts of pack-ages. They bring boxes into the garage and take everything else to Ezekiel's trailer. Then everybody stands around, probably hoping for an invitation to go inside.

Brother Paul is the only one to remain inside for several min-utes longer. When he finally emerges, he heads right to the silo.

He waves his arms at me. "Come on down. I'm going to take your place. Ezekiel wants to see you and Mother Rachel." His stony face tells me nothing.

I'm relieved to get out of the loft but I can't help feeling anxiety. What could he possibly want from me? But I scramble down the ladder, grateful to get off security duty.

When I pass the disappointed women still standing hopefully around Ezekiel's car, I find Rachel waiting for me at the trailer door. She doesn't seem to be worried. In fact, she looks thrilled. It's a compliment to be the first wife Ezekiel wants to see when he returns from a trip. But it sure doesn't thrill me.

Rachel rings the doorbell and we wait. In a low voice she says, "I'll ask Ezekiel to let us spend a full day in Boulder. Not for just the flea market and bead supplies, but to buy fabric for Mother Rebecca. The twins have outgrown their clothes, and she wants to make them new outfits for Christmas. Also we've got to get groceries."

Christmas is only three weeks away. We don't give presents but we do celebrate. Anyone who has outgrown or worn out an article of clothing will have it replaced before the Christmas service.

When Mother Esther lets us in, Ezekiel is pacing back and forth in the living room.

"Sit," he commands.

We make room on the sofa by moving a few packages and sit.

"It's good to have you home," Rachel says.

I smile at him but say nothing.

"Mother Esther and I were able to get all the guns and ammunition we need to protect Righteous Path."

A hot flash of anger makes me want to be bold. I want to ask him if he spent our food money on guns, but I hide my feelings by lowering my head.

When I look up, I see that his face is sunken and pale. His eyes are dull, and even his eyebrows have turned white. If this is because of the possible intruder, his reaction is certainly over-blown. I wonder if Ezekiel has a reason I don't know about that makes this information so alarming.

He's still pacing back and forth between the living room and dining room. "I want you two to keep going into Boulder to sell your jewelry and do the shopping, but you can't wear Righteous Path clothes. They make you look conspicuous."

Rachel and I look at each other, confused.

"If you were to wear Righteous Path clothing, someone could follow you home. Besides me, you will be the only ones to leave here until we're certain that we're safe. I want you to be alert and careful when you're in town. You cannot bring attention to the compound."

I'm careful to hide my relief and enthusiasm underneath a somber nod. It's not just selling jewelry and buying supplies; it's the idea of learning everything I can about the outside world and the enemy, who's scary and fascinating at the same time.

He digs through the packages and pulls out two green plastic bags. He hands one to each of us. "Mother Esther did some shopping at the Goodwill and found these."

Rachel and I exchange shocked looks. She pulls out a navy-blue, button-down sweater from her bag and a skirt in the same color. These really are street clothes. She nods—a carefully disciplined lack of emotion on her face—and reaches into the bag once again. As she takes out a pair of feminine-looking shoes, also in navy, I have to wonder what Mother Esther was thinking when she chose them. The shoes have heels! Small heels, but heels. Finally she pulls out a white blouse that has little ruffles going down the front.

"Thank you," Rachel says. Her cheeks redden when her eyes meet Ezekiel's. Mother Esther has come into the room and nods to each of us.

Ezekiel looks away as if the whole thing is an embarrassment.

I can't wait to open my bag. Regular clothes! I'll look like any other girl in Boulder.

Mother Esther repeats what we've been told by Ezekiel. "You'll only be wearing these clothes when you go to town, of course." Rachel and I both nod.

Finally it's my turn. I reach into my bag. The skirt is like Rachel's only in a burnt orange, and instead of a sweater, they've bought me a short burnt-orange jacket. The blouse is a bronze color and, like Rachel's, has soft ruffles down the front. My shoes are flat and a disappointing black.

"They're called loafers," Ezekiel says. He pulls the matchstick he's been chewing out of his mouth and replaces it with a fresh one that he takes from his shirt pocket. He drops the old one into a bowl on the coffee table and resumes pacing.

"Go try this stuff on in my bedroom."

"Can you believe it?" Rachel whispers when we get to the bedroom. But I'm too busy gaping. Ezekiel's bedroom is three times the size of mine. The walls are painted two shades of green. Three walls are painted a medium shade of green, and the wall with the bed against it is a darker green. I've never seen a king-sized bed before but I've heard the women talking, and it's every bit as large as they've said. I count nine pillows in varying shades of green and burgundy, just like the bedspread. His dresser takes up most of one wall with the largest mirror above it that I've ever seen. On each side of the bed sits a little table with a lamp on it. Ezekiel's cell phone and Bible are on the right side, so I imagine that's where he sleeps.

But I don't want to think about where he sleeps or anything else that may happen in that bed.

By the time I start changing my clothes, Rachel is almost dressed and looking in the mirror. She bends her arm so that her hand touches her hip, then pushes the hip out. I giggle, then clap a hand over my mouth to stifle myself.

"Shhhh!" she says. "We can't let Ezekiel hear us laugh."

I nod. "You look great," I whisper.

"So do you. Look," she says and pushes me in front of the mirror.

I don't know the person wearing these clothes. The burnt orange brings out my green eyes. The bronze blouse seems to make my auburn hair shine more. I think I might actually look pretty.

God forgive me for my vanity, I quickly pray.

"Ezekiel is right—no one would ever guess that we're members of Righteous Path. But these aren't exactly the kind of clothes teens are wearing on the streets of Boulder either," I say.

"The word is 'dowdy,'" Rachel says. "Thank goodness anything goes in Boulder, and at least we won't be dressed exactly alike."

"You look so retro," I say, imitating the lady in the bead store. I still don't know what "retro" means.

A sharp knock on the door pulls me out of my reverie. It's Mother Esther.

"These were left in the car." The package contains two pairs of tights, one for each of us. She looks us up and down. "Well, it works. You two certainly look common. Come show Ezekiel. Don't worry about the stockings now."

Ezekiel quickly looks us up and down, scowls, and motions us to go away. "They're fine for the heathen world. But I can't bear seeing you two look like sluts. Take them off!"

Rachel and I practically stumble over each other racing to the bedroom to change. This time I'm too ashamed to look in the mirror. I cannot unbutton the blouse fast enough, and it's a relief to get back into my everyday clothes.

"Much better," Ezekiel says. "Now, you'll keep your heathen clothes in my garage. You'll change there when you go into town so the others won't have to see you. Understood?"

"Yes, sir," we both say.

"Rachel, I need the rest of the money you took in at the flea market."

"No!" I blurt. Too late, I realize what I've done. "Sir, forgive me. It's just that we gave you everything except the money we need to buy more supplies."

The look on his face makes me cringe. He is so furious that I expect him to hit me. I'm the one holding the money, so I reach inside my skirt pocket and pull out the wad of bills.

He grabs it from my hand and points his right index finger less than an inch from my nose. The sulfur smell makes me a little sick to my stomach.

"*You* do not decide how money is distributed. *You* decide nothing!"

My knees buckle and I find myself unintentionally back on the couch.

When he finishes counting the money, he swings around to face Rachel. "*You* are entrusted with the money, not her." I feel like scum again.

"You made a lot last time," he says. "Good job." Again he directs the compliment to Rachel as if I don't exist. My stomach lurches and I'm afraid I might throw up.

"So how are supplies? Are you completely out?"

"We're down to practically nothing, but we do have a few pieces we made from scraps while you were gone."

"Buy inexpensive supplies to keep your costs down, then sell high." He hands some bills to Rachel. "Be creative, Rachel. And remember that it is *you* I've put in charge."

As we walk out, he glares at me again. I shudder at the thought that he's holding a grudge.

Thirteen

"Eva, are you asleep?" Annie asks.

"Yes," I say, wishing it was true. I'm wide-awake, worried about the Community Concerns Meeting tomorrow. Ezekiel is so mad at me. He could punish me for trying to control the jewelry money. But if he stops to realize that I'm the reason we made so much, maybe he'll let it go. *Please, God.*

I didn't tell Annie what happened. If she got worried, that could trigger an asthma attack. But more likely she wouldn't be sympathetic because everyone knows I need to learn my place and not speak in boldness.

Annie giggles. "Well, if you wake up, I have something to say."

"Go ahead. I'm listening."

"I've been thinking about the Community Concerns Meeting tomorrow."

"Me too."

"I'm worried," Annie says. "I think Ezekiel may know about Jacob. How he feels about you."

Volts of anxiety practically electrocute me. I sit straight up. "What are you talking about?"

Annie sits up too. "Eva, Jacob's smitten with you. Can't you tell?"

"What makes you say that?" I bite the inside of my lip so hard that I can taste blood.

"He follows you around. Sometimes he looks at you like he adores you or something."

"Oh no!" It's all I can manage to say. I take a moment to think.

"I can't believe how you tune in to stuff like that. I just figured out that he liked me." I bite the inside of my cheek. "Do you think anyone else has noticed?"

"That's what I'm worried about. If someone reports him, or Ezekiel knows, it will be really bad for Jacob. For you too. Do you like Jacob, Eva?"

The light from the waxing moon surrounds Annie's face and softens her so that she looks angelic. Her eyes are wide and innocent as she waits for me to respond.

I sit up straighter and make my voice strong. "No. Not like a boyfriend. Jacob is my friend—that's it."

It's true. I've thought about it a lot since the hayloft, and I realize that I liked being kissed but I'm not interested in Jacob.

"Good," she says. "I didn't think so. I never see you look at him in that way. I couldn't stand it if you liked him. If you did, I'd never get any time with you. Now maybe I'll get some sleep."

"Right," I say. "Get some sleep."

But sleep for me is even more elusive than before. Now I realize that Jacob's been acting obvious about his feelings for me. I pray that no one else has noticed or there'll be hell to pay.

When it's finally time for Community Concerns, I'm so frazzled that I almost don't care what happens. Anything has to be better than all this nervousness.

Before the meeting starts, I take a minute to look around the little chapel. Everyone seems tense, and they divert their eyes when anyone looks at them. This is the way it is when Ezekiel's in a bad place—fear tramples any loving feeling.

We begin by saying a prayer for each member to be honest and courageously examine their faults. When the prayer is over, Ezekiel asks for confessions.

I know that I have to confess my impertinence with Reverend Ezekiel, but I can't seem to find my voice. To my horror, he looks right at me. He shifts from one leg to the other. I stand up before he calls me out.

"I confess that I was impertinent with Reverend Ezekiel yesterday." My legs are jelly but I keep my face flat, free from emotion. I hardly recognize my scared little-girl voice.

Oh dear God, please don't let him beat me. I did the right thing; I confessed. Surely he'll take that into consideration.

"Come up here, Eva," he says.

My Jell-O legs somehow make it to the pulpit.

"Sit," he says, pointing to the only chair. His voice is almost gentle, much to my relief. The only sound in the room is the old chair creaking as I sit down.

"Eva, tell the congregation what you said to me that was impertinent."

I want to say something, explain, make him understand, but when I open my mouth, nothing comes out. I try again and again but my voice remains frozen.

A loud thud startles me into jumping, and I land crumpled on my knees. He hits the podium with a closed fist for a second time. My head jerks in the direction of the thud. The source of the noise must have been his fist hitting the podium. It is still clenched. I'm pulled into the vast darkness that his eyes have become, swallowed by his rage. This is the rage that he poured over the traitors who walked away during the big trial. It's the rage that he drowned Jacob in when he beat him so hard. It's the hatred that envelops him when he talks about the evil government and the fate of the Branch Davidians.

If my feet would only work, I'd run. But every cell inside me is frozen, as if the witch of Narnia has me under her spell.

"I hope that woke you up, Eva. Now explain what you did," he demands.

To my amazement, my body actually obeys and I am able to scooch back onto the chair. When I start to talk, I squeak like Mother Rose. "I said no to Reverend Ezekiel when he said he was going to keep all the money from our jewelry sales."

The shock is audible. Even Annie lets out a little gasp. That stings.

"I didn't mean it like it sounds. It's just...we needed money and..." From the looks I get I can see it's pointless to try and defend myself.

"Are you hearing this?" Ezekiel says to the group. "Eva wants to tell *me* how Righteous Path funds should be used."

Several of the mothers shake their heads or "tsk" in response.

I sink into the reality that he's right. They're all right. I'm willful. I'm impulsive. As scared as I am, I know that I deserve to be

punished. My eyes inadvertently wander to the paddle on the wall.
I'm betting that it will be at least as bad as the one Jacob got.

"We must help Eva learn obedience. We must help her finally
surrender to God as her Lord and to me as God's chosen minister."

Dear God, help me to bear this. I struggle to breathe.

"Did you bring what I asked, Mother Esther?"

She nods, stone faced and sad eyed. "It's on the podium."

My heart is beating faster than I knew it could. Ezekiel returns
to the podium and picks up a pair of scissors. When he holds it out
for everyone to see, I feel faint.

I cover my head with my arms as if I can protect myself this way.

One of the women, probably Martha, starts to cry. Others
whisper; someone moans.

"No, please!" I beg. "I'll be good. I'll be obedient. I'll take anything else for punishment."

"Say yes, Eva. Yes to this punishment. Show us that you are
willing to learn obedience. Show God that you will say yes to His
will, that you will be submissive."

He grabs a handful of hair. I'm sobbing. "Please…"

"Say yes to obedience, Eva." He yanks my hair hard.

"I'll change. I promise!"

He cuts a handful of hair close to my scalp. My shoulders heave
with sobs. My hair. Not my hair. But it makes no difference. He
keeps cutting.

"Yes!" I scream, praying that the word will make him stop.
It doesn't.

"Say it again," he demands.

Long waves of auburn hair—my hair—cover the floor in front

of me. "Yes!" I scream. My head feels naked. "Yes, I'll obey. Yes, I'll submit." All of the energy drains from my body. I go limp. Ugly now. So ugly. I want to hide.

He returns the scissors to the podium and admonishes Mother Martha for her interference by crying so loudly.

Earlier I'd noticed how good Mother Martha looked today. She had color in her face, and if it weren't for the big bump of a tummy, she could have been her old self, healthy and happy. Now all the color is gone, and she shakes as she looks at me and mouths the words, "I love you."

Ezekiel lifts my chin and forces me to look at him. His eyes are softer now that his anger is spent, but they hold no kindness. "Let the shame of this help you change. I believe you are capable of becoming the obedient girl you're called to be."

His words turn a switch in me. I lower my eyes, not out of the shame he wants me to feel, but because of the risk that my anger will show.

Sometime during the night when I finally drift into sleep, Mother Martha awakens me with a kiss on the forehead. She places a finger over her mouth and motions me to follow her. We go into the bathroom where we can have a bit of privacy. She holds me as I sit on the side of the bathtub. I bury my head against her big tummy, and she rocks me back and forth.

For a time I feel safe and loved in her arms. When I finally pull away, I see that her eyes are red and puffy as if she too has been crying all night.

"I'm sorry," she says. She repeats it over and over. "I should have...I never should have..." She doesn't finish either thought, and I haven't the energy to try to figure out what she's saying. Her hands stroke the nubs of hair on my head, and another wave of grief brings me literally to my knees.

Again she rocks me. I don't want her to ever stop but she finally straightens up, gives her head a little shake as if to wake herself up, and takes a comb out of her pocket.

"You know, I used to be good at doing hair. If you'll let me, I can shape it up for you, even it out some."

I shrug my shoulders. Most of my hair feels one or two inches long, but a few shoulder-length strands remain. I must look totally ridiculous. I wonder how she thinks she's going to do anything to make it look better.

She pulls small sewing scissors out of her pocket and motions for me to sit on the toilet lid. She snips and combs, snips and combs. My almost-bald head is cold without hair. When she's finished, she suggests I look in the mirror. I shake my head. The thought makes me feel like I might throw up.

"Think of the girls you see in town," she says, wearing a faint smile. "Don't you think some of them look good with short haircuts?"

I do, actually, but I never dreamed I would wear mine short.

She takes my hand and nods toward the mirror. I look down, but she raises my chin and holds firm. Finally I draw enough courage from her determination to play peek-a-boo with my reflection. In several quick glances, I see that the hair on the top of my head sticks up straight, like the twins' cowlick. The sides and back are a bit longer, maybe three inches.

Just when I think I'm all cried out, tears spring to my eyes all over again.

"I'm so ugly!"

Mother turns my face toward hers so that I have to look right at her. "No, Eva, that's the thing. You're not ugly. You're beautiful. It would be a strange-looking haircut for most people but it looks exotic on you."

I look but I can't see what she's talking about. My eyes are red. My cheeks are blotchy. My neck seems too long. And with the chopped hair, I look like a boy.

"I used to have a picture of me when I was about your age. I had a short haircut too. People would tell me that I was beautiful and I couldn't see it either. But looking at you, I finally see what they were seeing. You've got big, expressive eyes, and look at your eyelashes. They're long and beautiful, as if you're wearing mascara."

I hug my mother again and think about how brave she is to have slipped out of her trailer to come to me tonight.

"I didn't think you thought about things like beauty," I say.

Mother gets a faraway look in her eyes. She kisses me on the forehead. "You're beautiful," she says, as if it's final.

She leaves then, as quietly as she came.

The first morning light filters through my bedroom window when I finally return to bed. Ezekiel can make me say yes when I mean no, I think. He can make me submissive and obedient, but he can't control everything. He can't control my thoughts or memories. Like my book, *The Lion, the Witch, and the Wardrobe*. He burned it, but it will always remain in my heart. I can't hold it or read the words again, but the story is a part of me.

I picture Narnia and Aslan the Lion. He's come back to Narnia and winter is giving way to a beautiful spring. He's so big, so strong, so beautiful. In his eyes I see how much he loves. His love is so gigantic that it swallows me up. And when he looks at me, I feel like I'm somebody.

The scene changes in a flash. Aslan is sprawled on a slab, his beautiful mane shorn, sadness blocking out the light that usually fills his eyes. Nearby, the White Witch is laughing her haughty laugh, reeling in her success at bringing him down.

I run to him and hold him. I try to return some of the love he gives so freely. He touches my head with a soft paw and weeps. He is not weeping for his own naked head, but for mine. I know this. I can feel it.

It's all so real—brighter than a dream, more perfect than reality. I feel loved. And I finally fall asleep, nestled next to him.

Fourteen

The next several days are terrible. I know it's the sin of pride to be this crushed by my appearance, but I can't seem to pray my way out of it. It's another mealtime and the twins gape at me again, even though they've been corrected over and over by one or another mother for staring. "Is she a boy now?" David asks. A room full of "shhhhhh's" is followed by complete silence.

I lose all interest in eating.

Whenever I see Ezekiel, I wonder again why he chose such a severe punishment to teach me a lesson. Did it have to do with Jacob? Did he want me to be less attractive to Jacob? If so, it worked. Jacob avoids me completely now. I know I asked him to ignore me after he kissed me, but now I think he can't bear to look at me like this.

Unlike Jacob, Ezekiel looks at me all the time. His attention makes me smolder inside. At first his eyes and mouth told me he was satisfied, that he was glad about the horrible punishment he chose for me. But yesterday he went out of his way to walk next to me on the way out of chapel. He let me know that he was glad that the jewelry I made is so popular with the heathens. He let me know that my work was providing a service to help Righteous Path.

My body stiffens and my guts roil even now when I think of it. Is he trying to say he's sorry? Is he trying to win back my love? I'm not sure about much anymore, but I'm sure that I feel no love for him.

Something keeps gnawing at me. If Aslan and Jesus are supposed to be alike and Ezekiel is getting messages directly from Jesus, then why is Ezekiel so harsh and Aslan so loving? I know that Aslan is just a character in a book, but there is something so true and right about the way he loves and protects and teaches and forgives. The author, C. S. Lewis, must have seen God as loving, or he would have made Aslan different.

That awful lump takes over my throat again, and I couldn't speak if I wanted to. Is this God's way of telling me that my thoughts are heresy? Or am I choking on beliefs that no longer fit for me?

I give up trying to eat my oatmeal but it would be sinful to waste it, so I have to see if someone else wants it. Mother Martha is actually here this morning, and she looks pretty healthy. I approach her table with my bowl. "Any chance you're up for seconds?" Her smile is a healing balm.

"Sure," she says. "It's great to have an appetite again."

Ezekiel and Jacob are talking in the doorway to the dining room, and I feel trapped inside until they move. I have no idea what they're talking about, but they seem animated and relaxed, which is a long way from where they were a few weeks ago. I'm happy for Jacob. He's always craved Ezekiel's approval.

Ezekiel catches me watching the two of them. "Go get Annie," he says. "You girls are going to learn how to shoot today."

Oh no. I hope he doesn't plan on participating. I head to the barn where I know Annie's doing chores.

"Well, who's going to feed these poor animals?" Annie complains. She hates it when somebody uproots her day, and she's certainly not happy about the idea of shooting a gun.

"Don't worry. We'll tell someone," I reassure her.

"I wonder how Brother Paul can give us shooting lessons when he's patrolling the property," Annie says. The mystery is solved as soon as we get back to the dining room.

"I've heard that Jacob is quite the marksman," Ezekiel says. "I want to see him shoot, then I'll watch him teach you two."

"Yes, sir," Annie and I both say.

Jacob breaks into a wide smile that he shares with Ezekiel and Annie. He avoids looking at me. He walks a few steps behind Ezekiel, with Annie and me trailing behind him. Annie chews on her fingernails the way she does when she's nervous. I take it as a cue that I should try to lighten things up so she doesn't go into an asthma attack. But under the circumstances I can't think of anything to do, so I just squeeze her hand and smile.

I don't really care if I can shoot well or not. I just want to get through the lesson as quickly as possible and away from Ezekiel and Jacob.

We walk about a half mile into the hay fields to the place Brother Paul has set up for target practice. I expect to see the same kind of target that was on the side of the outhouse when we first moved in. Brother Paul said it had been there since he was a kid. That target had circles and a bull's-eye. But these targets are different. They're attached to trees at various distances, and they are drawings of human bodies with holes all over from previous shooters.

Jacob attaches new pictures of human forms to each of the targets. "Where do you want me to start?" he asks Ezekiel.

"At the beginning," Ezekiel says.

Jacob gives a little nod. "This one's going between the heathen's eyes." BAM! The hit is perfect. He aims toward the next target. "This one's going into the heathen's heart." Another perfect shot.

Ezekiel paces back and forth while Jacob is getting set up.

Jacob hits the first three targets just the way he called them. The first one between the eyes, the next two straight through the heart. I sneak a peek at Ezekiel. A thin smile threatens to break through his seriousness. "Continue," he says. "But go ahead and skip to the farthest target. And this time hit him between the eyes."

"Yes, sir," Jacob says. He pulls out the other gun from his two-gun holster. And though the target is so far away that I can barely pinpoint the space between the target's eyes, Jacob hits it.

I'm surprised. Instead of the loud bang the other shots made, this one makes a little "pop" sound and that's it.

"Aren't those silencers amazing?" Ezekiel says. "You wouldn't know what that was if you were ten feet away." He lumbers over to the wooden box that sits on the ground near the first target and opens the lid. Inside is a collection of items Brother Paul put together for shooting practice. From where I'm standing, I see a roll of papers with the outline of a body, a hammer, nails, and a can of red spray paint. Ezekiel picks up the paint and walks well beyond the targets to a huge maple tree. He sprays an *X* the size of a small orange on the trunk. "Can you hit this?" he asks Jacob.

"I think so," Jacob says. Ezekiel resumes his position, pacing behind Annie and me, and watches as Jacob aims and shoots.

"Perfect!" Ezekiel hollers. "Absolutely perfect! Take a look at that, girls."

Annie and I stand in awed silence as we look at Jacob's work. I run my fingers over the bullet holes, and goose bumps run up and down my arms and legs. If these were real people, they'd be dead.

I don't want to shoot anyone. I don't even want to shoot a paper person.

"How in the world did you learn this?" Ezekiel asks.

"I don't know," Jacob says. "Brother Paul says I'm just a natural. And he's let me practice quite a lot."

"God has given you this gift so that you can protect Righteous Path, my son."

I've never heard him call Jacob his son. And Jacob instantly looks taller. He's so happy.

"I want you to teach the girls how to shoot. Do you think you can do that?"

Jacob responds with an enthusiastic yes.

"Good, because Brother Paul has spent so much time with you shooting that these two haven't had one lesson."

It's the moment I've been dreading, but I want Jacob to continue to shine so I listen carefully to his instructions and follow them closely. He still avoids eye contact, but I can't blame him with the way I look and with Ezekiel right here.

After twenty minutes I get a bit more comfortable shooting, but

I haven't hit anywhere near the heart or the head. I hit the left leg once, the chin another time, and I graze the right shoulder once.

That's a lot better than Annie. It's hard to know where her bullets end up. After several efforts, it's clear that she's only becoming more upset, so Jacob takes the gun from her and suggests that he give her a lesson another day.

Ezekiel gets irritated with Annie—not because of her shooting, but because she cries so easily. "If we get attacked," Ezekiel says, "you're dead meat. You've got to toughen up, girl."

But to Jacob he says, "You are a good teacher. Your instructions are clear. You know when to push and when to stop." He pretend-punches Jacob's shoulder, smiling.

I'm happy for Jacob. He's found himself a niche and Ezekiel is finally proud of him. I just wish I hadn't been turned into an ugly person so that Ezekiel could stop worrying about Jacob and me wanting to be together.

"Eva," Annie says that night, "is Ezekiel making you go to Boulder tomorrow?"

"Yes."

"It must be horrible for you to be seen in public right now."

"Don't worry," I say as if it's no big deal. But it is. This will be the first time I'll be in public since my hair was butchered. Rachel went bead and grocery shopping without me on Monday because I simply couldn't face it. I had to pretend I was sick and gave Rachel detailed instructions about the beads and supplies I wanted. She was great about it. But she hated having Mother Esther as her partner. Mother Esther didn't like it any better. She had to squeeze into my street clothes, which she referred to as an "abomination." Rachel said that I would have gotten a good laugh if I'd seen her.

I dip my toothbrush in the dreaded baking soda that we now use instead of toothpaste. I begin brushing my teeth vigorously, looking at Annie's face to avoid the mirror. I shrug my shoulders and spit in the sink. Then I turn on the faucet and quickly catch some water in cupped hands to get rid of the awful taste.

"Rachel said she'd make me a scarf if I want."

Annie's eyes grow huge. "She could get in so much trouble for that!"

"Oh, she wouldn't make it without permission." I add to cover my tracks. I'm a bit surprised at Annie's reaction. It's not like her to make a big deal out of a little infraction. There was something else I was going to share with her but now I hesitate. It's that Mother Esther told Rachel that the money Ezekiel gave them for groceries was the end of our savings from the ranch contract last summer. Rachel said that even Mother Esther wondered aloud if maybe they shouldn't have bought so many guns.

But now I decide not to share this with Annie. Because she seems skittish about the rules.

Actually, I'm not as upset as Annie thinks about going to Boulder. I'm nervous about my hair, but it's the first time I'll get to wear the heathen clothes Ezekiel and Esther picked out for me. I was actually looking forward to fitting in, but now that my hair's been chopped, I'm afraid I'll look like a freak. For some reason, Trevor, the guy from the Wi-Fi Café, comes to mind. He'd be so shocked to see me like this.

Now Annie puts her arm around my waist. "I think you're still beautiful."

Tears sting my eyes. I stare down at her gorgeous head of hair. Perfect hair—long, black, shiny, never dry or frizzy. She's been careful to wait till I'm in bed to brush it herself these past few days. I've been touched by her kindness, but tonight when we get to our room, I reach for the brush on our shared dresser and motion her to sit on the edge of her bed. She loosens her braids and lets her hair fall over her shoulders. I start brushing.

When I kneel beside my bed and try to say my prayers, I picture God as angry, the way Ezekiel often portrays him. My whole body starts to tremble. After a while I give up trying to pray and crawl into bed. When I close my eyes, Aslan is there again. He seems to live right beneath my eyes when I close them, as real as real can be. We're back in Narnia. The land is thawing.

After so many years of winter under the control of the White Witch, the land is waking up, remembering spring, all because Aslan has returned. In this Narnia, the air is warm, the snow is almost gone, and streams that had been frozen for so long are flowing freely. As far as I can see are green meadows. Clusters of wildflowers pop up everywhere, and I actually witness them growing right before my eyes. I could sit here forever drinking in their perfume.

I drift into a peaceful sleep.

Fifteen

When I meet Rachel in the garage for our trip to Boulder, I find her in a rare mood.

"Too bad we don't have some of the stuff heathens put in their hair to make it stand up straight. A little gel would make your hair perfect for Boulder," she teases.

I'm so happy to be getting away from all the tension on the compound that I'm not even worrying about my hair. I scrunch up one leg of my tights the way Rachel does, then sit on the floor to stretch them over one leg, then the other. I love how soft and warm the fabric feels, but they barely cover my thighs. When Rachel sees my stricken face, she erupts into giggles.

"You have to stretch them up a tiny bit at a time starting at the ankles. Then they'll fit."

Rachel laughs hysterically, watching me dance my way into them.

"I can't believe any fabric can stretch this much. Whew! I'm glad you've had experience in the outside world."

For some reason, after that we giggle over every little thing on the way to Boulder. It's the lightest I've felt for a long time and it feels good. The mood keeps up all the way to town, since the roads are thankfully decent today.

We don't get serious until we start setting up our booth in Boulder. Now that the weather has gotten so cold, the flea market is no longer outdoors. It's in the basement of a library. But we've still been getting lots of business. It helps that Christmas is right around the corner. When we're all set up and have been selling for about a half hour, I notice that Rachel looks pale.

"Cramps," she tells me. "And I'm totally unprepared." She excuses herself to use the bathroom.

At first I panic. Left to sell by myself, I'm self-conscious and humiliated about my appearance. But it gets busy suddenly and the only ones who pay attention to my appearance are regulars. Shocked, they look me up and down to take in the new outfit and new almost-bald head. Thankfully, no one says anything, so I resist the urge to crawl under the table.

Because we had so little money to invest in the project, I got the idea to buy cord and leather laces as well as sterling silver chain so that we could space out the expensive beads and keep the costs down. We did save money and the jewelry is still beautiful, but it's different from what we'd sold before. It doesn't take long for people to notice.

"Where are those necklaces I saw here last week?" a middle-aged blond woman asks. "I'm looking for the one with lapis and crystal, but I don't see it."

I recognize her. She's back with her darling little girl and tiny dog. The dog has bows on her ears and wears a jeweled collar. She is so white that she looks like she has a bath every single day. I've never seen anything like it. Even when the woman studies a piece of jewelry, she continues to hold the dog or hands her over to her daughter to hold. I wonder if either of them knows that dogs can walk.

"We don't have anything like that this time," I apologize. "But we do have lapis earrings, and this chain necklace has a few lapis stones."

She groans but continues examining each piece, setting aside a few things to buy when she's finished looking.

By the time I look up and see Rachel returning, I have already sold a number of pieces. Rather than running back and forth to the cash box with each purchase, I'd simply slipped the money in my pocket for the last several transactions.

Rachel motions me to her when she reaches the booth. "There are no supplies in the bathroom," she whispers. "I have to find a store. Can you handle this by yourself a while longer?"

My heart sinks a little. I wish I could be the one leaving. I could use a break. But there's nothing to be done so I agree.

It's strictly against the rules to be without a partner in public, but there is no better option. I force a half smile and begin waiting on a customer. Rachel stops to count the money in the cash box. I want to tell her about the money in my pocket, but I can't without interrupting my client. When she's done counting, she holds up the five-dollar bill she's taking for her personal supplies and mouths "good job." I smile, knowing that she'll be even more pleased when she finds out how much I've really taken in.

I'm searching for a specific bracelet under the table when Annie begins to wheeze. Then I remember that Annie's not here. When I look up, I see that the little girl is doing the wheezing.

The woman drops her stack of purchases on the counter.

"Oh, Tiffany," the mother says. She holds the dog out in front of me. "Would you hold Shapoopsy while I dig out Tiffany's inhaler?"

Shapoopsy can't weigh more than four pounds and she smells like flowers. She licks my hand and cuddles against my chest like it's the most natural thing in the world to be passed from one person to another.

Tiffany's asthma gets bad fast. Her mother routs around in her handbag while talking in a soft voice to her daughter. After what seems an eternity, she pulls out a plastic contraption. It has a wide top. Tiffany opens her mouth and breathes in the substance when her mother pushes down on the top. I can hear the little puff emitted from the inhaler. They repeat the process. This time Tiffany manages a deeper breath. I pet Shapoopsy and watch in amazement as Tiffany's breathing continues to improve over the next couple of minutes.

I must look as shocked as I feel because the woman laughs when she sees my face. "You've never seen an inhaler before?"

I shake my head and repeat the word inhaler.

"The marvels of modern medicine!" she says, smiling brightly. "I don't know what we'd do without it."

She takes sleeping Shapoopsy back from me and hands me two one-hundred-dollar bills. I count out fifty dollars in change and hold it out to her.

"No, honey, that's for you," she chirps. "Merry Christmas! And keep making the beautiful gemstone pieces!"

A Christmas gift. For me? And it's fifty whole dollars. I have to give it to Ezekiel, of course. But the *idea* of someone giving me this much money to spend any way I want—it's wonderful! By the time I open my mouth to say "thank you," they've already moved on. I holler "Thank you!" anyway and hope they can hear me through the crowd.

I can't seem to let go of my gift. Instead, I place the money in my left skirt pocket, keeping it separate from the jewelry money in my right pocket. I add up all the jewelry money, except for my gift, and discover that we have more than six hundred dollars. Since there are no customers at the moment, I collapse into one of the folding chairs Rachel and I brought from the compound and imagine what I could do with the fifty dollars if I kept it.

After all, Rachel used tip money to pay for our lunch that day. There's so much I could do with the money. I could find a way to buy extra food for Mother. I could buy more expensive beads and make gorgeous pieces to sell. Maybe I could even get one of those inhaler things for Annie.

It was a miracle how that inhaler worked on Tiffany. One minute she couldn't breathe. Then she used the inhaler, and she could breathe normally after only a couple of minutes.

"Modern medicine," the woman had said lightly. It made me want to cry. If Annie had modern medicine, she wouldn't suffer so much. "Annie is suffering for her sins," Ezekiel always says. But it's hard to imagine why God would want Annie to suffer while Tiffany is able to get instant relief. If modern medicine could do this for asthma, what more could it do for Mother's difficult pregnancy?

Ezekiel's argument is that all women must suffer in childbirth because of Eve tempting Adam in the Garden of Eden. I remember him announcing that he named me Eva to remind all members of how Eve stole the Garden of Eden from Adam and the rest of the world by tempting him. I felt so ashamed. For weeks I cringed each time someone said my name.

I shrug off the old feelings of shame. Instead I close my eyes and picture Aslan.

If God is loving like Aslan, he would want Annie to be healthy. If God is loving like Aslan, he wouldn't want Mother, or any women, to suffer in childbirth.

I jerk into the present moment when I hear a male voice.

"Excuse me, would you happen to know…"

I look up into the shocked face of the waiter from the Wi-Fi Café. "Trevor!"

"Eva?"

He looks me up and down. "You've changed!"

The world is frozen in the moment. I'm happy to see him, but in a flash, I remember what I look like. In my worst moments I've imagined the horrified expression I'd see on Trevor's face when he saw my shorn hair. Instead, Trevor explodes into laughter. He looks me up and down.

I bristle, thinking he's making fun of me. But he's not. I realize this because his eyes are sparkling and his smile is warm. In fact, he seems delighted. Seeing this, my legs recover strength and my heart slows down its racing.

"I thought you must have skipped this week. I've been up and down these booths three times. I just didn't recognize you because of your new look."

He scans my hair, my clothes, and my shoes, which happen to be killing me. "Look at you! That funky hairdo is going to take a little getting used to, but I think I like it."

"Funky?" I search my mind, trying to remember if I've heard that word before.

"You know, cool. Funky." He leans across the table. "Have you left the, the…"

"Righteous Path." I shake my head.

"Righteous Path," he repeats. "So that's the name of your religious community."

My stomach does flip-flops. I have just given private information to this, this outsider. Rachel and I discussed what to say if a regular customer asked about our clothes. Now it comes back to me. "Our community is becoming more modern." My words come out sounding practiced.

"You've changed too." I nod toward his hair. Where he flaunted a single pink streak on the left side of his head before, now his hair is dyed in two streaks of blue. Where he used to wear one earring in his right ear, he now wears two.

Trevor smiles. It's an easy, confident smile, like someone who never has to worry about going to hell. "Do you like it?"

I smile back and turn his own words back on him. "It'll take a little getting used to, but I think I'll like it. I don't see a lot of blue hair."

"I bet you don't," he says. His eyes scan the booth. "Where's Rachel?"

Oh. Disappointment sinks heavily inside my chest. He's interested in Rachel, not me.

Stop it! If he likes someone, it's not important.

"She'll be back soon," I say lightly. I look around as far as I can see. Come to think of it, she's been gone for a long time.

Trevor pulls out his cell phone. "Eleven twenty. I have to meet someone for lunch downtown at noon, but I wanted to talk to you two about getting your beading supplies online. I remember you said you couldn't because you didn't have a credit card, and I thought I could help."

Two college-aged girls stop at the booth to browse. I hold up a finger signaling to Trevor to wait a second while I attend to them.

Why is he doing this? He seems so nice, too nice. I can hear Ezekiel warning me to stay pure. He'd tell me Trevor was from the devil. I have to get rid of him before Rachel gets back. This has to be God testing me.

"We're just looking," one of the girls says.

"Let me know if I can help you with anything," I say.

To my surprise, I find that Trevor has placed a small computer on the table and is tapping away.

The crowd is thinning, and there's still no sign of Rachel. She's been gone for hours. Two booths down, the man selling local honey and homemade sausage is already folding up his table. My mouth waters at the idea of sausage, and a second later my stomach grumbles. But I can't have any food. Not in the middle of a fast.

"What are you doing?" I finally ask.

He looks momentarily puzzled. "I'm looking up some beading stuff for you."

"Why?" I ask.

"Just a second," he says. He hits a few keys and drums his fingers on the table impatiently while he waits for something to come up on the computer. "There!" he says, turning the screen so that I can see it too. "I wanted to make sure I could order the wire and chain too. I noticed you're using quite a bit of both along with the beads."

The screen is filled with different widths of silver chain. Prices and quantities are in big red letters. I gawk, amazed again at how easy it is to shop on a computer and how inexpensive everything is if you're willing to buy in quantity.

Trevor looks me straight in the eye. "Hey, it's an easy thing for me to do, and it's impossible for you to do without help."

His face is honest. He seems sincere.

"Plus," he continues, "I've never known anyone from an alternative religion before, and honestly, I figured it would be interesting to get to know you."

An alternative religion. Is that what outsiders call us? "I never thought of Righteous Path as a religion, or an alternative religion. It's just the right path for the chosen."

Trevor breaks into a wide smile. "That's what's so interesting. Right there. You've been so sheltered that you don't know anything about other people's beliefs."

"I've never known anyone who's not in Righteous Path. Since I was five anyway." And I've always wanted to know a heathen. But that part I keep to myself.

"Okay, thanks. But I still don't have a credit card," I add.

"That's okay because I have one."

A guy in a brown leather coat stands in front of me holding out a sausage and jar of honey. I recognize him from two booths down. It's the booth with the brightly colored sign that says *Homemade Sausage and Local Honey*. "Merry Christmas," he says, placing them on my table. And he's off.

I holler "Merry Christmas!" to his backside and look longingly at the sausage.

This is my second gift of the day from generous people. The third gift, if I count the one Trevor is offering me. From heathens. From people Ezekiel says are damned for eternity.

Trevor closes the top of his computer. "I don't want to pressure you, Eva. You can think about it and I'll come back another time."

"Wait!" The idea of him leaving wakes me up. I want this. Not just the cheap beads so the community will have more money, but the chance to learn more about the outside world from someone as kind as Trevor. "It's just that, it's that...You..." I blurt it out. "You have no idea how much trouble I could get into. If Rachel finds out, she could turn me in." I've been gesturing, and now he notices my trembling hands.

"Turn you in?" His face registers shock.

Silence.

"What would happen if Rachel turns you in?" He voice is soft now, so sympathetic I almost cry.

"Reverend Ezekiel punishes us to keep us pure for God. We have to perfect ourselves on earth so we can be saved." Automatically, I bring my hands to my hair, touching what little is there. His eyes open wide, and I see a flash of something on his face—an immediate understanding, shock, horror.

He knows. I can tell that he knows. I've said too much again, and now he knows that Ezekiel lopped off my hair as punishment.

I drop down on the chair, exhausted, and look around again for Rachel. Thankfully she's still not in sight.

Trevor offers a thin smile. "I'm so sorry, Eva. I had no idea that your community was so harsh. I'd never want to be the cause of you being punished. I should leave."

I shake my head vehemently. I can't let this chance pass me by. He could help us. He could help me. I could learn from him, even if he is a heathen. Especially if he's a heathen.

If I spend Righteous Path money on beading supplies, I will betray Ezekiel and all Righteous Path members. But I can't trust that Ezekiel will use the money for food or supplies.

And Mother Martha looks puny from not getting enough food. She needs good food for herself and for the baby. I have to take control over some of the money if I'm going to make sure she gets fed enough.

There, that's it. That's exactly it. Some kind of sickness has swept over Ezekiel—a kind of sick in the head—ever since Rachel and I told him about the stranger asking about a cult. That was weeks ago and we've heard nothing from the stranger, yet here we are stocking guns, learning to shoot, patrolling the grounds, ready to attack. Attack what? Attack who?

If I want there to be enough food for the winter, I have to take this opportunity Trevor is handing me. I pick up the sausage and honey, and hide them inside my coat.

Trevor stands in the same spot, watching me intently.

"I want to do this," I say.

"Really, you're still interested? Because I'd just put it on my credit card and you could give me cash when I get the bill. It would make your profit margin a lot higher. If—if it's not too dangerous."

I bite my lip, thinking. "We can't have a package come to the compound. Could the beads come to your house and we could meet somewhere for me to pick them up? We shop on Mondays and sell jewelry on Saturdays. So Mondays would be the best day to meet."

"What about Rachel?" Trevor asks.

"If she's with me, we'd have to be really sneaky, but I bet I could get her to go to Costco while I'm buying beads. It's more practical. Otherwise it takes all day for us to buy beads together and then grocery shop together. Especially now that we're the only ones going into town. We end up with lots of extra errands."

"We could meet at the library across from the bead store," Trevor says.

"Perfect," I say. The library. The idea of all those books and everything I could learn, maybe even about how to help Mother through her labor. Something shifts inside me, and though I'm about to take the biggest risk ever, I feel as if I'm standing on solid ground for the first time in my life.

I look around again. Rachel's still not coming. It's been something like two hours, and I can't imagine what's taking so long.

Trevor laughs. His face lights up. "This is turning into an adventure. I love adventures." His eyes cloud over. "But it wouldn't be worth it if you got hurt." He drums his fingers on the table again, thinking.

I could get hurt. Ezekiel would be furious and would punish me in ways I don't even want to imagine. And I could also get hurt by Trevor. He could run off with the money. If Ezekiel's right, Trevor's a mere heathen condemned to hell, not someone I should trust. But Ezekiel's beliefs are becoming harder to believe than Trevor's kindness. And the idea of someone like Trevor burning in hell for eternity doesn't make sense to me.

Even if Trevor does run off with the money, at least it won't be spent on weapons that destroy lives. "Let me show you what I want to order," I tell him.

Once we've done that, I reach into my pocket before I can chicken out. I pull out the fifty that was given to me as a gift and take out a hundred-dollar bill from the bead money. He looks shocked when I hand it to him. I watch him slip it in his backpack.

In the nick of time.

"Hey," Rachel says in a weak voice. "I'm so sorry. I was sick and fell asleep in the car." When she sees Trevor, she stops and registers surprise. "Oh, I remember you. Trevor, right?"

Sixteen

When we get to the van, Rachel is so sick with cramps that she can barely drive. She makes it out of Boulder but she pulls into the lookout minutes later.

"You're going to have to drive. I can't."

"But I don't know how!" She opens her door and throws up. She's so weak she practically falls to the ground.

"Oh, Rachel!" I jump out of the van to help her.

"You've gotta drive," she repeats.

My belly flips and I feel sick myself. Rachel gets sick with almost every period. I've even seen her faint. I have no choice. I have to meet this challenge. I exchange seats with Rachel and study the buttons and controls. "Please try to stay awake so you can supervise. I don't want us to go over the side of the mountain or crash Ezekiel's van into a tree."

"Of course," she says. "And I'll pray for you."

Rachel struggles to stay awake long enough to give me a lesson. Before we leave the overlook, I practice accelerating and slowing down, stopping and steering. The scariest thing is backing up. It's basically the same as the tractor Brother Paul let me drive a few times last summer, but everything's so sensitive. I barely touch the steering wheel and the van turns. It's the same with the gas and the brakes. After a few minutes of this, I take a deep breath and turn my signals on. I wait for a chance to pull onto the road.

While waiting for two cars to go by, I suddenly remember the money I gave to Trevor. *No!* I have to put that out of my mind. I need all my concentration for driving. The cars have passed and I ease onto the road.

"Good job," Rachel says in a barely audible voice. She drifts off to sleep almost immediately. I slam on the brakes the first time I see a sharp curve ahead. The guy behind me almost smashes into me, but he manages to brake first. He's mad, though. As soon as we're around the curve, he pulls up next to me, rolls down his window, and holds up his middle finger. I've never even heard some of the words he shouts. It shakes me up to think I made him so angry! I hug the side of the mountain, feeling safest as far as I can get from the drop.

Rachel is sound asleep. She barely responded when I slammed on the brakes.

I'm terrified. I decide to drive slowly, even if that means making people mad. They can pass me and yell obscenities and make their weird gestures, but I'm just learning to drive and I'm taking it slow.

Lord, please help me drive safely. Be my hands on the wheel. Be my eyes seeing clearly and my ears hearing.

I realize I've never said a prayer like that. Normally I would pray for Ezekiel to see and hear God's voice clearly.

The drive goes on and on. Slowly I gain confidence. I'm getting better at taking curves, getting the feel for how fast is safe, when to brake, and when to forge ahead. It helps that the farther we get from Boulder, the less traffic is on the road. When there's a straight stretch of road, I relax my grip on the steering wheel and even hum a little. But when I see a large icy patch on a narrow curve ahead, I'm terrified all over again and slam on my brakes. Rachel wakes up and I explain that the ice scared me.

"Never brake on ice. You'll lose control of the van. We're getting pretty close to Grand Hill." She drifts back to sleep.

"Really?" The knowledge of how far we've come makes me almost giddy. I begin to take in the beauty around me. Rays of sun make the snow glisten. I can see deeply into the pines, where light and shade make everything magical. There are no cars anywhere now, and we could be the only people in the world.

But suddenly a doe darts out in front of me. I hit the brakes, causing both of us to lurch forward. I'm literally inches from the doe. She freezes. She looks right at me with surprised eyes. So innocent, so sweet. "Go on, little doe," I say, my voice cracking. But she stays frozen.

"Turn the lights off," Rachel says. It takes me a bit to find the light switch, but when I turn them off, the doe comes alive and scampers away almost immediately. But it doesn't stop my tears. Where's her mother? Where's her family? She's so young to be her own.

"It's okay," Rachel says. "You're doing so well."

But it doesn't feel okay. I almost killed that deer.

We drive through Grand Hill without any problem. Now it's only three miles to the compound. But it takes another twenty minutes to get there because the road's so steep. When I can see the entrance, I'm so relieved that I speed up. Then I'm on ice. I forget and brake, and the van slips into the bank.

"Don't panic," Rachel says. "I think you can back out if this."

I look behind me. All I can see is the drop-off. "You're kidding! We'll plunge to our deaths."

Rachel holds her head. "Don't be so dramatic." She opens the door on the passenger side and steps into snow to her knees. "There's more room than you think. I'll direct you."

But I can't. Not until I see for myself. I force my door open and manage to get out. She's right. There's room if I ease out. But I'm not sure I'm in control enough of the gas to ease out.

"You do it."

"No, Eva. It's better for me to direct you."

Lord, oh Lord, please help me. Guide me.

Back in the van, I give it a try. The van moves back a few inches but then rocks back to where it was before. I try again. Same thing. I try a third time, but we simply rock like before.

"Give it more gas," Rachel says.

Sure. She's not the one who's going to die.

Don't abandon me, God. I'll do anything you want, be anything, but help me live.

I stretch my shoulders and arms because I'm so stiff. This time I give it more gas, and miraculously we're out. Rachel cheers in a weak voice and gets back in the van. It still takes a while to get the van turned around, and I'm exhausted when we turn into the compound.

I wave at Jacob, who's riding Berthoud, patrolling just inside the gate. He's got to be jealous seeing me in the driver's seat when he's never been allowed to drive. But he only smiles. His newfound position as protector must be making him feel—what's that word Mother Martha uses all the time?—magnanimous.

I drive straight into the garage because of wearing heathen clothes, but I'm so concerned about getting Rachel out of the van that I forget to close the garage door. Within a minute, half the mothers are inside, along with Annie.

The women are shocked to see me driving, but that quickly gives way to disgust when they see that we're wearing heathen clothes. After several gasps, everyone starts talking at once.

"What are you wearing?"

"Why are you wearing those slut clothes?"

"Does Ezekiel know?"

"Yes," Mother Esther yells over the other voices. "Ezekiel knows. It's for our protection. But he didn't want to subject the rest of you to this."

The sour faces of the women make me cringe. It's awful seeing myself through their eyes.

A moan from Rachel seems to wake everyone up. She has managed to open the passenger-side door but is crumpled against it, unable to get out.

The mothers rush to help.

"Oh, honey, is it your monthly?" Mother Rose asks.

Rachel nods.

"I'll run and get Rachel's regular clothes," I say. But Mother Esther puts her hands out, palms up, in a signal to stop me.

"We're not supposed to walk around the compound in heathen clothes," I remind myself. Mother Esther shakes her head. "She's too sick to change her clothes. You can run and get her a blanket from the bottom drawer in Ezekiel's room. We'll cover her with that, but then it's straight to bed for her."

I get the blanket, and after the women wrap it around her, Rachel leans heavily on Mother Rose.

"Wait," Rachel says. "I have to get this to Ezekiel." She holds up her purse with the earnings of the day.

"Give it to Eva. She'll get it to him," Rose says.

Everything stops, and it gets completely quiet. I drop my eyes, embarrassed.

"Oh, I'm sorry, Eva. I forgot you aren't allowed to handle money," Rose says.

Esther takes the envelope from Rachel. "I'll give it to him," she says.

At bedtime, anxiety pushes through my exhaustion. What was I thinking, giving Trevor that money? Maybe I made a grave mistake with Trevor. But I push it away when I think about the gifts I have for Mother, and I feel better knowing how badly she needs food. There will never be an opportunity to give them to her during the day, so tonight is the time.

When I'm sure that Annie is sleeping, I tiptoe into the hallway. I wait until I can no longer see light seeping from under the door of Mother Rose's room. Then I sneak down the hall, carrying my boots so they won't make noise on the floor. When I get to the door, I sit on the wooden bench in the hall to strap them on.

No one is in sight, so I dash across the courtyard to where Mother's trailer is situated in the farthest corner. The snow crunches under my feet. Usually I love that sound, but now I pray no one hears me or happens to be looking out a window.

Mother's window is too high to reach, so I throw a snowball against it, then another and another until she appears. Her mouth gapes open in shock.

I smile impishly, but she shows nothing on her face. She offers me a hand, but I don't want her hurting herself so I hoist myself up onto the ledge and climb through the window. A warm blast of air feels good after the cold.

She looks left and right out the window. "What are you thinking, coming here?" she scolds. But she hugs me fiercely. "We can't let anything happen to you," she whispers, still not letting me go.

My fear evaporates in the luxury of her embrace. "I have something for you!" I beam. I reach inside my coat, victoriously retrieving first the honey, then the sausage. I put them on her bedside table.

Her mouth gapes open, and she stares at the gifts as if I had pulled them out of thin air.

"Where? How? When?"

I hold my mouth to stifle my giggles. "At the flea market. This nice vendor gave them to me for Christmas!"

Mother stares at the sausage and honey and swallows. "I shouldn't...Oh, Eva." She looks at the food longingly. But doesn't take it right away. She shakes her head and covers her mouth with her hand. "I shouldn't thank you. I should shake you because this is so dangerous. But God knows I'm weak from hunger. And if this baby's going to make it, I need more food."

Sitting on the edge of her bed, I watch as she reaches inside her bedside table for scissors to split the sausage skin. "God knows this baby is hungry too." She takes a big bite of the sausage. "I wish Ezekiel didn't expect God to feed it. With other things, he says, 'God helps those who help themselves.' I don't understand why this is different."

As I watch her eat, it's as if my own body is being nourished by the food she takes in. I try to refuse when she offers me a small chunk of sausage, but I'm too hungry. The gift feeds me like Holy Communion, touching me deeper than regular food can reach.

Until now I hadn't noticed how much Mother's stomach was protruding, but it's a perfect ball at five months.

"Won't Ezekiel allow you to have extra food?" I ask.

She shakes her head. "At first I'd get a bowl of oatmeal at lunchtime during our fasts, but now Ezekiel says that God is nourishing this baby and that I must fast along with everyone else. I still get extra milk and tea, but that's all. And we're fasting so much!" She sighs. "I worry about how the other kids are doing, and you're still growing."

"I'm okay," I say. "I get hungry but it's not as bad for me as it is for some people. Ezekiel has increased the fasting. We're fasting at least three days a week."

Mother's eyes look far away. "It didn't used to be like this," she says, her voice resigned. But panic flashes in her eyes as they connect with mine. It's like she's realizing that we don't dare discuss these things. I don't know if she feels she is committing a sin, or if she's more worried about what will happen to us if she gets caught.

But I'm grateful that she's talking to me. And even more grateful to see her eating. I want to know her deeply. To know if, like me, there are cracks in her beliefs about Ezekiel.

I want to ask her a million questions—like what made her follow Ezekiel and why my father allowed me to leave his life, and if I did something wrong because he never came for me, and if she ever thinks about him anymore. I want to ask her these things right then because I worry we won't have another opportunity to be alone for a long time. But I can see by the worry lines on her forehead that any more forbidden discussion would just cause her more distress.

Life was so simple when I didn't question Ezekiel. It's lonely not to be able to raise questions out loud without fearing punishment for lack of faith.

I kiss her one more time before sneaking back out the window and returning safely to my room.

At breakfast the next morning, Rachel looks much better and I tell her so. She gives me a warm hug.

"You were so brave to drive yesterday. Thank you. I don't remember much about it, but you must have done okay because we got back here safe and sound."

"You're welcome."

"You know that our whole bead schedule is getting messed up because of the holidays," she says.

"What?"

"Sure, next Monday is Christmas so we won't be going bead shopping."

I lean on the table for support.

"Then the following Monday is New Year's Day and the bead store will be closed again," Rachel continues.

Somebody must have just punched me in the stomach. "Will we go to the bead store on Tuesday then?" I asked weakly. "What day will we go?"

Rachel looks at me strangely. "Relax, Eva. It doesn't really matter. We have two weeks to figure that out. It'll be nice to have a little break—unless we run out of food or something. We're fine. We get a little break. And Ezekiel says we earned enough for a good Christmas brunch."

"I'm glad you feel better," I say and excuse myself. I hurry to the bathroom off the kitchen, where I lock the door and collapse on the toilet, letting the words sink in.

Had Trevor realized about the holidays? Maybe the plan to meet me on Monday was always a sham. Maybe he just stole the money and took off. Of course! I should have known. Ezekiel has warned us hundreds of times.

Christmas

Seventeen

Annie plops down on the empty chair next to me in the dining room. "Are you sick or something?"

"No!" I say, not meaning to sound defensive.

"Well, what's wrong with you, then? It's Christmas, for heaven's sake!"

I manage a smile. "I know what day it is. Wasn't the service beautiful this morning? I love all the extra singing we get to do on Christmas. Especially the carols."

"But you hardly ate anything! This is the best meal I've ever had, and your plate is still full."

It's true. The mothers did an incredible job with the brunch. They made scrambled eggs and bacon and coffee cake for the breakfast part of the brunch. For the lunch part, they made roast beef, mashed potatoes, green beans with slivered almonds, and French rolls. In this room, right now, is more food than we usually eat in a week. Thank God Rachel and MaryAnne managed to go grocery shopping before the blizzard hit.

"This feast is incredible, Annie. I'm just taking my time to appreciate every morsel," I lie. In truth, I'm in such agony over the mistake I made giving Trevor the money that I don't feel I deserve this feast. I have to figure out what I should do about my betrayal of Righteous Path. Should I find a way to pay the money back? But doing something behind Ezekiel's back would be another disobedience. Should I confess at the next Community Concerns Meeting and risk being thrown out? Or should I try to let it go, forget about it, and resolve never to do anything disobedient again?

"Well, eat up. We're practically the last people here," Annie says. "We have the whole afternoon to play, and I don't want to miss any time."

I look around. The only other person still eating is Mother Martha, who smiles at me and dives into a piece of beef. I pick up my plate and walk over to where she's seated, motioning Annie to follow. "I really don't think I can eat all of this. Can you two help?"

Annie looks at my plate greedily. Even with a feast like this, the portions are small and seconds are not allowed.

Mother Martha is hesitant. "Are you okay?"

I nod. "I think my stomach has shrunk from all the fasting."

"I don't mind stretching mine some!" Annie says.

"Me neither," Mother Martha says, pointing to her big belly.

We all laugh. I hand Annie my unused spoon and Mother uses her own utensils. Between the three of us, the food is gone in no time at all.

Mother Martha stands. "Now, I must excuse myself and take a nap."

I give her a quick hug and a kiss on her forehead. She smiles. It's great to see her looking fairly strong, and her color is good.

Annie looks a bit irritated. "You better be careful," she says.

I'm surprised. The kiss I gave Mother on her forehead is the only thing that's "special." And no one saw me. I made sure the mothers in the kitchen couldn't see. I wonder if Annie is jealous. Mother Rose never tries to spend time with Annie. In fact, nobody would ever guess that Rose was Annie's mother. Rose is like a little mouse, with her squeaky voice and nervousness. She wouldn't break a rule unless Ezekiel commanded her to.

But I can tell that Annie wants what I have. I've seen how she looks longingly at her mother at times.

"So, are we going to spend our special afternoon together or not?" Annie asks.

I actually forgot about the free afternoon we get on Christmas. "Sure, what do you want to do?"

"I don't know," Annie says. "It looks like Jacob won't be with us, though. He's going shooting with Brother Paul." She shakes her head. "Things are sure changing around here."

"I know," I say. "Let's think of something special and fun."

Annie brightens. "We could do the Noah's Ark puzzle."

From the dining-room window, I can see that the sun is out and it's gorgeous outside. What a welcome relief after three days of blizzard conditions! "Let's do something outside, Annie."

She doesn't respond right away. I see Brother Paul and Jacob walking out of the barn, and I'm inspired in a flash. I swing around to face Annie. "Let's see if Brother Paul will let us ride his horses!"

Annie hisses. "Not *his* horses. Aspen and Berthoud belong to Righteous Path now."

I'm taken aback by her anger. "Of course. But Brother is still in charge of them and he's the person we need to ask."

"Okay, let's go ask before they go off to the shooting range. It's not that cold today, and the snow is still white and sparkly."

We hurry outside and flag down Brother Paul and Jacob, just as they're headed toward the range.

"Go ahead," Brother Paul says. "But stay on the driveway. We've got deep drifts in the fields."

I can't hide my disappointment. The drive is only a half mile, and I want to ride and ride and ride. "I wish we could go outside the gate," I blurt out without thinking.

Brother Paul looks alarmed. "Don't be crazy. Ezekiel would have your neck. Besides, I doubt that the roads are plowed. We might not even make it to the shooting range." He gives me a knowing smile. "I understand. I get claustrophobic myself. Try running the drive two or three times to get it out of your system."

He helps me saddle up while Jacob helps Annie. I'm glad to see that Jacob is wearing the warm gloves and hat the mothers picked up for him in town. He was one who sure needed a Christmas gift.

"See you later," I say to Annie as Berthoud and I speed ahead.

"Wait!" I hear her yell. But I don't slow down. Berthoud and I fly through the snow, the cold whipping my cheeks. I feel alive. Exhilarated. Free.

Berthoud and I pass Annie several times as I run him back and forth, back and forth on the half mile. I catch the dirty look Annie gives me when we fly past for the third time, but I can't seem to stop myself. It isn't until poor Berthoud is panting that I slow him down. The snow mutes the sounds of Aspen trotting leisurely behind us. But I can hear Annie making clear tsking noises. Berthoud and I stop so they can catch up.

Just as Annie almost catches up, the chapel bell begins to ring urgently. I strain my eyes to see that Mother Helen is ringing it.

"We have to go in already?" I complain to Annie. "I thought we'd get the whole afternoon."

"And I thought we were going on this ride together," Annie says, sounding huffy.

This isn't like Annie. I'm taken aback. "I'm sorry. I needed to feel the freedom of racing for a while. I thought you'd join in."

"I wanted to *talk* to you. We can't talk if you're racing." She shakes her head. "You're in a different world lately."

"I know. I'm really sorry, Annie." I am sorry and I can't think of anything else to say.

Everyone seems to be hurrying toward the chapel. Mother Esther cups her hands over her mouth. "Hurry, girls. Chapel. Right away." She rushes inside.

Neither Annie nor I pick up the pace. I can see that Annie's truly distressed. We trot along in silence as we see everyone else race into the chapel.

When Annie speaks again, her voice is hushed and serious. "I had a dream last week," she says. "I dreamed that you went somewhere in the middle of the night and I couldn't figure out where you were."

My veins are filled with ice. "That's a weird dream," I say, trying to sound normal. We are almost to the barn. "How did it end?"

"It ended okay," she says. But her words are careful. "In my dream I woke up and you were in your bed as if you'd been there all night." She gets down off Aspen to open the barn door.

"Thanks, Annie," I say, sliding off Berthoud. I close the barn door behind us, but when I see Annie's face, I know the situation is dire.

"I was relieved that it was just a dream," she says. "If it were real, I would have to report you."

I'm so cold that I begin to shiver. And I know that the chill is not from the weather.

In the chapel, Ezekiel bounces to the altar as if he has springs in his shoes. He pulls the matchstick out of his mouth and places it on the pulpit. Whatever the Lord has said to him has given him more energy than usual. But I'm still so shaken by Annie's words that even his jubilance doesn't hold my attention completely.

"Alleluia, the Lord has spoken on this Christmas day. Praise the Lord!"

"Praise the Lord," we all repeat.

I want to look at Annie, but I don't. What happened to our understanding? It was never spoken, of course, but we always talked out problems. We never reported each other, or threatened to. If one of us stumbled on the path, we'd encourage the other to make it right. Like the time I sneaked an apple for each of the horses. She didn't have to say a word to correct me. I told her I would give up fruit the next four times we were offered it, and she had smiled her approval. Maybe she senses that I've lost my fervor. Maybe I crossed a line this time.

"Our dear Lord has blessed us with good news today," Ezekiel proclaims.

I can hear little sounds of delight from behind me, stifled giggles and sharp, surprised breaths. What a Christmas present to see Ezekiel with his old exuberance back!

"The Lord came to me when I was settling in for a nap. 'No rest for the wicked,' He said. At first I was frightened that He saw me as wicked, but then He laughed."

I hear snickering from several people, including Annie who's right next to me.

Ezekiel begins to pace back and forth, his hands clasped behind his back. He's thoroughly enjoying himself.

"I wish you could have heard His laughter. It was like thunder—not too loud or too close—and a flash of lightning at the exact same time. The Lord said, 'Ezekiel, you are not wicked. I have made you my prophet for all those who have ears to hear.'"

Now Ezekiel's voice becomes timid, and he seems slightly embarrassed. "God said 'From now on, your flock is to call you Prophet.'"

The congregation breaks into applause. Several people practice the new title, "Prophet Ezekiel." Their voices are filled with awe. Annie notices that I haven't said the title, and she glares at me. I quickly join in. Behind me I hear MaryAnne say, "Of course Ezekiel's a prophet." Suddenly everyone is talking, making supportive comments. It's clear that the group is delighted.

Ezekiel holds out his hand, signaling for us to stop. But he's laughing. "One at a time," he says. He signals to MaryAnne to repeat what she said.

"Our Ezekiel's a prophet! Of course he is!"

Everyone claps again.

Ezekiel acknowledges another hand. "I didn't know God laughed and joked," Annie says. "It makes me so happy."

He walks over to where Mother Martha is sitting and pats her tummy. "The Lord also told me about the child Mother Martha carries," he says.

We take in a collective breath.

"She will have a boy."

More clapping, of course. This time I clap enthusiastically. The sounds all around are joyful.

"And this boy child will be a prophet as well."

The room erupts into cheers.

"As a child he will be taught by me. When he is an adult, he will go out in the world to gather those who are yet to be saved."

I raise my hand and Ezekiel calls on me right away. "I'm so grateful to God that the baby will be all right, but Ezek—Prophet Ezekiel, um, did God tell you if Mother Martha will be all right as well?"

"I didn't ask him that, Eva, because I know she'll be fine." His face softens and he takes Mother Martha's face in his hands. "You will be fine," he repeats. Mother Martha smiles and tears stream down her cheeks. I'm touched by seeing how much he cares for her.

After a moment his attention returns to the congregation. "Any other comments or questions before we move on?" Ezekiel asks.

"It sure sounds like we don't have to worry about the world ending anytime soon if God is sending a baby prophet who will grow up and carry on Prophet Ezekiel's work," Rachel says.

I had thought of the same thing. Twice we've been given signs that the world was coming to an end, and twice God changed his mind at the last minute.

"Now I understand," Mother Cecelia says. "I mean, I still don't get why God makes the decisions He makes—like having you stop seeking souls when we counted on that income. But I do see that He has a plan, and that plan is unfolding bit by bit. My faith is strengthened."

"God always has a plan. We have to trust that plan," Ezekiel says.

I squirm a bit and notice that several people look uncomfortable. Cecelia just brought up something we never discuss, the fact that our primary financial support has always come from the monies and possessions new members brought in. Ezekiel would be gone for weeks at a time, often returning with a new member. But that practice abruptly stopped a few years ago after he came home from an unusually long trip exhausted and anxious. When a few of the mothers asked if something had happened, he refused to talk about it.

"I'll take one more comment or question, and then we'll pray," Ezekiel says.

We hear the timid voice of David from the back of the room. "I have a question," he says. "Since you are a prophet and the baby will be a prophet, who will be in charge, you or the baby?"

This brings a fresh round of laughter, especially from Ezekiel.

"We don't need to worry about that for a long time. I certainly won't take orders from a baby."

Ezekiel silences us again by holding out his hands, palms up, head bent slightly. "Praise God for great news and great gifts," he says.

"Praise God," we repeat.

Eighteen

The day after Christmas, I wake up before the sun and tiptoe to the window. Another whole week before we go back to the bead store and I'll know for certain whether Trevor is a thieving heathen or the kind man I thought he was.

Everyone was so happy yesterday when Ezekiel shared his visitation and the news that God gave him. I loved seeing the women's excited faces when they learned that the baby would be a boy and a prophet. No one hesitated when we were told to call Ezekiel "Prophet." No one except me. I'm totally confused. If Mother gave birth to a healthy baby boy, would I be back on track with Ezekiel? If Trevor came back with beading supplies or the money, would I believe that Ezekiel is wrong about the heathens?

I don't know. What I do know is that I long to be back in a life that is simple. I used to know what to do and when to do it. Being obedient wasn't always easy, but at least I knew what was expected of me and what to strive for. Now everything is one big question. I'm jittery inside and so very lonely. No one can know my doubts and fears. But I am no longer thinking of turning myself in to the Community Concerns Committee. No good can come of a confession. And I'm sure I'd never see Mother Martha again.

I stare into the darkness and pray for strength. Little by little the sky begins to lighten. I love this part of the day. I love how the dawn takes on the darkness and gradually forces it to surrender to daylight. It reminds me of when Aslan brought spring back to Narnia. If God can bring light to the whole world, surely he can bring the light of truth into my heart and soul. This is my prayer. I say it over and over.

Suddenly a dark figure sprints down the driveway toward the dining hall and chapel. As the person gets closer, I see that it's Jacob and he's wearing a holster with two guns. He dashes to the chapel and urgently rings the bell.

Lights begin to shine in room after room as people hurry to their windows. Nobody's dressed yet, of course, so instead of joining Jacob in the courtyard, we all open our windows to hear what he has to say. He says something but I can't make out the words.

"Use the megaphone!" Ezekiel orders.

Jacob races into the dining hall and returns seconds later with the megaphone.

"We had an intruder," he says. Now his voice is loud and clear. "Don't worry. I got rid of him and taught him a lesson." His voice sounds totally grown-up. He's no longer the kid he was two months ago.

Jacob holds out the arm that isn't holding the megaphone to quiet the chatter. "We're not in danger now. He was trying to climb over the gate, but he got a shock and fell back. I ordered him to leave. But he didn't move fast enough so I shot."

"You *shot* him?" Ezekiel roars.

"No. I shot toward him to let him know I meant business, but I only hit his car. I think I took out one of his mirrors."

I can't help wondering why it's such a shock to Ezekiel that Jacob shot at the intruder. If someone tries to enter, shoot to kill. That's what we've been taught.

"Did he say anything?" Ezekiel asks.

"Yeah. Just one thing. He said he wanted to make sure everyone was all right."

"Okay," Ezekiel says. "Everybody get dressed and we'll have our morning service. Brother Paul, I want you to go to the gate in case there's more activity. Make sure you're armed. Use your whistle to let us know if you need backup."

I take in a half breath and move away from the window to get dressed. "Prophet Ezekiel doesn't sound terribly distressed, so that's good."

"You're right," Annie says. "And Jacob too. He actually sounded excited."

A dreaded knowing settles in the pit of my stomach, like lead. The news will probably involve fasting, heightened patrols, even bloodshed. This is not good for any of us, but especially Mother Martha, who's having enough trouble with her pregnancy.

And I'm right. The next hour is spent in the chapel as we listen to Jacob getting interrogated. Jacob seems to handle the interrogation, but it sends shivers through me. When he describes the outsider, he mentions blue in his hair and something sparkling on his ear.

He could be talking about Trevor. No, that can't be. Trevor doesn't know where we live. Out of guilt, I consider confessing about Trevor, but I see Mother Martha's pale face and instantly change my mind.

For a moment Ezekiel considers the idea that maybe the intruder knew Rachel and me. But Rachel is quick to refute this and suggests that, with all the shooting going on here, someone probably heard and decided to check it out for himself.

"It's better that he decided to check for himself rather than call the police," Mother Esther says.

Ezekiel stands up straighter, and he looks frightened all of a sudden. "He could still call the police. He could report that Jacob shot out his mirror."

"But he was on our property," Jacob says. "Didn't you say that trespassing was against the law? Why would he call the police when he broke the law?"

Ezekiel seems to relax some. He tells us that we will need to pray and fast, but Mother Cecelia reminds him that we have lots of Christmas leftovers that will go to waste if we don't eat them. Considering this, Ezekiel decides that we will begin a fast on New Year's Eve. In the meantime we will have an extra chapel session after lunch each day.

New Year's Eve is a beautiful winter day. The sun is shining, and much of the snow from last week's blizzard has melted. There have not been any more incidents with an intruder, and in spite of the fast we are now starting, the mood at Righteous Path is almost cheerful.

The best thing of all is that Ezekiel has already given permission for Rachel and me to make a trip to Boulder the day after New Year's. I'm not even thinking about seeing Trevor. I've let go of that possibility. Besides, Rachel and I have to bead shop and grocery shop so it will be busy. This morning Mother Mary Anne joked that we don't even have enough food to go on a fast. Plus several of the mothers are in need of personal items—shampoo, deodorant, and soap.

My secret hope is that I can sneak to the corner store on the Boulder mall and buy Mother Martha something nutritious to eat.

New Year's Day is not a holiday for us, so we go about our normal activities. In evening chapel Ezekiel wears the first smile I've seen since the attempted break-in. Good. Maybe he'll talk about something else for a change.

It's so tiring to hear the heathen horror stories, especially the ones about how the government may try to murder us like they did in Waco. I'm also tired of the idea that everyone outside Righteous Path is bad. Even if Trevor doesn't turn out to be a good person, I've still seen enough goodness on the outside—the friendliness of vendors and customers at the flea market, the gifts two people gave me for Christmas—that I can't lump everyone into the "bad" category.

But Ezekiel is in a great mood today. The only thing that makes me nervous is that he keeps smiling at *me*. After prayers he makes an announcement. "God has spoken to me once again. We must remain aware of the heathen, but God says that we are not in any danger now. The heathen who tried to break in has gone away, and God said we didn't need to think about him anymore."

I boldly turn around to see how everyone is reacting to Ezekiel's mood change. Annie always wants to sit close to the front so we're in the second row, which is really the first row since no one ever wants to sit that close to the pulpit. She seems more relaxed than usual. Behind me and to my right sit Rachel and Mother Martha, who both look relieved. In fact, Rachel looks downright happy.

I find Jacob in the end of the third row. He's been moving closer and closer to the front ever since he became the star gunman. He seems to be frowning. I think he's disappointed that he hasn't had a chance to use his skill more. And Daniel and David remain in the back along with Mother Helen and Brother Paul. The rest of the mothers are in between.

"And he gave me good news." Ezekiel pauses dramatically.

Every muscle in my body tightens as he smiles at me again. I'm pretty sure I know what's coming.

"I am to marry Eva."

The response is mixed—some make happy sounds; others sound shocked.

I am too numb to respond, but I know it's a grievous error not to appear happy.

I recognize Mother Martha's voice, though it sounds shaky. "Prophet Ezekiel, Eva is only fourteen years old."

"She will be fifteen in a few months," he counters. His voice is clearly angry.

Mother Martha begins sobbing. Ezekiel looks as though he wants to slap her, but she doesn't stop.

"Why would you want to spoil this moment?" he yells.

"I'm sorry," she says. "It's just that Eva's so young."

"You would argue with *God's will?*"

Mother looks as if she might faint. She leans against Rachel.

Rachel laughs. She actually laughs! "Prophet Ezekiel," she says, "it's just hormones. She's not realizing what a huge honor this is for Eva." She faces me. "How exciting!" Her smile is huge, but there is a warning in her eyes that I can read perfectly.

I do the impossible. I smile as happy a smile as I can manage. And I turn toward Mother Martha to make sure she sees my face.

Ezekiel approaches me. I force myself to look in his face, keeping the fake smile in place. He takes my hands in his. Everyone around us claps politely.

Miraculously Prophet Ezekiel has calmed way down, and Mother Martha is silent. I'm in awe of how great Rachel is with him.

"My dear, your hands are way too cold," he says. He blows his sulfur breath on them. The smell makes me sick to my stomach.

"Stay in chapel after the others are dismissed so we can talk."

He says a closing prayer and everyone files out. A few people stop to congratulate me, but mostly they just leave in silence.

He sits next to me in the pew. I know that there's nothing I can do. If he says God has proclaimed the marriage, then the marriage will happen. But it occurs to me that I need to delay it somehow.

"May I speak, Prophet Ezekiel?" I ask. He considers this for a moment. Maybe he's afraid that I'll protest.

"Yes, go ahead."

"Did God tell you when we should be married?" I ask.

"He did not give me a date, but I'd like to do it as soon as possible."

"With your permission, I'd like to make a suggestion."

He nods.

I strive to be like Rachel—offering a bright smile and enthusiasm. "I would love to have a Promise Ceremony the way you did with Rachel. It was beautiful. And we could have a spring wedding."

He looks like he's about to protest so I quickly continue. "If we married in spring, Prophet, we could celebrate the wedding and the baptism of the baby at the same time. The wildflowers would all be up by then and it would be beautiful."

He looks to be considering the idea, so I keep going. "I'm thinking about Mother and her messed-up hormones." I chuckle a little, making it light like Rachel did. "In the spring she'll have had the baby, and I'll bet she'll feel better about it then."

Ezekiel is silent for a bit. He paces, deep in thought for what seems an eternity.

"Okay," he says finally. "We'll have the marriage and baptism together, but I want the Promise Ceremony tomorrow night."

January

Nineteen

The Promise Ceremony is a big deal. I have always loved it. When I was little, I saw a couple go through it, and of course, Ezekiel went through the ceremony with each of the mothers. But I mostly remember Rachel and Ezekiel's Promise Ceremony because Rachel was so young and excited and in love. There were only two women he married without the Promise Ceremony, and that was because their husbands objected and Ezekiel felt the marriage needed to happen immediately.

I meant it when I told Ezekiel I wanted to have the ceremony. It wasn't just to buy time so Mother Martha could have the baby safely.

When I imagined myself in the ceremony, I never pictured going through it with Ezekiel. I imagined a disciple I hadn't met yet who was young and handsome. And I pictured myself in love, like Rachel.

The whole congregation sits in our little triangle chapel. I wear the same lavender smock that all the mothers wore. It is plain except for the embroidery around the neck that consists of one small row of dark purple crosses and another of intertwined vines in various shades of green.

Rachel did my hair. I don't have the long, flowy hair that is usually a part of the ceremony, but Rachel placed silk lilies in my hair and managed to make it look nice.

None of the lights are on in the chapel. It is lit by candlelight alone, which makes it feel warm and sacred. I sit in the first pew with Mother Esther next to me. The congregation is behind me, and Ezekiel waits in the back.

Brother Paul and Mother Esther are the chosen assistants, which is convenient because they were also the assistants of Rachel and Ezekiel, and we didn't have time to change the names on the scrolls.

The ceremony begins with a loud knock on the chapel door. Esther gets up and approaches the door. She wears a plain black smock and opens the door in silence.

Brother Paul enters, wearing a brown hooded smock. The hood is down. He carries a scroll that he unfolds. Everyone has a written script so they know their lines. He reads from the scroll.

Brother Paul: "The Servant and Prophet Ezekiel has been called by Our Lord for the duty and honor of marriage."

Mother Esther: "Will you please come forward, Prophet Ezekiel."

Prophet Ezekiel comes forward, walking with a light step. He too is wearing a tunic. Like mine, it is a light lavender. Instead of embroidery on the neck, his has a large cross embroidered on his chest.

Brother Paul: "The woman Eva May has been called by Our Lord for the duty and honor of marriage."

Mother Esther: "Will Eva May please come forward."

I walk to the altar. I feel so pretty in my lavender smock. I let my smock swirl just a little so everyone can appreciate it. None of this seems real. It's like I'm playing a part in a skit, like we used to do as kids.

Mother Esther: "The duty of the husband is to love, support, nurture, and serve as the spiritual guide and master to the promised for her earthly life and life in the hereafter. Are you willing to accept these duties and promise this to Eva before God and your congregation?"

Prophet Ezekiel: "I promise to marry Eva and to take on the duties of a husband after marriage. I make this promise before God, Eva, and my congregation."

Mother Esther turns to me: "The duty of the wife is to love, support, and nurture her husband; to accept his authority as spiritual guide and master; to obey him; to lay with him; and bear his children, God willing. Are you willing to accept these duties and promise this to Ezekiel before God and your congregation?"

I am floating somewhere beneath Ezekiel's smile and above the congregation. I am watching the amber glow of the three candles twinkling on the altar and noticing the shadow cast over Ezekiel, who stands just an inch outside the light. I strain to read my line in the dim light.

Eva: "I promise to marry Prophet Ezekiel and to take on the duties of his wife when we become married. I make this promise before God, Prophet Ezekiel, and my congregation."

Mother Esther now goes to the pulpit where she pulls out a purple satin ribbon. It's about an inch wide. She ties one end around Ezekiel's left hand and one around my right hand. "This ribbon symbolizes that you are bound together by your promise. Please hold up your arms so that the congregation can see the symbol of your promise."

We hold up our arms with the ribbon intact. Everyone is smiling at us. Even little David and Daniel.

Mother Esther takes a seat in the front row, and Brother Paul motions to the congregation to read the next part. They do so in unison.

"We, the congregation, witness this symbol of Ezekiel and Eva's promise of marriage made before God and this congregation today."

Brother Paul: "Now we must hear from each congregant individually."

One by one the members stand up and read the line on the scroll: "I, Mother Rebecca, am witness to this sacred promise of marriage between Prophet Ezekiel and Eva May." When it is Mother Martha's turn, her voice cracks. I carefully avoid looking at her out of fear that I'll burst into tears.

Before the service began, I had decided to go through the motions without thinking about what was really happening. So far, it's been easier than I expected. I just have to know my lines.

When everyone has witnessed the promise, Brother Paul goes to the podium and brings out a pair of scissors.

I freeze.

I picture myself back in the chair at the Community Concerns Meeting. I reexperience the horror of Ezekiel chopping off my hair and screaming at me to say that I will obey. I look at him now in his robe, a gentle smile on his face as he gazes lovingly at me.

The spell is broken.

This is the man I just promised to marry. My heart races, but my feet remain frozen to the spot. I want to run. Just in time, I stop the scream that makes its way to my throat.

Where is Rachel? I find her face. She looks concerned, but when she sees me looking at her, she smiles and mouths, "You're fine."

I think I nod slightly. When I hear the snip of the scissors as Brother Paul cuts the ribbon that binds me to Ezekiel, I almost stumble, but I keep my eyes on Rachel and manage to stay standing. She is the source of my strength.

Brother Paul: "I now cut the ribbon because the two remain separate until the wedding. But each of them will now tie the ribbon around the wrist of the other, and they will continue to wear the ribbons until they marry in the spring."

I manage to tie the knot on Ezekiel's wrist so that it fits loosely. He ties mine uncomfortably tight.

We sit in two of the chairs behind the pulpit. I hear Brother Paul lead the congregation in prayer. Thankfully, I know all the words and can easily mouth them while my head and heart go away.

Aslan now has a full mane. I nestle against him, drawing comfort from his presence.

Twenty

Rachel and I make small talk while we dress for Boulder the next morning. I want to hug her and thank her for how she saved me and Mother Martha when Ezekiel proposed to me. She saved me again yesterday when she showed me how to respond to the Promise Ceremony. I think her actions mean that she understands me. I think they mean that she has her own doubts. She was manipulating Ezekiel, especially when she said that Mother's concerns were just hormonal. Manipulation is a sin.

She's done other things that are against Righteous Path rules—like deciding we could spend money on lunch that time—and she breaks the rule of two. She asked if I'd mind doing the bead shopping by myself each week, so she could do the shopping to save time. I'm excited, but it is breaking the rules, so maybe Rachel has doubts about Ezekiel and Righteous Path.

Does she believe that what he says comes from God? Does she believe that all the outsiders are damned? Does she believe that the baby will be a prophet and that Mother Martha will give birth safely without medical help? Does she ever question marrying Ezekiel or think about leaving?

None of these are safe topics.

Dear Lord, please give me a sign that tells me whether or not it's safe to talk honestly with Rachel.

I'd love for her to be my confidante, but it's probably way too dangerous. I don't even feel safe about expressing doubts to Mother Martha.

The roads are pretty icy again, so Rachel concentrates hard and we don't talk. But when we get to the paved part and the road is dry, Rachel visibly relaxes.

Finally I think of something safe to ask her. Something I really need to know. "Rachel, now that I'm promised to Prophet Ezekiel, is anything going to change between now and the day we get married, or should I expect some things to be different?"

"Oh, that's right," Rachel says. "You were only eleven when I was promised."

"Yeah, I didn't pay much attention."

"Well, the changes may not look big, but they are. You'll get a lot more respect from the mothers even though they'll be struggling with their own jealousy. You'll be let in on more of the gossip, so you won't have to try so hard to listen in."

I laugh. She's got that right.

"Ezekiel will want to spend more time with you. He'll probably want to sit with you at dinner and will talk to you more. He may even take you to town with him, though he hates driving on icy roads. And, let's see...that's pretty much it until you're married."

Rachel stops the van in front of Beads Galore. It's a relief to see the green-and-gold sign, but I'm sad about betraying Ezekiel by giving Trevor money. With all that's happened in the last few weeks, it's great to get my mind back on something that is certain. In the last couple of days, I've been coming up with images of new pieces I'd like to try making. I push the button on my seat belt and practically leap out of the van.

"Hang on," Rachel says, laughing. "I haven't given you any money yet."

"But I'm not allowed to…"

"Hush! That was before the Promise Ceremony. None of that matters anymore."

Shocked, I take the money envelope and begin to open the door. But I hesitate.

"Rachel"—I struggle to talk without crying—"I just want to say thank you. You helped me so much these last few days. I'll never be able to repay you."

Rachel looks from me to the steering wheel. "You're welcome," she says in a quiet voice. "But I did it for Prophet Ezekiel. See, I love him. And I didn't want to see him hurt, not by Mother Martha and not by you. Do you understand?"

Perfectly. An invisible boulder just rolled off the mountain and smashed all my hope. None of her actions had the meaning I thought they did.

I say nothing. I just get out of the van and start to go inside.

Rachel calls after me. "I forgot to tell you. It'll be between three and three thirty when I get back. So, take your time in there. It's almost noon now. Don't get lost in too many choices," she teases.

I nod again and manage a smile.

Inside the store, the bubbly clerk who helped me with all the spilled beads welcomes me and signals me to the checkout counter.

"You're Eva, right?"

"Yes," I say, almost as if I'm asking a question.

She looks at me like we share a secret, reaches into her pocket, and pulls out a slip of paper. "He said that if you were alone, I should give you this number."

"What?" I'm so surprised that I look down at the folded paper without taking it from the clerk for a long time. Finally I reach for it and unfold it. I stare for a long time. *Trevor 303-722-0419*, it says. Ten numbers shine up at me like the sun.

Maybe this is pretend. Maybe it's a dream.

The clerk keeps talking. "I've been holding on to it since before Christmas. I thought you'd *never* come in." She leans in to me with peppermint breath and the stale smell of cigarettes. "Do you have a cell phone? Because if you don't, you can borrow mine." My head nods no before I even think about it.

I mumble a thank-you to the clerk when she hands me the cell phone, but I don't start dialing right away. I've only used a phone a couple of times in my life and never a cell phone. This one looks exactly like the one Ezekiel carries, so I flip the top up like I've seen him do. There's a green button and a red button, numbers and symbols. I feel like an idiot, but I finally ask the clerk to show me how to use it. She looks surprised, but she helps me.

"No problem," she says. "You push the green icon of the phone and then punch the numbers." I do what she says and look to her for further instructions. "Now hold it to your ear. It should be ringing."

She's right. I wait as it rings again and again. Then I hear his voice say hello, and my shaky one responding.

"Eva? What's up, girl?" He chuckles. "With all our planning we forgot to factor in the holidays, so I had no idea when you'd be back. Are you at Beads Galore?"

"Yes," I say. I can't believe this is happening.

"Are you alone? Can you meet me at the library?"

"Yes," I tell him. I hang up. In five minutes, my hopes about Rachel have been dashed and the hope I had for Trevor is blossoming.

Finally, after all these years, I'm inside a real library. The lobby is huge. It smells like the pews in our chapel right after they've been polished. I look at all the people milling around—a few standing in line at an enormous desk holding stacks of books in their arms, others sitting in comfortable-looking chairs and leafing through books of all sizes. A lady holds a finger in front of a little boy with a warning look when he pops a bubble with his gum. I'm self-conscious. I don't know what to do or where to go. Even though I'm in my heathen street clothes, I bet the people around me can see that I don't fit in.

Do I want to fit in with the damned? No, I shouldn't think of them as damned. A strange idea crosses my mind. Maybe God is in the library, not just in Righteous Path.

I feel a tap on my shoulder and swing around too fast, practically knocking Trevor off his feet. He recovers quickly and his smile is electric. Maybe it's his hair that's now dyed a sunny yellow on one side and partially shaved on the other, but the world seems to be changing from black and white to vibrant colors the instant I see him.

"Hi, Eva," he says, pulling me into a hug.

"Hi," I say back, hoping I wasn't too stiff when he hugged me.

He catches me staring at his hair and laughs. "You like?" His laughter is a song. "My hair shocked you, huh?"

I nod.

"Sorry," he says. "But, hey, I'm in Boulder now instead of the Podunk, Iowa, town where I grew up. Why not have a little fun?"

"Okay," I say, returning his smile. I don't understand why it's fun to make your hair like that, but it sure is colorful.

"Let's find a conference room and I'll show you what I got." He points to the backpack he's holding.

I follow him up the wide, winding staircase, and he ushers me to a small room with a table, four chairs, and three glass walls. He starts digging in his backpack before either of us sit down.

"You got the beads?" I say, half question, half statement.

"Of course." His eyes study my face. "Oh man! You didn't think I'd rip you off, did you?"

"Well, yes. I'm sorry but I did."

"Oh, Eva. You must have felt terrible. But don't go getting all paranoid on me."

I have no idea what the word *paranoid* means, but I've heard it before. It's the same word that Ezekiel used when he was talking about what outsiders might think if they knew we were stocking guns. "But I am *not* paranoid," he had said. "I'm just making sure we're protected so the government doesn't burn us out like they did the Branch Davidians. I won't let that happen to us."

My eyes are drawn to the crystals spilling from one of the plastic bags Trevor has taken from his backpack. I begin to separate them. They're multicolored and a variety of sizes. I hold up a bag of sterling silver clasps and another of findings that are used to separate the beads and make all kinds of designs. These too are sterling silver and consist of shapes I've never seen before. This one an elephant. That one a lion. "They're beautiful!" It's what we ordered—and more.

He pulls out several more small bags. I open one after another, computing what they'd cost if I purchased them at Beads Galore. "You got all of these for a hundred and fifty dollars?"

"No, actually it was a hundred and fifty-one dollars and twelve cents." He flashes me another smile. "You owe me."

I plunk myself down in the nearest chair and really look at Trevor for the first time. His eyes are blue like mine. And the blond—no, sun-yellow—hair makes them stand out even more. In spite of the strange things he does with his hair, he's good-looking, taller than Jacob, taller than Ezekiel. More importantly, he's not the thief I convinced myself he was. He is nothing like the heathens Ezekiel taught us to fear.

"Thank you, but why?" I ask. "I still don't understand why you're doing this for me."

"I thought we went over this at the flea market," he says. "I think it's a real disadvantage for anyone over the age of three to not know how to use a computer. Plus, you seemed really interested in learning, especially since you were paying too much for jewelry supplies. And…I thought I could help, you know?"

I continue staring at him, taking it all in, thinking about what he's saying.

He pulls his lips inside his mouth like he doesn't want to say what he has to say and studies an empty spot on the table. If I didn't know better, I'd think we were at a Community Concerns Meeting and he was getting ready to confess something.

"I'm a religious studies major so I'm interested in learning about alternative religions and what things people in cults believe and stuff," he says. "But if it makes you uncomfortable…"

"No," I say too quickly. "You did tell me that. I'm afraid that my upbringing has made me a little suspicious. We're taught not to trust any heathen—er, anyone outside of Righteous Path."

He smiles.

I think about the terms "religious cult" and "alternative religious group." I think about how kind it was for Trevor to get me all these beads and how I understand his curiosity about me and my world because I am just as curious about him and his.

"Thank you!" I say finally. "You have no idea how helpful this is for me."

He studies my face, his eyes sympathetic. "I probably don't. But, hey, I want to know all about you and what your beliefs are and stuff. But—anything you want to tell me is fine."

I want to tell him everything. I've wanted someone to talk to for a long time. I want to ask questions that I'd get in trouble for asking at Righteous Path and share thoughts that would make Ezekiel furious. But an image of Ezekiel, furious and vengeful, silences me. So I repeat, "Thank you," and change the subject. "Are you still willing to teach me computer?" I ask.

"Of course," he says.

According to the wall clock, it's one thirty. "I have about an hour, then I need to be back at the bead store to be on the safe side."

"That's great," Trevor says. "Where do you want to begin?" he asks.

"First I want to know what you mean by 'religious studies major.' Then I want to look up the words *cult* and *paranoid*."

"Okay!" Trevor says. "That's kind of random but I'll bite. Let's fire up Google." His face is one huge smile. "But don't forget we need to pick out the beading stuff for the next order."

A wave of excitement swooshes through me. Finally, I can learn about anything that interests me.

"Eva, look." He points to a row of desks on the library's main floor. Each desk has its own computer. "You can use any of those computers anytime you visit."

"By myself?" I count as many computers as I can see from where I'm sitting. Six, no seven. And four of them are free at the moment. I stand up and can see nine more computers—all vacant. The whole world is in my reach all of a sudden.

My hands shake when Trevor shows me how to position them on the keyboard.

It takes me a while to find the letters Trevor instructs me to enter. It would go faster if I could type with one finger, but he insists that correct fingering is worth learning.

Half the battle is figuring out the key words to enter so the computer looks up what you want. Trevor suggests I enter the words "religious education major at CU" to get the program he's in.

By the time I finish my computer training, I know more about Trevor and college programs. I know that Righteous Path is one of hundreds of cults, each claiming to be the one way to God and salvation. I know what it means to be paranoid. And I know that the description fits Ezekiel.

March

Twenty-One

The winter has been tough. It has been snow and more snow and more snow. The snow is impossible to navigate when it gets too deep, and lately it's been so bad that even the devoted ranchers to the east and west of us haven't plowed. That means no bead shopping, no flea markets, no fresh food.

It's just Annie and me in the barn doing chores because Jacob is off with Ezekiel, shooting. The two are always together these days. They're either giving shooting lessons to the reluctant mothers, cleaning guns, or strategizing about an attack. Jacob walks a little taller with self confidence, enjoying Ezekiel's favor.

"I hope Jacob's having fun while we do all the dirty work," Annie complains. She's been complaining about one thing or the other the whole time we've been in the barn.

"You can be thankful he's not giving you another lesson," I tease, remembering what a terrible shot she was in our first lesson.

"I don't want to be good at killing," Annie says. "Even for self-defense." She sounds indignant. "Just because you've gotten pretty good at shooting doesn't mean you should like it. No, I'd rather let the invaders shoot me dead and go straight to heaven."

Annie's been so crabby lately. I don't know what it's about, but it's getting on my nerves. It's hard enough to see the promise ribbon all the time and try to keep sane knowing what it means. I struggle to pretend to be happy while I dread every minute of being around Ezekiel. Annie's moods don't help.

She hasn't said a word to me about the promise ceremony or marrying Ezekiel. And I'm not going to bring it up.

I notice that Bessie is restless in her stall. "Oh, Bessie, I forgot that Brother Paul wanted me to milk you guys for him." I hurry to get the pail off its hook to start milking.

"I forgot too," Annie says. "I'll help milk."

"You can't," I say. "Jacob has the other stool at the shooting range for some reason. Go ahead and feed the chickens. I'll manage."

"Tomorrow will be April first," Annie whines. "When will it stop snowing?"

"I don't know," I snap. "I'm not a prophet."

Annie looks hurt. I immediately feel a pang of regret, but I don't follow her as she scurries out of the barn, bucket in hand, to feed the chickens. I'm as sick of this weather as she is, and I don't want to hear about it.

It's been three weeks since Rachel and I have been off the compound because of the heavy spring snows and ice-packed roads. I need to get out of here. I need to get back to my lessons with Trevor, earn some money, and buy beading supplies and food. I'll scream if I have to eat one more bowl of rice.

I miss Boulder. I miss Trevor and the lessons. We have fun and laugh all the time. Plus I'm learning so many fascinating things from the computer and from our conversations. I especially miss the talks we have about what he calls "comparative religions." What amazes me is the number of alternative religious groups that are convinced you have to be a part of their group to be saved. They differ in what they think God wants, but in other ways they are the same. Sometimes it ends in disaster, but I now understand what Trevor means when he talks about a self-fulfilling prophecy. The leader and members expect to be attacked, then do things to make that happen. Another big thing is sex. A lot of leaders believe they can and should have sex with all the women.

My eyes wander to the last stack of hay where I've hidden the books I borrowed from the library last time. I'm so ready for new books.

When I get discouraged or feel trapped in my situation, I move my leg, just so, and can feel the little spot on my thigh where I have wedged my most precious possession between my long underwear and skin.

My own library card.

With my real name on it.

From the first time I entered the library, I dreamed of getting my own card. But I knew it was impossible. Yet I stared at Trevor's card each time he used it, even held it, and once, for fun, slipped it in my pocket.

The last time I was at the library, Trevor and I were sitting in a cubicle surrounded by a dozen or so other cubicles when he finally said something.

"Why don't you get your own library card?"

"Because I can't." I looked away and bit the inside of my lip to contain my feelings.

"Yes, you can. Come on, we'll go do it right now. It only takes a minute." He took my hand and pulled.

"No!" I said way too loud. Several people from surrounding cubicles peeked out to see what was going on.

To the surprise of both of us, I burst into tears. Embarrassed, I tried to turn off the tears, but once the waterworks started, it was too late. Trevor escorted me to one of the little rooms, and I continued sobbing for some time. He rubbed my back.

"I can't," I repeated. "Ezekiel would kill me."

Trevor looked puzzled. "Wait. You manage to take full-sized books home and keep those hidden, and you think you couldn't hide a little card?"

"It's not that." But I didn't have words to express what I wanted to say. I just knew that a library card was a way bigger offense than reading books.

"The scary thing," I'd told Trevor, "is that it kind of makes me a part of the heathen world."

He'd frowned, pretending to be offended, while his eyes showed that he wasn't. "I really don't think of myself as a heathen. How about we call it 'the broader society' instead of 'the heathen world'?"

"The broader society." I liked how that sounded. It didn't make anybody wrong or bad.

"You don't have to do this, Eva. And you don't have to try and explain."

"Okay, thanks," I said. But over the next few minutes I couldn't stop thinking about it. I wanted my own card. I loved to imagine the freedom of coming to the library on my own, without even the help of Trevor, picking out books, and with the magic of the library card, walking out with as many as I wanted. I could use any of the computers whenever I wanted. Well, not "whenever," of course. I still had to sneak. But once here, I was free to learn.

Freedom. That's what the card represented. Freedom to learn as much as I could.

"Come on. I'm not going to be afraid anymore. I want a library card."

Trevor had taken my hand, and together we walked to the checkout desk where Mrs. Jenkins sat smiling.

"I–I would like…Could I please get a library card?"

"It's about time!" She beamed, pushing up the purple glasses that had slipped down on her nose. She pulled a purple pen from behind her ear and handed me a form with questions typed on it. That's when I noticed that she was dressed from head to toe all in purple. She saw me noticing and laughed. "You seemed to have noticed. Purple is my theme for the day."

Her rainbow-colored theme days and friendliness always made me feel good. I braved looking at the questions. But the first one tripped me up. *Name.* I didn't want to put "Eva." That was Ezekiel's name for me, and I couldn't put down my real name. I simply couldn't!

After a minute Trevor suggested we sit at a table. "You're whiter than a sheet," he said once we were seated.

"I want to use my real name, but I can't do it."

"Of course you can! Here, just say it. I'll write it on the form."

Memories of getting paddled, spending hours in the corner, wearing tape over my mouth, all for referring to myself as Lily, made it impossible to say.

I pull the form back in front of me. Better to write it than say it. With unsteady hands and terrible penmanship, I scrawled out my name: Lillian Rose Wells.

The next line stopped me as well—*Address*. I didn't remember my childhood address and certainly didn't want to use the address of Righteous Path, so I was stuck.

"For that line, you can use my address." Trevor said. I hesitated again at *Phone Number*, but Trevor suggested I enter "none."

I used the real names of my parents too.

When it was finished, I handed the form to Mrs. Jenkins.

"Stand right here and smile for the camera," she said.

Mrs. Jenkins paused before taking the picture. "Lily, you look terrified. Could you smile for your picture?"

I managed a brief smile that she captured on camera. It turned out all right as long as you don't look too closely. The eyes show how afraid I am.

Actually it captures me perfectly where I'm at—the eyes show my fear of stepping off the Righteous Path and the consequences I'm just beginning to see. The half smile shows my hope for the possibilities in the unknown.

I look up from the cow I'm milking to see Mother Martha *in the barn.* She's walking straight toward me.

"What are…?" I say

Before I can finish, she holds her index finger to her lips. "Eva, we have to talk."

"What's wrong, Mother?" I ask. But from the corner of my eye, I can see that Annie is returning with the empty feed bucket and heading straight toward us. Mother Martha must see it too, because she holds up the tin cup she's been hiding in the folds of her skirt.

"Good morning, Mother Martha," Annie says. Her voice is strained, and I know she is suspicious that Mother Martha and I are seeking "special time."

"Good morning, Annie dear. How is your day going so far?" Mother Martha's voice is steady and warm, immediately diffusing the situation. She holds the cup up so Annie can see. "Pregnancy cravings," she says. "We're out of milk in the kitchen."

Annie watches as I dip Mother's cup in the milk bucket and hand it back to her. Mother Martha drinks it down in three gulps.

She pulls a handkerchief from her pocket and wipes her lips. "Thank you, girls! That's just what I needed."

She holds up her cup, and as she turns to leave, her shawl slips from her shoulders to the ground. I stoop to pick it up, and as I gently fold it over her shoulders, I see a blood spot as big as a grapefruit on the back of her skirt. I make sure the shawl covers it up.

"You need to be in bed, Mother," I say.

She nods significantly and takes her leave.

"Yuck," Annie says.

"Yuck what?" I pray that Annie didn't see the blood spot on the back of Mother's skirt.

"I could never drink warm milk like that."

I shrug my shoulders. "I don't mind it warm."

My head is swirling with the implications of what it means that Mother Martha is bleeding this late in her pregnancy. It takes me a while to realize that Annie is quiet. Her silence is shouting at me to apologize for my attitude earlier.

My mind is a calculator. I realize that if Annie's mad, she's more likely to make a big deal out of Mother Martha coming to talk to me.

"Annie, I'm sorry for hurting your feelings. I guess we're both tired of this weather."

"And yet *you* were the only one who was rude," Annie says.

Her coldness is a knife. "What happened to us? How did we get so far apart?" I don't say this to manipulate her. My shock is real.

"We're far apart because *you've* changed," Annie says, her voice as accusing as her eyes. "We used to talk about everything. Now you don't tell me anything. You keep secrets. And I'm supposed to be your best friend! You get to do all that bead stuff while I'm in school with the same boring books and the same boring lessons. And you get to go into town twice a week. And now you're promised to the Prophet."

Her last statement makes me reel. "Annie," I ask, "would you want to be promised to the Prophet?" I say it softly, careful not to betray my horror over the upcoming marriage.

"Well, no," she says, looking as if she's just tasted something bad. "Because I'm not old enough. But now that you're promised, the mothers treat you like a grown-up and they still treat me like a kid. And you're promised to the holiest man on earth so you know you'll have one of the highest places in heaven."

I bite my lip to avoid blurting out how much I question these beliefs. I think about how Trevor reacted when I told him what it meant spiritually to be promised to the Prophet. He'd swallowed hard and looked away. I asked what he was thinking, though I wasn't looking forward to the answer.

"I'm thinking that if you refuse to marry Ezekiel, you are damned to eternal hell, but if you marry him you're assured of the highest place in heaven."

"Yes," I told him.

"That sure gives him a lot of power."

I had shrugged. "If you believe he is who he says he is, then you figure he's following God's will." But even as I said it, I could feel cracks in my beliefs regarding Ezekiel.

Now I tell Annie that I'm glad we're talking again. "Let's try to get our friendship back on track." She lets me hug her.

Bessie starts shifting her weight and mooing. She should have been done milking a while ago. I stroke her body and plunk back down on the stool to finish.

Annie laughs. "We can talk more tonight," she says. She gives me a little wave and walks backward toward the front of the barn. "I'll do the sweeping, then we can brush the horses together."

I lean my head against the cow's warm body as I continue to milk. The familiar smells of sweet milk, pungent manure, and hay make me feel safe for the moment. Annie and I will be all right, I think, as long as we keep talking. But Mother Martha. Did she let that shawl slip on purpose so I'd see that her pregnancy was in trouble? Was she warning me? Because if that baby isn't born healthy, all hell will break loose.

Twenty-Two

I'm grateful that it is me and not Annie who brings the fresh milk to the kitchen, because when I get to the refrigerator, I discover a pitcher half-full. Mother Martha is clearly desperate to talk to me. I rack my brains all day to find a way to be alone with her, but she is never alone, and any ideas I come up with would put us both in danger.

I reluctantly get ready for bed at the usual time. For a minute I actually think about trying to sneak out to Mother's room after Annie falls asleep, but she's a light sleeper and after her threat on Christmas, it's not worth the risk. I beg God to provide me with an opportunity to speak with Mother tomorrow.

Annie releases her braids and reaches for her brush to comb out her hair. I manage to get the brush first and begin brushing it for her.

"It's been a while," Annie says. Her face is somber, her voice wistful.

"I know," I say. I let myself enjoy the ritual that we've had for years. I've been afraid to relax with Annie, afraid I might say or do something that would reveal how much I've changed.

A too-familiar crackling sound emanates from Annie's lungs and my heart sinks. Another asthma attack.

"Oh, Annie," I say. I try to rub her back to calm her but she wriggles away.

"Don't!" she says.

Stunned, I back away. She's never refused my help before.

"This is punishment," she says. "God"—she wheezes—"is punishing...me...for...my sins."

"Annie, don't say that. You're going to make it much worse."

She looks at me like I'm a stranger. "*No!* You don't say that. God *is* punishing me," she says. "Of course...He is. Are you...questioning Prophet...Ezekiel?"

"I think that if you put those thoughts out of your mind—"

"You *are* questioning Ezekiel."

"Annie, I just want you to calm yourself so the attack can go away."

"Maybe it's...suppose...ed to be...bad," Annie says.

I'm silent. Helpless. Anything I say to comfort her she'll see as going against Ezekiel. Annie no longer trusts me. There's nothing I can do about it.

"I con...fess my sin"—she sucks in as much breath as she can—"of jealousy. I'm jealous...because...you and...Jacob are treated... like...adults...now."

"Okay," I say, "I forgive you." Her breathing gets more jagged, and I pray she'll stop talking because it only makes the asthma worse. I want to cry. "And I'm sure that God forgives you too."

"You...don't know that," Annie snaps. "You're not a prophet."

Tears sting my eyes. "Of course I'm not. Annie, I'm sorry if I sounded like I was putting on airs."

"That's what I don't understand. He's marrying you, and you're a…fake," Annie says. "You act…all…sweet, but…you don't want… marriage. You don't…believe…in him…like I do."

"It's about obedience, Annie. I'm finally learning obedience. I guess that looks fakey to you."

Oh, how easy it is to lie when the consequences of not lying are too great to handle.

"Really?" Annie asks. Her face begins to relax.

"Really," I reassure her. I look right into her eyes as if I'm the same trustworthy person she's always known. I have reached a new low.

Annie's always been religious, but she's become zealous lately. She continues to struggle to breathe for some time. For once I stay silent. There are no stories that will help her right now, no words of comfort that she'd believe. Little by little, her breathing returns to normal. I'm almost asleep when she decides to start a conversation.

"I'm thinking about the baby prophet," she says. "I want to be ready. I want my heart to be pure, my thoughts too. I want to atone for my sins so that I'm worthy to be in the baby's presence. Do you think I'm grown up enough to be his nanny?"

Her devotion is sweet and simple. I want to reassure her, but with all the other women whose arms are hungry to hold a baby, I doubt she has a chance. I say the only safe thing I can think of. "I'd be thrilled if Prophet Ezekiel chose you for the honor."

When Annie finally goes to sleep, she's wearing a smile. And when I wake up hours later to use the bathroom, she's still smiling.

Oh, to be so certain about everything.

Twenty-Three

At breakfast, Rachel approaches me all excited. "We're going to town. Brother Paul and Jacob drove a ways down the road. They said it's still icy but if we're careful, we should be fine. I'll start loading the van."

I can't match her excitement because Mother is not at breakfast again, and if I'm gone all day, it will be at least tonight before I have another chance to talk to Mother. I decide Rachel must be as stir-crazy about being stuck on the compound as I am.

Jacob leans across the table and says something to Mother Helen. He looks tall and confident. Mother Helen is puffed up with pride. Her son, who is not supposed to be special to her, now holds a special role in Righteous Path. He wears a gun and holster all the time these days. Instead of school, he spends his time patrolling the property on horseback or doing important tasks with Prophet Ezekiel.

When Jacob sees me, he gives me a polite nod and a half smile. I return the motion. It's the only way we interact. Any feelings he had for me seem to have vanished and I'm glad. He is like a brother to me. Anything else would be wrong, not to mention dangerous. But I'm glad we shared that kiss. Now I know what it's like to be kissed.

I hurry to finish my oatmeal so I can fix a tray for Mother before someone else does. But I'm too late. Rose is almost out the door with a tray when I stop her. "Let me take that for you, Mother Rose," I say sweetly. But she holds the tray more firmly.

"You have your own jobs to do," she squeaks. "Now let me do mine."

I ignore her scolding tone. "How is Mother Martha doing? She's so rarely at meals anymore."

Rose purses her lips as if it's none of my concern, but she answers. "She's pale and tired, but she knows that she's in God's hands and accepts His will. You need to do the same."

The whole time I'm dressing for town in the garage, I'm fuming silently about Mother Rose. I'd love to say to her that if she understood mother-daughter love, she wouldn't try to stop me from being with my mother at every turn. I'd love to tell her that Annie would be a much happier person if Mother Rose cared about her the way Mother Helen cares about Jacob and Mother Rebecca cares about Daniel and David. I'd love to tell her about the families I see together in Boulder, mothers and fathers laughing and talking with their kids.

The fireworks inside must show on my face because Rachel whistles. "What's gotten into you?"

"Nothing," I say. I change the subject quickly so she doesn't ask more questions.

"How much of the jewelry money did Ez…er…Prophet Ezekiel give us back for materials?"

"He gave me two hundred for groceries and just one-fifty for beading stuff. But I'm not worried. Do what you always do, and we'll be fine."

Dear God, I hope she doesn't know what I always do. "What's that?" I ask as casually as I can sound.

She laughs. "I don't know, rub two crystals together, say some magic words, pray, whatever you've been doing to more than double our monies."

I relax a little.

"I don't know if Prophet Ezekiel realizes what a bright head you've got on your shoulders, but besides creating great designs, you're a natural at business."

"Thank you, Rachel." It's unusual for her to be this complimentary. It's unusual for anyone at Righteous Path to be this complimentary. I can't think of anything else to say so I bask in the warmth her words have given me.

We drive in silence for a long while. I'm intrigued by Rachel's skill in negotiating these treacherous roads. She slows down before hitting a patch of ice but keeps a steady pace when we're actually driving on one. I'm grateful I can't get a license until I'm sixteen. The steep curves still scare me. It's truly a miracle that I got us home safely that time.

"Where's my satchel?" Rachel asks, her voice sounding rattled.

"It's on the floor." I lift it up to show her. "What do you have in this thing? It's so full," I say. She pulls it away from me and rifles through it, driving with only one hand.

"I don't feel the wallet. The wallet's not in here!" It's rare for Rachel to panic, but I hear it in her voice now.

"I'll help you look," I say, sticking my hand inside.

"No!" she says and moves the purse next to the door on the driver's side.

"Let me look on the floor," I say, more curious than offended. "Maybe it dropped out." I look on the floor and reach under the seat. Immediately I feel the soft leather of the wallet and something else too. Something metal. I hand her the wallet and watch as she guzzles air in relief.

The metal thing turns out to be a gun. We both gasp. "It's loaded!" I say.

"Good Lord," Rachel says. "Put that back. I swear somebody's going to get killed."

"Somebody's going to get killed," I repeat, wondering if she disagrees about Ezekiel gathering guns and making us all learn how to shoot them. But I don't dare ask her. If that's not what she's implying, the stakes could be high.

When Rachel stops in front of Beads Galore, she says, "See you around three thirty."

I'm surprised because it's only eleven a.m. and that's more time than she usually takes to go to Costco. Maybe she forgot to mention other errands she plans to run. She pulls away wearing a cheerful smile.

How ironic. The one time I want nothing more than to be back on the compound to find a way to speak with Mother, I'm offered the longest time in Boulder.

Twenty-Four

"Hello, Eva." It's the voice of Mrs. Jenkins, the nice librarian who helped me get a library card. Even though she knows my real name is Lily, she calls me Eva because I asked her to. It's too scary to go by my real name. "Eva," she calls again. I look all over but I can't see her.

She laughs. "Look up," she says.

Now I see her. She's high on a ladder arranging baskets of flowers on the top of the bookshelves. Three baskets of flowers sit on the floor next to the ladder.

"Hello, Mrs. Jenkins." I stifle a giggle. She's wearing red glasses with little white dots on them that go with her ladybug shirt and red skirt. "I bet you have a hundred pairs of glasses."

She flashes a bright smile. "Not quite a hundred, but I'm getting there. Several of my patrons are keeping count." She points to the flower baskets on the floor. "Would you mind handing me those?"

Even though the flowers are plastic, the colors brighten my mood. Handing them to her, I feel a lightness I haven't felt for a long time. Nothing is light at Righteous Path.

When we're finished, I gather the courage to ask for a favor. "Could I please use your phone?"

"Sure," she says. She points to the one on her desk. "But you have to dial nine first."

After the fourth ring Trevor starts talking. I interrupt him to say that it's Eva and that I'm at the library but he's not listening. "Please leave a message after the beep."

Oh, it's an answering machine. He told me he had one of those. *Beep.*

The idea of talking into a recorder makes me so nervous that I open my mouth and nothing comes out but "um."

Just then Trevor picks up the phone, sounding out of breath. "Eva? Are you at the library?"

"Wow, you recognized my voice from me saying 'um'?"

"Yup. You have a very distinctive way of saying 'um,'" he says.

We both laugh.

"Yes, I'm at the library," I tell him.

"See you in ten minutes," Trevor says.

Mrs. Jenkins approaches the desk. "Is there anything I can help you with?" she asks.

My hands feel clammy all of a sudden but I make myself ask her anyway. I lean in close enough so she can hear my whisper. "Is there anything on the computer about what might go wrong with a pregnancy?"

Her eyes automatically drop to my stomach.

"Oh, it's not for me. It's for my mother." I hope my face isn't as red as it is hot.

"What makes you think she might have a problem?" Mrs. Jenkins asks.

"She had a tough time when she had me, and she's been pretty sick during this whole pregnancy."

"How far is she into her pregnancy?" she asks.

"Eight months," I tell her.

"What does her physician say?"

"She doesn't have a doctor."

"Oh," she says, "a midwife then."

I remember that Mother Esther said that all the mothers would be midwives. "Yeah, she has midwives. But they don't say anything except to trust God."

She leads me across the room to the computer on her own desk. She sits down at her chair and motions me to pull up a chair next to hers. She types "pregnancy problems, third trimester" onto the Google bar, but pauses before she hits Enter. "Eva, do you know much about pregnancy—about fetal development and the birth process?"

"Yes," I say but instantly feel guilty. I can tell by her half frown that she knows I don't know much about either.

Finally she sighs. "How about I stay right here and answer questions if you have them."

"I can do this," I say. But her offer touches me deeply.

She could be my friend. Funny that the two people I can trust are both heathens—or people from the larger society.

Within minutes my head is spinning with new terms like "placenta previa" and "gestational diabetes," along with other terrifying concepts. Trevor dashes through the front door so I immediately close out the screen. I don't want him to see me looking at this pregnancy stuff.

We exchange hugs. "You don't look so good," he says. "Are you okay?"

I motion him to follow and hurry up the winding stairs to our favorite room.

Trevor hasn't even pulled off his backpack before I drop into a chair and start wiping away tears. "It's my mother."

He pulls a chair up right next to me and takes my hand. His forehead is all scrunched in concern.

I let him pull me into a hug. I'm beyond tired of keeping things inside, and Trevor has been more a friend to me than anyone at Righteous Path. At least I don't have to worry about him turning me in.

Suddenly I'm blubbering out the whole story, how Mother Martha is pregnant with the next prophet, how we're not allowed to get medical attention, how she almost died having me and has been sick her whole pregnancy, and how she came to me in the barn, a place she never goes, to tell me we had to talk but we were interrupted. I even tell him about the blood on the back of her skirt. "I didn't have an opportunity to talk to her because talking in private would mean we were trying to have a special relationship and we'd get punished."

The shocked look on Trevor's face intensifies with each of my statements.

"I think if she went to so much trouble to talk to me, something must be wrong. But if there's a problem with her pregnancy, there's nothing I can do because we're not allowed to get medical help."

"Whoa!" Trevor says. "I gotta back it up here."

I let myself breathe in some of the air I missed during my big outburst, while Trevor looks thoughtful. "Ezekiel says that your mother's baby is going to be the next prophet?"

"Yes. Prophet Ezekiel had a visitation from God." I realize that I'm saying this as if it were fact—as if Ezekiel really did have visitations from God, as if the baby would really be a prophet, as if I was talking to someone at Righteous Path where you didn't dare express doubts. But I can't make my lips form the words that say I don't believe him. "The baby will be a boy, of course."

"Right." Trevor rolls his eyes. "Ezekiel can't imagine a female prophet, can he?"

I'm confused by his sarcastic tone at first. But then I remember what Trevor once said about men and women being equal. What an interesting concept!

Trevor shakes his head. "No way Ezekiel knows the gender without a medical test." He leans forward. "You guys don't use doctors ever? Not even when somebody breaks a bone?"

"Not for anything," I say. "I don't want her to die."

His mouth is locked in a strange open position. I can tell he's horrified.

In a sad way, Trevor's reaction feels good to me. I've had to hide my own horror so many times. It's the feeling I squelched when Jacob lost his front teeth at the hands of his father when he tried to protect his mother. Ezekiel had said to pray for a miracle, and God might let his front teeth grow back. I prayed like crazy. We all did. But he never grew new teeth.

It's the same feeling I have every time I look at Mother Miriam with her left arm dangling uselessly at her side. She broke it several years ago and wasn't allowed to get it fixed. For months she spent every extra minute in the chapel praying for a healing. It's the feeling I have now, knowing that Mother Martha may be in trouble with her pregnancy and I can't do anything about it.

"But why?" Trevor asks.

I open my mouth to respond but he interrupts.

"Never mind. I know why." He holds up his thumb using it to count. "One, it's God's will that we suffer. Two..." He adds his index finger to the first. "Whatever the suffering is, it is punishment for your sins." I nod emphatically. "Three, if you pray hard enough, God will heal you."

"Exactly!" I blurt out.

"Four," he continues, "if God doesn't answer your prayers, then you're not worthy."

He puts his hand down and looks disgusted.

"Five," I say, "medicine is from the devil."

Trevor sighs. "Eva, do you believe all this?"

"No," I blurt out. Suddenly I freeze. I cannot move or breathe or speak. I said I don't believe. Now something terrible is about to happen. I know it.

"Are you okay?" Trevor says.

I can't respond. "I'm not sure what I believe, but I know my mother can't die having this baby."

"Do you think a loving God would want his chosen people to suffer while he gives the rest of us the gift of science?"

A loving God—like Aslan. The gift of science. I let the words roll around in my head, remembering the little girl and her inhaler.

Everything in the outside world is topsy-turvy from Righteous Path. The opposite of what I've been taught.

"You look terrified," Trevor says. "But you haven't done anything wrong, and there's nobody who will hurt you."

"Prophet Ezekiel will hurt me. And if Ezekiel's words are really coming from God, God will hurt me too."

I think about Trevor's confidence that God is a loving God. "Trevor, how do you know that God is loving? Did you read *The Lion, the Witch, and the Wardrobe?*"

"By C. S. Lewis. Sure, I read it."

"Oh, that's how you know."

"What?" He shakes his head. "I take it *you* read *The Lion, the Witch, and the Wardrobe,* and that's how *you* know that God is loving. But most Christ-based religions see God as loving—and not as eager to punish."

"God is loving." I let myself say the words. "I *know* this inside myself. And that makes me think"—I whisper these next words— "that Ezekiel is not really hearing God's voice."

I cannot look at Trevor's face. So he lifts my head and I have to see him. He's smiling. A huge, mouthy smile that gives me courage.

"Ezekiel is wrong," I say out loud. "He's wrong about a lot of things—like refusing to let us use modern medicine. My mother deserves to see a doctor." I study Trevor's face carefully.

"Of course she does. Where do you think medicine comes from?"

I shrug my shoulders. "Ezekiel would say it comes from the devil. But I think maybe it comes from God."

Trevor nods. "I believe—and lots of other people do too—that we're partners with God. God gives us intelligence, and we are responsible for using it. He gave us mold, for instance, and the intelligence to figure out how to use it to make antibiotics."

I look at him puzzled.

"Antibiotics are used to fight infections."

"But we can invent bad things too, like bombs," I say.

"Right. I think that the biggest gift is love, and if we use our intelligence in a loving way, we invent stuff that's for the good of everyone. If we miss the love part, we invent things that are bad for people."

"Whew! You've given this a lot of thought, haven't you?"

"Yeah." He laughs, then gets serious again. "Eva, your mother needs to get to a doctor."

According to the wall clock, I have less than an hour before Rachel returns. We haven't even started to order the beads, but I don't care.

The room is quiet for some time before Trevor speaks again. "You could just leave and tell the police that your mother is being held prisoner," he finally says. "You could walk out of this library with whatever money you brought to buy beads, and we could get you a home through Social Services. Or you could even search for your father. Have you thought of that?"

I stare at him. It sounds so easy, so terrifying.

I shake my head. "I can't leave Mother. Especially since she's in danger."

More silence.

"What would happen if I simply drove out to the compound and we brought your mother to a doctor?"

"No!" My heart beats wildly and I think I might faint. "They'd shoot us dead."

Trevor looks stunned. "They'd actually kill us?"

"Yes. Mother Martha is carrying the next prophet. No one is going to get near her. Plus, Ezekiel is convinced that we will be attacked at some point. But you can't tell anyone about the guns. I'll think of a way to get her out of there and to a hospital."

"Well, at least we have another month before the baby's due," Trevor says.

"Right. And circumstances change," I add. "Maybe Ezekiel will go on a trip. Pray for the perfect opportunity to get her to a doctor."

I excuse myself to use the bathroom. Maybe if I splash some water on my face, I can take down the swelling in my eyes and pull it together a little better.

When I return, Trevor is on his laptop. But I don't care about beads right now. I lay my head on the table, my arms folded underneath like a pillow.

"Look," he says. "If I type your father's name on the Google bar, we might find some information. But I need his first name."

I don't move. "I can't, Trevor."

"Why not?"

"Because he left me. He never called or wrote or visited me before we joined Righteous Path. And he didn't try to find me when he got back from China."

"How do you know that he didn't try?"

"Because. Mother told me. Ezekiel told me. Ezekiel said my father was evil." I raise my head, thinking. "Maybe Mother lied to me. She was so angry at Daddy. Maybe she lied." I picture Daddy lifting me up and twirling me around the way he used to. We're both laughing so hard. Then he hugs me close. With my head pressed against his chest, I hear the strong thump, thump, thump of his heart.

This was a daddy who really loved me. Why did he leave me?

"Maybe Ezekiel and your mother were better at hiding you than your dad was at finding you."

Finding out about him doesn't mean I have to get in touch with him. Still, I'm terrified to say his name. Punishment is always swift and severe at Righteous Path for saying the name of the damned. I type it onto the Google bar: Charles Wells.

"You have to push Enter," Trevor says.

I hesitate. I know that finding out anything about my father will change my life, and I have no idea what that change will look like.

I do it anyway.

Twenty-Five

Rachel is late picking me up. Really late. I have looked at every jewelry magazine in Beads Galore for the last two hours, and she's still not here. Not that I've been paying any attention to the magazines. I have way too much on my mind for that. What I learned about my father is foremost on my mind. He's tried to find me for years. Mother must have lied when she said he never sent a letter or tried to call.

I lock myself in the store bathroom for the third time since I've been in the store. The privacy is an amazing luxury that I cherish, almost as much as the article that I read over and over. When we narrowed the search to Charles Wells in Chicago, up popped an article from the *Chicago Tribune*.

FOUR-YEAR SEARCH FOR MISSING DAUGHTER YIELDS NOTHING

University of Chicago professor Charles Wells last saw his daughter, Lily, four years ago on her fifth birthday. In what Wells describes as a "contentious divorce," he and former wife,

Margaret (Lang), were granted shared legal custody. Mrs. Wells was to maintain physical custody for the next two years while Dr. Wells took a sabbatical to do research in China.

"My former wife and I agreed that I could speak with Lily weekly while I was in China, but when I made those calls, she never once allowed me to speak with my daughter. I sent letters weekly as well. I have no idea if my daughter ever received them."

Wells reports that the phone was disconnected the third month he was away. At the time Wells was convinced that his wife changed the number to a private one out of spite but remained confident that his ex-wife had remained in the Hyde Park home.

"That's when I made the biggest mistake of my life. Instead of returning home immediately, I redoubled my efforts to complete the research early. I returned after thirteen months to find that the house with all of the furniture had been sold in a cash deal and that Lily was long gone with her mother."

Wells reports that he instantly began a search but that no one, not neighbors or friends, had information about his ex-wife's or daughter's whereabouts.

I jump when I hear a knock on the bathroom door, sure that it's Rachel at last. "Just a minute," I say. I fold the article in quarters, hug it against my heart, and hide it in my skirt, next to my library card.

When I leave the bathroom, a lady holding the hand of a very uncomfortable-looking little girl rushes her inside.

"I'm sorry I took so long," I say.

"Don't worry about it," the lady says. "Small bladders, you know."

I decide to leave the store and sit on the little bench two stores down. I take out the copy and finish reading it. The rest of the article describes Dad's efforts to find me through a detective, a website, an email address, and a phone number. There's a picture of Mother and another of me blowing out candles on my birthday cake. I looked adorable back then—certainly not the tall, nearly bald, almost fifteen-year-old that I am now. My heart sinks. Maybe he wouldn't like the me that I am now.

But maybe he'd want me and Mother too. Maybe he'd forgive her for her lies and we could be a family. I picture the three of us having lunch in a restaurant. We're laughing and having a great time.

It's like I've been under some kind of spell all these years and am just now waking up. I should be furious with Mother for lying to me, but I'm too worried about her to be mad.

Part of me thinks, *Of course he loves me. Of course he wants me in his life.* I had to bury that hope deep inside all these years because it wasn't safe to hope, not safe to love someone I was told was evil. But I don't think I ever really closed the door to him. It never made sense that he would go from adoring me to nothing.

It's a little after five p.m., and Rachel's still not here. Something is wrong.

I decide to walk the two short blocks to the parking lot Rachel would most likely use since there's never any street parking. There's a van parked near the front that looks like ours, but I don't see Rachel. Maybe we walked past each other and now she's at the bead store. But something tells me to check the van out first.

As I approach, I have no question that it is ours because of the distinctive dent on the driver's side that Ezekiel never got fixed. We were never told how it happened.

On the front seat is a note with my name on it. She left me a note? My heart begins to race. Surprisingly the door is unlocked. Even before I read the note I know. Rachel is gone. My shaky hands make it harder to read her writing.

Eva,

I'm sorry. I can't go back. I just can't. Ezekiel may try to look for me. He shouldn't. I'll be long gone by the time he realizes that I'm missing.

I love you and everyone at Righteous Path. But this is what I have to do. I'm so sorry to leave you to make it home yourself, but I know how capable you are and that you'll be fine.

Love, Rachel

My tears splatter the ink on the note, but I don't care. Her note is almost illegible by the time I crumple it into a little ball and throw it on the passenger seat.

Reality sets in slowly. Rachel ran away. She's not coming back. She left me! She left Ezekiel, and she said she loved him. Now I have to make it back to Righteous Path by myself. Now I have to face Ezekiel alone. How could she do this to me? I would never have left her alone like this.

In spite of how angry I am at her, I miss her already and I'm a little awed that she's made herself free. Rachel is free! She's free of Ezekiel telling us what to think and feel and act. What to believe. She can do whatever, be whatever, believe whatever she wants now.

Her reaction to the gun really was because she disagreed with Righteous Path having guns. She should have told me. She should have trusted me.

And something else—her bag was so full and she wouldn't let me go through it.

It's almost dark. The only time I've driven in the dark was that time Rachel was so sick, and it was light out until just before Grand Hill. I don't have a driver's license. If I get stopped by a cop—the very idea sends shivers down my spine—he'd lock me up and I'd be forced to tell him about Righteous Path. And it would be my fault when the police were gunned down by everyone.

"You can leave any time," Trevor had said to me.

I *could* leave. I could go back into the library and borrow the phone again to call Trevor. But then I'd end up living with a stranger and I couldn't help my mother. I could call my dad too, but then everything would change, and again, I'd be abandoning Mother Martha.

I consider calling Ezekiel. That way he might come and get me, and I wouldn't have to take the treacherous journey back up the mountain by myself. But he'd bring other members to start searching for Rachel, and then she wouldn't be free. She might even end up dead.

No matter how I look at it, the conclusion is the same: I have to go back. I have to be there for Mother. I may not be able to do a thing to help her, but at least I'll be with her and she'll know I care.

The keys are tucked under the seat, just as I suspected they'd be. I fiddle around with the buttons and, after three or four tries, manage to find the lights.

As I pull out of the parking lot, I notice that the van clock reads 5:16. Everyone will be sitting in the dining room right now. They'll all be anxious because no one knows where Rachel and I are. Maybe, if Ezekiel is upset enough, he'll make everyone skip dinner and pray in the chapel until we're home safely. Jacob will surely be on horseback near the entrance to the compound so that he can signal everyone as soon as he sees the van.

The drive home is every bit as hard as I imagined. Thankfully, a man in a pickup truck pulls in front of me on the west side of Boulder. His lights give me more light and I am able to literally follow in his tracks up the mountain. But when I'm about halfway home, he turns into a drive and I'm suddenly on my own.

It's actually harder than the last time I drove this because there's much more ice. I clutch the steering wheel at every curve, and when my headlights shine on a steep drop, I'm careful not to look at anything but the road ahead.

My attention is completely on the road except for brief moments when I worry about how Ezekiel will react. He'll be shocked about Rachel and probably crushed. But he'll also be angry with me, especially if he realizes that we broke the rule of two by doing our chores separately.

I'm only going about twenty miles an hour when I take an icy curve and the van starts sliding. I slam on the brakes, forgetting I'm not supposed to do that, and the van spins, getting closer and closer to the drop-off. *God save me! I'll follow your will, I'll do anything, but please save me.*

The van stops. I'm turned in the opposite direction from the one I was traveling, but for the moment, I'm safe.

It's probably ten minutes before I'm able to move, and then I only do because a car can't get by. The owner of that vehicle gets out and guides my turn.

"I'm going to Grand Hill," he says. "How about you?"

"A little farther," I say.

"Do you want me to follow you or drive ahead of you? I'll do whatever is most helpful."

"Oh, thank you," I say. "Please drive ahead of me."

"Okay, good luck!" he says.

Here it is again. Another so-called heathen acting out of kindness.

I drive very slowly and manage to make it, first to Grand Hill, where I wave good-bye to the good man, and finally to the ranch. But I take little comfort because of what I know will come next.

The minute I see the property, I see Jacob on horseback. He sits rod-straight, shoots the 42-caliber pistol once in the air to let everyone know that I'm home, and then approaches the car. He motions me to roll down the window and I do.

"Where's Rachel?" he barks.

It seems ridiculous for him to talk to me this way, like he's a soldier for God who is going to find and destroy all that is evil.

"She's not here," I say. I don't owe him an explanation.

"Where's Rachel?" he screams louder.

I hit the gas pedal and swerve around him. I drive straight toward Ezekiel and everyone else gathered in the common area. The way Ezekiel looks surprises me. He seems a little hunched over and tired.

I know that my best course of action is to avoid being defensive. "I'm home. I'm finally home," I say as I get out of the van. My attitude seems to throw Ezekiel off balance for a minute.

"Where have you been? Where's Rachel? What happened?" Ezekiel shoots the questions, leaving no time for me to respond.

I hand him the crumpled note Rachel left for me.

"This isn't for me. She wrote this note to you. This is all blurred like it got wet. I can't even read it." His voice sounds puzzled, hurt. "Why? Why would she do this?"

He looks at the note. Suddenly his face contorts and his shock turns into rage. He steps within inches of me. "How did this happen?"

"I don't know," I say.

"Where were you when she left?"

A whimper from the back of the group draws everyone's attention to Mother Martha. She's leaning against the door to the dining room. Under the stark light from the single bulb above her head, she looks deathly white; even her lips are pale. Esther and Alice each take an arm and help her inside. Ezekiel follows them into the dining room where they help Mother into the closest chair.

Everyone else remains where they are standing, but the door is wide open and we can hear Ezekiel ask Mother Martha if she's in labor. His voice is gentle and loving, and I am washed in guilt because I want so badly to leave him.

"I don't think so," she says. "I'm just overwrought. Rachel has left us. But, thank God, Eva is safe and remains righteous."

Ezekiel tells Mother Esther to bring Mother Martha some tea, and she toddles off to the kitchen. He whispers something in Mother Martha's ear. Whatever it is, the words make her eyes well up with tears.

"To the chapel," he commands, gesturing to the rest of us.

I bite the insides of my mouth. His interrogations could break anybody down.

"Brother Paul and I could go look for Rachel," Jacob offers on the way into the chapel. But Ezekiel holds up a hand in dismissal.

This surprises me. I had expected him to start looking immediately. But since it's been several hours, maybe he has no idea where to begin.

He fires questions at me, and I lie my way through them. I say that Rachel and I had just gotten to Costco when she said she had to go to the bathroom. We were in a hurry so I continued picking out produce instead of going with her. I say I got so absorbed in getting the stuff on the list that it took me fifteen minutes or so before I realized that she hadn't returned. I say that even then I figured she was just in a different section of the store. I looked and looked for her, I say, and after an hour or so, I realized she was gone. I left when I couldn't find her.

"You left without the groceries?"

"Yes. She had the money." Immediately I realize my mistake. I never checked the back of the vehicle to see if there were groceries. I assumed Rachel never went to Costco, that she just left the note and took off. The fear in my eyes must show because Ezekiel looks at me suspiciously. He directs Brother Paul to look in the van.

My heart beats practically out of my chest while waiting for Brother Paul to return. Ezekiel paces back and forth until Brother Paul announces that there are no groceries.

I'm weak with relief.

"So she not only left me, she stole money from me as well," Ezekiel says bitterly.

The word "me" shoots fire through my body. "She stole money from *me*," he said. Never mind that the cupboards will be bare for a week and every one of us will go hungry—even the little kids and Mother Martha. Ezekiel sees it as an offense against him, and only him. Rachel has hurt his pride, pride that would be punished if anyone else showed it.

"You had no right to let her go to the restroom by herself," Ezekiel barks. My eye catches Annie's. She looks away. My throat tightens with unshed tears.

When I look back up at Ezekiel, I see that he is clearly in a rage. The next thing I know, my head is hitting the base of the altar and the pain above my right eye is so sharp I can barely breathe.

"Get up," he demands. But the world is spinning too fast for me to get up. I vaguely realize that the cause of my pain and dizziness is that Ezekiel has hit me. Little flickers of light break through the darkness, and when my eyes can focus again, I see Ezekiel's hand poised to hit me again. Blood from my forehead trickles into my eye. I try to push myself up but my elbow slips in the puddle of blood on the floor.

I must pass out because when my awareness returns, gentle hands are lifting me into a chair. When my eyes can focus, I see that it is Brother Paul.

A piercing scream coming from another room startles everyone. Through my pain, I realize what it means: Mother Martha is indeed in labor.

Twenty-Six

Prophet Ezekiel keeps us on a prayer vigil in the chapel. Because of my bleeding head, I'm allowed to sit in the pew and hold a towel to it. Everyone else is kneeling. It is a mercy so unusual for Ezekiel that I can't help wondering if it's from regret or guilt. Is he sorry that he hit me so hard, or does he feel I deserved the punishment? Whatever the reason I'm grateful.

Mother Rose brings me two towels. One is filled with ice to keep the swelling down. The other is to sop up the blood that has slowed down to a trickle in the last hour. My entire body aches from the impact of hitting the altar, but my head throbs with pain. I don't look at Ezekiel for fear that my anger will show.

I've got to get into the room with my mother. I have to see how she's doing and what she needs. But the women are taking turns, two at a time, nursing Mother Martha in two-hour shifts. I'm sure they won't want my help because I'm not yet married. If I go to her, it will be seen as defiant.

Her screams continue, but they're farther away now that the women have taken her to her bed. Each scream tears me apart as if I'm the one going through the contractions. When the screaming stops for a few minutes, I'm exhausted.

Lord, help me find a way to help her.

Ezekiel interrupts our silent prayer every so often by praying out loud or giving short sermons to direct our prayer. During the first hours, he prays as much about Rachel running away as he does about Mother Martha and the baby.

"Lord, make Rachel see the errors of her ways and return to the fold," he prays.

But over time his prayers become hardened toward her. "Let she who has chosen to abandon your ways burn in hell along with the heathens. Do not punish us for her sins, Lord, but know that we have cut her out like a cancer. We shall never speak her name again."

He raises his head to us. "Hear this commandment, my people. She who has run from us is no longer a part of us. Her name is poison and will not be spoken again by anyone here."

I pray that no one will forget this order because Ezekiel will punish us severely if we say Rachel's name. I crane my neck to see if David and Daniel are paying attention. Turning, I discover, makes the room spin and it takes a minute to discover that both are sound asleep, one on each side of Mother MaryAnne. I hope she remembers to tell them about not using Rachel's name.

They're not the only ones sleeping. Next to me, Esther jerks her head again. She's fallen asleep several times already. It doesn't surprise me, though. She's begun to show her age more and more in the last months and often sleeps when she gets a sit-down task.

An idea begins to take shape in my mind. When the women come in to change shifts, I'll get up to take a turn as if it's simply part of the plan for me to do so. If anyone objects, I'll remind them that I'm promised to Ezekiel, and of course I should take a turn. Esther will be the perfect partner for me. I'll let her fall asleep and finally get a chance to have time alone with Mother.

But I worry how well I'll be able to pull it off because the pain in my head is getting worse and so is the dizziness. I have to, though. I have to.

It takes forever before Cecelia finally enters the room to summon the next team of caretakers. I immediately stand up tall and nod to Cecelia. Then I gently tap Esther's shoulder. She startles and comes to attention.

"It's our turn," I whisper, bracing myself against the dizziness when I stand. Esther looks a bit confused at first, but she stands and follows me to the door.

Cecelia looks puzzled. She looks to Ezekiel for direction, but her concern gives way to a smile when we both catch Ezekiel's nod of approval. I hurry, not wanting to give him the chance to change his mind.

I'm not prepared for what I encounter in Mother's room. The first thing that hits me is the rancid smell of sweat and blood combined. Mother's eyes remain closed. Her face is whiter than bleached linen hanging in the sun. She looks fragile. I'm about to take her hand when her face contorts and a strange guttural sound comes from her mouth. Mother Rose holds a blood-soaked washcloth in her hands.

"She's too weak to scream now," she explains. She dips the

cloth into a bucket, wrings it out, and wipes Mother Martha's leg under the blanket. When she pulls the cloth out again, it's saturated with blood.

"Oh, Eva, you shouldn't be here," Mother Rose says in her mousy voice.

I fight the feeling that I might faint. "Yes, I should," I say.

"It's our turn," Esther adds as she takes the bucket from Rose.

I struggle with every ounce of energy to keep my composure. I'm vaguely aware that Rose has left the room.

"Mother, it's Eva. Can you open your eyes for me?" I can't disguise the sob in my voice.

Her lips form a weak smile, and after a moment her lashes begin to flutter. Slowly she opens her eyes. They flash with anger when she looks at the gash on my forehead. For the first time I think about what I must look like.

"What did he do to you?"

Her words are furious and uncensored. I notice the startled expression on Esther's face, but there is nothing I can do. I squeeze Mother's hand gently.

"I'm okay, Mother," I say.

I direct my attention to Mother Esther. "It looks like she has some strength left," I say.

Mother Esther nods. Her hands are under the sheets. "Spread your legs a little further, dear. I need to see how far dilated you are." It isn't until I hear Mother Martha moan and see Mother Esther remove her bloody hand that I realize what's happening. That hand was actually inside of her.

"She's hardly dilated at all," Mother Esther says, shaking her head.

I think I might really throw up. Instead I rest my hand on Mother's shoulder. "You're going to be all right," I say. Our eyes lock. She knows my determination. I cannot let her suffer like this any longer.

I pretend I'm kissing her cheek, but instead I whisper, "I'm going to get you out of here."

Twenty-Seven

I hand Esther a towel so she can dry her hands after "cleansing" them in the bloody water. "I'll get us some fresh water," I say. I pick up the bucket and move toward the door.

"Thank you," Esther says. "We're running low on towels too. Could you stop in the laundry for those?"

"Sure."

Mother groans. I squeeze her hand and reassure her that she'll be okay.

It's hard to walk without swerving, hard to stay focused. I lean against the van that remains in the courtyard until the dizziness quiets down. I have to get Mother to the hospital. Can I really rescue her when I'm hurt myself? The answer is a shout inside me. *She'll die if I don't.*

The keys are still in the ignition. Good, but first I need to get inside Ezekiel's house. I remove the garage door opener from the visor and trudge along as quickly as my uncertain legs will carry me. The whole way I pray. *Please God, let the door between the garage and house be open. Please.*

It is.

I scurry to Ezekiel's bedroom and pray that his cell phone will be on his bedside table like I remember from the first time I was in his room.

It is.

God *is* answering my prayers! My knees go weak as I dial Trevor's number and the dizziness gets worse. I want to rest on a comfortable bed, but not Ezekiel's bed. The thought is repulsive. Instead I lean against the wall for support.

Even though I know Trevor's number by heart, I misdial twice. "Answer! Answer! Answer!" I whisper into the phone.

"Hello?"

Finally! His voice is sleepy.

"Mother's in labor. Tell me how to get to the hospital in Boulder."

"What? Eva?"

"Yes. It's me. Trevor, please. I need those directions."

"Wait! Let me call 911. They're better equip—"

"No! If anybody comes here, they'll get shot. I'm not joking, Trevor. Ezekiel's got everybody trained. We're supposed to shoot to kill anyone who tries to enter."

"I know," he says. "Then you're in danger trying to get out of there."

"Don't worry about me. I have a plan. I'm okay."

I wish I had a *better* plan, but all I can think of is to get Mother into the van and drive as fast as I can safely drive.

The only sound is breathing. His are deep, considered breaths; mine are rapid, too rapid. I have to calm down. Finally he breaks the silence. "The directions are easy. Turn left at the second stop-light in town. It's about a half mile on your right. Use the side door that says 'Emergency Room.'"

"Thank you." I start to hang up.

"Wait!" he says. "Do you even know how to drive?"

"I'm fine." I repeat. If he only knew. "I've got to go." But as I close the phone, he gets in two more words, "Be safe."

Back in the garage, I stare at the guns stacked on the shelves. Somehow, until this minute I hadn't fully realized that they were purchased for killing people. They're not just for shooting bottles or targets that look like a person. These guns are here for violence, for blood and guts and the death of anyone who's not a Righteous Path member. Maybe even me, now that I've become a traitor.

I have an idea, one that may save Mother's life and my own. I scurry back into Ezekiel's bedroom, ignoring the increasing pain in my head and the dizziness sudden actions seem to cause. On the bedside table, right next to his phone, are his keys to the BMW. I take both with me.

When I return to the garage, I open the trunk and shove armloads of guns inside. I know that Ezekiel and Jacob have guns on them, but getting rid of the rest means fewer bullets fired. This could save lives if it comes to that.

As I pick up the last armload, I hear a pop. A gun has gone off, one with a silencer. I look down to see the air whoosh out of the tire on the back driver's side.

The whole situation is so bizarre that I laugh. I laugh until tears stream down my cheeks. Ridiculous, hysterical laughter. Somehow it calms me, and the calm sparks another idea.

I pick up the gun that went off. It hadn't occurred to me that any of these guns would be loaded. I face it toward the front tire and shoot. Pop, whoosh. Two more times—pop, whoosh, pop, whoosh—and the tires are flat. Even if Ezekiel has another set of keys, he won't be able to follow me now. I make sure that the trunk and car doors are locked before pocketing the keys.

I'm dizzy. I'm nauseated. And something more: I'm filled with a sense of power I've never felt before.

But when I look at Ezekiel's disabled BMW, I realize the implications of what I've just done. There is no going back now. No changing my mind and deciding to stay in Righteous Path. I need to get out of here as much for my own survival as Mother does for hers.

If God is the God Ezekiel portrays, I am surely damned. But if he's the God who feels so right in my heart, a loving and forgiving God like Aslan, then I'm doing the right thing.

The thought gives me courage to continue. I close the garage door behind me and scramble to the courtyard where I've left the empty bucket.

In the kitchen I stagger to the sink and vomit.

Oh God, if you want me to get Mother out of here safely, please help. I can't do this alone.

I take deep breaths to calm myself and fill the bucket with warm, soapy water before I return to Mother's trailer. Fortunately Esther's eyes are closed. Mother looks paler than before, and the sheets are blood soaked. I glance at the wall clock and realize that forty-five minutes of our precious time have gone by. When I set down the bucket, Esther startles awake.

I force a smile. "Rest, Mother Esther, it's fine. I can take care of Mother Martha for a while.

"I'm not resting," she snaps. "I only close my eyes because it helps me pray."

She signals me to come closer. *Please don't smell the vomit*, I think. When I approach, she whispers in my ear. "This is going badly. She's not dilating. It will take hours, maybe even days, and she could…" She stops herself from saying the word I so fear.

I return to Mother's side and place the back of my hand on her face and forehead. "She's burning up! Is it normal to have a fever during labor, Mother Esther?"

Her face looks grim. "It's not good."

When Esther nods off again, I squeeze Mother's hand. "Will you be able to walk to the car?"

She shakes her head. "Don't do this. Too dangerous. He'll kill you."

"I'm. Getting. You. Out. Of. Here."

Her lips stretch to form a thin smile. "Thank you," she mouths.

Esther springs forward again in her chair. "Did you say something, dear?"

I want to scream. She's such a light sleeper. I'll never get Mother out of here unless I get Esther out first.

"Oh dear, we've got to get her cleaned up." Esther looks around the room. Her eyes focus on the one towel remaining.

"Where are the towels?" she asks.

"I'm so sorry, Mother Esther, I forgot them." I hesitate a minute, hoping she'll offer to go, but she doesn't. "Would you like to stretch your legs a bit and go get them?" It's bold of me to ask an elder to do something. She scowls slightly when she stands up but proceeds stiffly toward the door.

"Tea," Mother Martha says. "Please, some tea."

"Of course," Esther replies. She stands up a little straighter and walks with purpose.

I kiss Mother's forehead. "You just bought us ten extra minutes. But we've got to go now."

When I try to get Mother to stand, I discover she's dead weight. I lose my balance, and we both end up in a heap on the bed.

"Sorry," she whispers. "I'll try harder."

Seeing her this way breaks my heart. This time I brace myself and we manage to get her on her feet. Her weight is almost entirely on my shoulders, but she manages enough strength to step forward. Twice she almost ends up on the floor, but step by painful step, we somehow make it to the van and into the backseat. Once down, she's too spent to move.

"They'll hear you," she whispers.

Out of the corner of my eye I see figures leaving the chapel. I duck down. Does this mean that Ezekiel is letting everyone go to bed? But I hear nothing more, and when I peek through the window, I see MaryAnne headed toward the trailer with little David on one side and Daniel on the other. Apparently Ezekiel is just letting the kids go.

When I peek out the window again, I'm greeted with the shocked face of Mother Esther. She lets the tea slip from her hands. The cup breaks when it hits the ground. "What are you doing in that van?"

"Shh, they'll hear you." I will myself to keep a calm voice. "Just returning the van to the garage."

"You left your poor mother alone to do something no one asked you to do!"

"I'm sorry, Mother Esther, but it was wrong for me to leave the van here, and it will only take a minute. Why don't you make more tea while I clean this up?"

She gives me a hard, angry look, turns, and starts for the kitchen. But she stops suddenly and swings around toward me.

"No! You can make the tea this time, and you can clean this up. I'm getting back to your mother."

When she discovers Mother is gone, she'll be screaming in a matter of seconds. I'm out of time. I jump into the car, tell Mother to brace herself, and speed down the long drive as fast as possible.

The first shot rings when we're almost at the gate. It's either Jacob or Ezekiel since they're the only ones with guns. I knew this would happen, of course I knew, but the fact that either one of them would shoot at *me*…It's still a shock.

"Mother, pray that the gate is unlocked." I consider plowing through it, but it's heavy and if it damages the van too much, we won't get out of here. Instead I screech the van to a stop inches from it. The gate pushes open easily, but the shots are close enough now that one hits the back window. When I scramble to get back into the van, another shot hits the window.

"Get back here, Eva. You won't get away with this." The voice is Jacob's.

From the rearview mirror I can see a swarm of people by the garage and know that they've discovered the tires and the missing guns.

"How are you doing?" I call to Mother once we're on the road.

"Eva, they'll be right behind us."

"No, Mother, they won't." I take in a breath knowing that what I'm about to say will shock her. "I shot out the tires of the BMW."

Silence. Then an unmistakable chuckle erupts from the backseat. When I peek in the rearview mirror, she's actually smiling.

"Only you," she says.

Her affection calms me. It helps to round the first bend because I can no longer see Righteous Path. I have the advantage since I'm driving the only operating vehicle.

I can't believe I'm on this treacherous road for the second time in one day. This time with a head injury. And with Mother and the baby.

I want to race down the mountain road, but it's too treacherous. When we're not on ice, we bounce along on stones. Mother moans with every bump and swerve. When I look back, I see that more and more of the white blanket is dark with blood. I force myself to go slowly so she'll bleed less and not suffer as much. "Hold on, Mother! Please hold on."

No one seems to be following us, much to my relief. But when the road eases into a straight line, I see flashing lights some distance ahead. Why lights? Police? They can't be for me unless Trevor…

The road dips and swerves again. At the point where the van is higher than the approaching cars, I see flashing blue-and-red lights on several cars. They practically blind me. I pull over to the left as far away from the edge as possible and wonder how they'll ever get by since the road is so narrow. But they don't go by me. They pull over ahead of me. Now I see that there are two squad cars and an ambulance in the rear.

An officer gets out of his car. He approaches me.

I'm frozen. *Police.* Everything I've been told about police is bad. They'll hurt me. Burn me like the Branch Davidians. Take me from my mother. Put Ezekiel in jail. Force me into a foster home. Take away my purity. Steal my salvation.

I lock the doors as if that will keep the police out. I tremble and the pain in my head soars. Mother is a silent lump in the backseat. Even as my head spins from turning and I must clutch the steering wheel so I don't throw up, I remember what is real and true. She'll die if we don't get her to the hospital. I will my voice into calmness.

"Mother, we have help now. An ambulance is here to take you to the hospital and you'll be fine."

Mother groans. "Thank you."

An intense light blinds me. The officer motions for me to lower the window. "May I see your driver's license and registration?"

I shake my head. "I don't have a driver's license."

God, I don't care if he puts me in jail. Just please save my mother.

The policeman shines a light on Mother, and his face looks like he's just seen something horrifying. I turn to see what he's seeing. She is almost transparent from the loss of blood, and her lips are blue.

It's too much—the motion, the bright light, Mother fading before my eyes, police. I vomit. All over the passenger seat.

"We've got the woman who's in labor and a young girl. The girl needs medical attention too. We need to move fast," he says into a little machine.

"Are you Eva?"

"Yes."

Now I *know* Trevor called. How else would this man know my name?

"Is anyone following you?" He points up the path.

"I think so. But they're on foot. Unless they decided to ride the horses."

"And they have guns?" He points to the hole in the back window.

"Jacob and Ezekiel have guns. But I locked the rest in the truck."

"What trunk?"

"The trunk of his BMW. And I have both sets of keys."

The officer smiles. "Clever girl," he says.

Three people with a strange-looking bed open the back door to help Mother.

"You'll need to step out of the car," the officer says. His badge reads *Officer Brad Snead*.

He's going to arrest me or hurt me. But the ambulance people have Mother on the bed with wheels. They're helping her.

Thank you, God.

The earth does not feel sturdy under my feet when I get out. I stagger.

He flashes that light in my eyes again. "Whew! That looks nasty."

I nod, which is the worst thing I can do, because suddenly I vomit again. This time it hits his shoe.

I hear Mother moan. She's on the rolling bed and is at the ambulance. They lift the whole bed, and amazingly the legs collapse underneath so now it's like a regular bed.

"Please, can I be with my mother?"

A commotion behind us demands our attention. Three

policemen point their guns toward something I can't see. They shine floodlights up the road and in and around the bushes.

"I bet they followed us," I say.

"How did you get hurt?" Officer Snead asks.

"Ezekiel hit me and I flew into the altar. He wants to kill me."

"Why would he want to kill you?"

"Because I took Mother Martha and she's carrying—well, Ezekiel says she's carrying—the next prophet."

"He's the leader, right?"

"Yes."

"Okay. He's not going to have an opportunity to hurt you again," Officer Snead says. "I'll see about getting you inside the ambulance. You've probably got a concussion."

He helps me sit down on the passenger side of the car and places his little talking machine close to his mouth. I miss what he says next because there's more yelling behind me.

"Put your hands up!" one of the policeman yells. I turn to see two officers up the road with guns pointed toward the bushes. Then an unmistakable voice.

I crouch down in the seat as far as I can and shake uncontrollably. The voice I hear is Ezekiel's.

Twenty-Eight

"I've been shot. Help me," Ezekiel yells.

It's his voice but he sounds so different—not the thundering, righteous man who rules Righteous Path. He sounds puny, whiney even.

"Drop those guns and raise your arms!" an officer yells.

"I can't. I've been shot in the shoulder."

My curiosity is greater than my fear, and I sit up to see what's going on. Even from this distance, I can see them both clearly under the glare of the officer's light. They walk almost together, Jacob with both arms in the air, Ezekiel lumbering slightly behind with only his left arm in the air. The only guns are those carried by the officers behind them and the one carried by the officer in front.

Officer Snead takes over. "Are you Leo Farmer?"

Leo Farmer? I think I heard that name once but I don't know where.

"I am Prophet Ezekiel." He juts his chin out proudly. "But my name doesn't matter. I'm bleeding here. I need an ambulance."

Jacob's mouth drops open like he can't believe what he's hearing. Neither can I. Now that Ezekiel's hurt, medicine is not only okay, it's his right!

"Who shot you?" Snead continues.

I suddenly realize that I have no reason to cower in the car. There's nothing he can do to me now. I ignore the dizziness and get out of the car.

Ezekiel sees me immediately. He points a finger in my direction. "That girl shot me."

Now it's my mouth that's wide open.

"What?" Jacob says. " C'mon, Prophet Ezekiel, you know that's not true. Why are you saying that?"

Something heavy weighs on my chest. It hurts to see Jacob waking up to the truth about Ezekiel.

"What did happen?" Snead asks Jacob.

"He shot himself. His gun went off when he was mounting Aspen, his horse."

"It doesn't matter *how* it happened. I need *help*," Ezekiel says. "I'll bleed to death without it."

"We'll get you help," Officer Snead says. "But you're not bleeding that badly and we have a bigger emergency to deal with right now." He points to the ambulance. "We're trying to save the life of a woman who may have already bled to death—because of you!"

I hear a scream and slowly realize that the sound is coming from me. "She can't be dead. No, God, please."

Somebody, an ambulance person, I think, puts an arm around me and says something. I'm not hearing her words, but her voice is caring and reassuring. She ushers me to the ambulance.

"She'll be okay, she'll be okay, she'll be okay," I reassure myself.

"And that young girl may have a serious concussion because of your physical abuse," Snead continues. "Now give us your real name."

"You have to help me, regardless of race, gender, or creed."

As the medic is about to lift me into the ambulance, Officer Snead asks me another question. "Can you identify this man?"

It takes me a minute to compose myself. Any respect I had for Ezekiel is gone. The terror I felt so many times is gone too, extinguished by his actions tonight. Not only was he willing to hurt or kill me to get Mother Martha back, but he demanded medical attention after denying it to all of us for so long. And he lied about me shooting him. I straighten myself up and walk right up to Ezekiel.

"I don't know if his real name is Leo Farmer. He's called himself Ezekiel since I first met him as a little kid. We are supposed to call him 'Prophet,' but I can tell you that he's not a prophet."

Ezekiel glowers at me, but he doesn't scare me anymore. "You're still promised to me."

"No, I'm actually free of you."

"Damn you," he says. And he spits in my direction.

Jacob has moved farther and farther away from Ezekiel. His face is stricken. "I'm sorry," he mouths to me, tears glistening in his eyes.

"I know," I mouth back. It's sad to see him so defeated, but I manage a smile so he'll know that I don't hate him.

A voice from inside the ambulance calls to Officer Snead.

"The patient here confirms that this man is Leo Farmer."

"He told me once," I hear her say weakly as I approach the ambulance.

Mother's talking. That has to be good.

"You have said it," Ezekiel says.

The attendant helps me into the ambulance where Mother, pale but alert, smiles at me.

Snead continues, "Mr. Farmer, I have a warrant for your arrest for the unlawful imprisonment and rape of one Marie Thompson..."

Marie Thompson—that's Rachel!

"You are also charged with two counts of embezzlement and four counts of fraud in the states of Arizona and Colorado. These don't include the charges you'll face for abusing this young girl, and God help you if the mother and baby don't make it. You have the right to remain silent..."

With that, the ambulance door is closed and I can't hear any more.

Mother has some kind of mask over her face. "For oxygen," the attendant says. She also has a needle in her arm with two bags on a pole above her. "We're giving her blood plasma and intravenous fluid," the attendant says. "That should give her some strength until we get to the hospital. But she'll need several blood transfusions."

"We're ready to take off," an attendant says.

Now that I'm back with my mother, everything else falls away. She smiles at me, actually smiles!

"The stuff they're giving me is helping," she says.

"I can tell." I laugh in relief, but the movement brings on another wave of dizziness and nausea. "You're going to be all right, Mother, and the baby will too. You'll both be just fine."

I'm jostled slightly as the ambulance begins to move, but the straps on Mother's cot keep her steady.

We're quiet as I try to breathe through another bout of nausea and Mother groans with another labor pain. After a few minutes she places her hand on my arm. "Are *you* okay? Does that gash hurt much?"

"Not the gash so much, the nausea and dizziness." Sadness washes over her sallow face.

"Honey, there's something I have to tell you." Her chin shakes and tears roll down her face. "The baby didn't make it."

I shake my head, not willing to take this in. "I'm sure he's fine."

"No, Eva. He stopped moving several days go."

My throat hurts too much to respond.

"I wanted to—I tried to tell you—in the barn."

"Is that why you have a fever?"

"Probably. I'm sure I have an infection."

The nurse-attendant places a cloth cuff around my arm. She explains to me that she's taking my blood pressure. I nod, although I have no idea what a blood pressure is. I'm too lost in my own thoughts to be curious.

It's a relief to not be driving and to be with Mother. It doesn't matter that the attendant is with us. No one's going to turn me in for anything I say to Mother. "I love you."

"I love you too," Mother says.

We ride in silence for a little while, Mother with her eyes closed and me biting the inside of my mouth against the pain in my head and all the worry.

I go back to thinking about Ezekiel's arrest. The policeman used Rachel's real name: Marie Thompson. Slowly the puzzle pieces fit together. When Rachel left, she must have gone to the police and reported Ezekiel. Maybe Trevor didn't call the police at all!

When Mother opens her eyes again, she quietly says, "I'm sorry."

I don't ask what she's sorry about because it doesn't matter now.

"No, please..." I say. I don't want her using all her energy.

"I thought Ezekiel would save our souls." She swallows hard. "And I didn't want your dad to have the chance to take you from me."

I don't want her to use up her strength but I can't help asking, "Why?"

"I wanted you just for me." She closes her eyes, and I can see by her face that she can't continue talking.

This is the talk I've wanted to have for so long, but not like this. She's far too sick to talk about this now. And it doesn't matter anymore.

"No," I say firmly when she opens her mouth to speak again. "You need to save your strength."

We go over the last big bump before we reach the paved part of the road, and Mother's eyes go wild with pain. I squeeze her hand again. Pretty soon she looks as bad as she did before she got the fluids. The nurse turns a button on a little machine. "I'm giving her more oxygen to help her breathe."

She stops responding, and I'm terrified.

"Mother, Mom...Mommy," I cry. "Stay. Here." I clasp her hand as tightly as I can. "Mommy, please."

The nurse checks her heart and her pulse. "She's hanging in there, and we're almost to the hospital."

That cavern inside me, that empty space where Daddy was supposed to be, is so deep now that I'm afraid I'll fall to the bottom and break apart.

Six Hours Later

Twenty-Nine

When we first got to the hospital, one of the ambulance people said that Mother had a pulse and was "hanging on." But they wouldn't let me go wherever they took her.

Meanwhile, I'm stuck in a private room, alone. And there's nothing I can do about it because I'm stuck in a bed that has side rails like a baby crib, and I have intravenous fluid going into my arm.

I have a button I can push if I need anything. Then a nurse comes in.

"I promise we'll let you know the minute we hear anything about your mother," they keep saying. But I can't help asking how she's doing. Somebody has to know.

If Righteous Path is an alternative religion, the hospital is a whole alternative world. It's weird. So many people in and out of my room—and they all ask me the same questions. There are IVs, tests where I get poked, and strange machines that take pictures of the inside of your head. I push the button in the bed to bring my feet up, then use another button to bring them down again.

I like the buttons for turning the television on and off and changing the channel, but as much as I've wanted to watch television forever, it hurts my eyes too much.

Each time I hear a knock on the door I freeze, thinking it's Ezekiel. I can't quite comprehend what the police said—that he'd get his shoulder looked at, but then he was going to jail.

This time when I hear the knock, I remember that Ezekiel is not here. "Come in."

It's Trevor. He takes in a noisy breath and groans when he sees me. Then his face turns to rage.

"Ezekiel did that to you? That bastard. I hope he's in jail for a long time."

The corners of my lips turn up into a smile. "Thanks. Everyone at Righteous Path thinks I'm a traitor."

I was mad at him about something, but now I can't remember what. By the time he gets to me, his face is washed clean of the anger I just saw. He hugs me and takes my hand.

"How are you doing, Eva?" The softness in his voice makes my eyes tear.

"I have a concussion, and I still don't know if Mother is okay."

I tell him everything that happened and how brave Mother was. "She was in such terrible pain, but she still had the courage to try the escape."

"But how did you do it?" Trevor asks.

"I blew the tires out of his BMW, hid the guns in the back of the van, and took his keys."

Trevor's eyes grow huge. "You did?"

"Yeah, so they couldn't get into a big shoot-out and kill people."

We're interrupted by a nurse. She uses a little light to check my eyes for a concussion. She also holds a needle with more medicine in it. "How's your head?"

"It hurts."

"And your nausea?"

"Better."

"Good. Do you think you could eat something?"

I haven't thought about food in all this time—not since breakfast yesterday morning. I shrug my shoulders.

"You can have whatever you want. Maybe your friend could help you pick something from the menu." She hands the menu to Trevor and sticks a needle in my IV. "Something for pain," she says.

"Somebody has to know something about Mother. Please! It's been hours."

She sighs. "Look, I understand that this is hard for you. But your doctor will give you a report as soon as she gets up here. Try to relax, and maybe get some sleep after you eat ." She doesn't sound like she understands at all. She peeks under the bandage that's wrapped around the top of my head. "Looks okay, but I'll bet it's really sore."

With Trevor's help, I order a grilled cheese sandwich.

The nurse takes her time typing notes on the computer. When she finally leaves, I blurt out the questions I have been waiting to ask. "Did you call the police and an ambulance?"

"Yup," he says without pausing, "I sure did." He sits up taller in his chair.

"You could have gotten us killed, Trevor."

"I did what I had to do. The police have training in handling these situations. You don't."

It's a challenge going from a sitting position to lying down. I make the transition very slowly, managing to keep my head from spinning again.

"You did so well. How smart to disable Ezekiel's car and hide the guns. That was inspired."

"I think so too. God was helping me. But it means nothing if Mother doesn't make it."

"Even if your mother doesn't make it, you're going to make it."

"Well, the police and ambulance attendants were wonderful. Not the horrible people we were taught they were. But I see why Ezekiel hates them so. He was already in trouble for fraud.

"Did you know that Rachel went to the police too? She told them she was an underage bride. She probably told them that he planned to marry me too."

Trevor buries his head in his hands and makes a moaning sound. "Of course he wanted to marry you. You're young and beautiful, and he's got to be sixty-something."

"How do you know?"

He quickly points to the television. "His face is all over the news. Should we turn the television on?"

The idea of seeing him on television makes my stomach turn. "No. I already know what he looks like."

A young girl walks in with a tray of food. But my head pounds when I try to chew the sandwich, and I give up after two small bites.

"I can't stay awake, Trevor, but I don't want you to leave. Will you stay with me?"

"Of course," he says. And I let myself drift off to sleep.

Thirty

In my dream, Aslan and I are in the same springtime meadow where we've been before. We sit next to a trickling stream. I watch how the sunlight makes the water silver shimmery. Suddenly my mother is right next to me. She's laughing and happy. We hug each other. "You're all better!" I say.

"So are you!" We hug and hug. Aslan laughs in delight over our joy.

"I had no idea it could be like this. I feel great here," Mother says.

"You forgot about God as love," Aslan says. He's pushing logs around in a fire I hadn't noticed before. Then he holds two sticks in his hands, each with a marshmallow he's toasted in the fire. The marshmallows are perfectly golden and not burned.

"Do you remember these?" he asks. I do remember. We used to toast marshmallows years ago at sing-alongs around the campfire. That was before Ezekiel changed—became so punitive.

The three of us are together for a long, long time, relaxed and happy.

When I'm ready to burst from the joy of so much love and beauty, Aslan says, "It's time."

Somehow I understand. I have to say good-bye to Mother and Aslan. My heart is breaking. But Aslan takes my hand, and without using any words, he lets me know this is what's meant to be. I know, too, that I'll be all right, just as Mother will be all right— more than all right.

A nurse invades my dream.

"Eva, I need you to wake up and open your eyes." When I do, she shines the light into my eyes like so many times before. "Okay, dear," she says when she's finished. "You can go back to sleep now."

I try and try to return to the dream that was more than a dream, but I can't.

"There's no going back," Aslan says inside my head. "Only forward."

It hits me then. Mother is really gone. She's with Aslan now.

A sob breaks through in my chest, forcing me to sit up so I can breathe.

"Are you okay?" Trevor's voice sounds alarmed.

I shake my head. I feel my face scrunch up in agony and hear a scream come from my own mouth. I'm missing some part of me, an arm or a leg—no, something from inside. Something has been wrenched from me, taken from every fiber of my being. I'm empty, hollow, and desperate for what's missing.

Trevor is suddenly next to me, his face contorted in grief for me. "What happened? What's the matter?" he asks.

"Mother's gone." I choke out the words.

Trevor takes my hand. He's crying now too. "We thought you were sleeping when Dr. Harris came with the news. I'm so sorry."

My tears fall silently. Part of me is here in the hospital with a head injury and an IV in my arm that's beginning to feel sore. Part of me is with Aslan and Mother back in my dream—or vision or whatever it was. It remains sharp and vibrant, yet with every passing second it seems further away.

How can I possibly survive without Mother, without Ezekiel and Annie and all of Righteous Path?

I cling to Trevor. Can he possibly make me whole? I can't let him go or I'll be totally alone. I *am* totally alone. He turns my face toward him. "You've got your father, Eva. Are you going to call him?"

"No!" I say. The force of my own voice startles me as much as it does him.

"Okay," he says, looking troubled. He lifts my chin and looks directly in my eyes. "But you've got to live somewhere. You won't be in the hospital forever." He points to a card on my bedside table. "The hospital social worker was here while you were sleeping."

"I could live with you," I say.

"I'd love that, Eva, but it will never happen. I'm twenty, and you're fourteen. Trust me, I'd get in big trouble if I let you live with me."

I turn away from Trevor, from the bedside table and the card. I think about Mother. That's where I want to live, with Mother. I've wanted to be with Mother for so long. Nothing can stop the sobs now. They're coming from somewhere so deep.

When I'm completely wrung out, I realize that I've heard nothing about the baby. I sit up. "Was the baby a boy or a girl?"

"She had a boy. A tiny boy, just over three pounds. But she died before he was delivered, and he'd already died inside her."

"He wasn't the next prophet, was he?" I don't know why I ask that. It sounds really stupid, and I can feel the heat rise in my face.

A flash of concern crosses Trevor's face. "No, Eva. He was just an ordinary baby who didn't make it."

"Of course he was," I say.

Trevor pulls up his chair as close to me as he can. "What do you need, Eva? How can I help?"

I shrug my shoulders. "You're my friend and that helps. Right now I need to sleep until my head stops hurting. I'll figure out what to do after that."

"Okay," he says. "I charged your cell phone so you'll be able to call me if you need me."

I lift myself up on one elbow. "What cell phone?" Trevor holds up Ezekiel's phone from—how long ago was that? Could it have really been only last night?

"The charger from my phone worked perfectly. But we'll have to get you your own charger.

"I don't know...This phone's not mine. It's Ezekiel's."

"I wouldn't worry about borrowing it, Eva. He can't have it in jail. They denied him bail this morning. Trust me, he won't need this."

"Okay," I say.

"I'll be back tomorrow, but I want you to call me if you need anything or just want to talk. Will you promise to call me?"

"I promise."

"Good. I'm going to take off, then."

"Wait!" I say as he approaches the door. "How did you know where to send the police and ambulance? I never told you where I lived."

He looks suddenly exhausted. "Maybe we should talk about that tomorrow."

I grab the side rails to steady myself against the room spinning again and turn to see him better. "Please, Trevor. Tell me now."

Trevor sighs, drops his backpack, and straddles a folding chair backward. "Okay, but this isn't going to sound good," he says. "See, when my class was assigned to research and write a paper about an alternative religion, one of the guys followed some Righteous Path members from Boulder to see where you lived. I think it was Ezekiel he followed. Anyway, he lost track of the vehicle in Grand Hill, but stopped to ask questions of some of the townspeople. They weren't very friendly.

"When he reported this to the class, my professor had fits and said we had no business intruding to do our research."

"No kidding," I say. "That's just what Ezekiel warned us about—nosy heath—I mean, outsiders following us." For a minute I'm confused. Here was something Ezekiel was right about.

"But Ezekiel thought they'd follow you in order to do harm. My classmate didn't mean harm."

"That's true," I say. And notice I can breathe again.

"So when you and Rachel came into the Wi-Fi Café a few days later, I had a chance to get to know you without being intrusive—at least I hope so."

"I'm glad I got to know you," I say.

"There's more. When I learned that Ezekiel cut your hair as

punishment, I started worrying about you. Then when we both forgot about the holidays, I couldn't stop thinking about you— afraid you'd gotten caught or confessed or lost faith in me. So I went to Righteous Path in the hopes that I could do something. Maybe I could talk to Ezekiel or rescue you or something."

"When?"

"The day after Christmas."

"Oh, Trevor. You were the intruder!"

"Yup, you know the rest. One of the guys shot at me. He missed, of course, but he did hit my car. He took out the light on the driver's side."

"Trevor, I can't believe you put yourself in so much danger."

"Why? You lived it every day. Anyway, I went to the police and made a report, and they hadn't followed up on it when I called them again because your mother was in labor."

I think about the guns, the training, the paranoia, the prayer sessions and fasts, and I want to cry.

Suddenly I can't keep my eyes open. "You should go. We both need sleep," I say.

Thirty-One

Sharp blades of light stab my eyes and make the pain in my head almost unbearable. For a moment I'm confused. Where am I? Slowly it all comes back: hospital, concussion. Mother is dead, Ezekiel arrested. I scream my anguish into a pillow so no one can hear me. Over and over I scream. When the pounding is too great to scream anymore, I reach around for the call button and push it.

"What can I do for you, honey?" Her voice is syrup. Sticky, icky syrup. "Hmm? What's wrong, honey?"

Mother calls me "honey." Only Mother. It's our secret. I don't even know this woman.

I point to the window. "The light hurts my eyes. Please close the blinds," I tell the nurse. She leisurely walks to the windows and closes them. "I need the bathroom too and something for this pain. Can I go by myself?"

The nurse shakes her head. "You're still getting dizzy spells, and you're on strong pain medication. But I'll tell you what, I'll walk you to the bathroom and stand outside the door. You call if you need help."

"Okay." I sigh.

She pats her uniform pocket. "I did bring you something for pain."

After the shot, I must fall asleep again because Dr. Wilson has to wake me up when she comes in. "How are you feeling?" she asks as she makes herself comfortable sitting on the edge of my bed.

She is so caring and maternal that tears spring to my eyes. "My head hurts really bad. I've never had such a bad headache in my life, and it won't go away."

"I know. I was pretty worried about your concussion. Your brain swelled quite a bit, and I thought I might have to cut open your skull to relieve the pressure. Fortunately, the tests show that the swelling is going down. We'll want to keep you for a couple more days, at least, to make sure you continue to progress. I'm sorry about your headaches"—she lays her hand over mine—"and so sorry about your mother and the baby."

I mumble a thank-you and drop my eyes, afraid I'll start to cry because of her kindness.

"I know you haven't seen any relatives for a long time, but could we contact someone for you about living arrangements?"

"No." I say it hard and fast. "My father would be the only one, and please, please don't contact him."

"Why?" she asks.

"Because it would break Mother's heart."

I think about Annie and the others. "Is that what's happening with Annie and Jacob and the twins? Will they go to relatives? Will they go to foster homes?"

Dr. Wilson shrugs her shoulders and holds out the palms of her hands. "I don't know, dear. I'm not working with any of them, just you."

She stands up. "Oh, Eva, I'm getting ahead of myself. Don't worry about any of this today. I'm sure your friends will be well cared for. And so will you. Just get some rest for now, and we'll think more about where you should live when you're feeling better."

It's like someone lifted a boulder off my back. It's so good not to have to think about the future right now. I begin to relax.

A little while later, a nurse comes in with everything I need for a sponge bath. When she leaves me alone to wash up, I continue to think about everyone at Righteous Path—how betrayed Annie must feel to learn that Ezekiel isn't a prophet. Or maybe not. Maybe she still believes in him and blames me for his arrest. Maybe all the women still believe in him. Maybe they'll all continue living together at the compound. Maybe I'll never know and never see them again.

When I've finished brushing my teeth and washing up, the tray lady knocks on my door. My mouth waters before I can even see what's under the dome. And when I see that it's a grilled cheese sandwich, tomato soup, veggie sticks, and apple pie, I dive right in. This is the first solid food I've had since I've been here. And it's delicious.

Out of the corner of my eye I catch a glimpse of someone at my door. When I see who it is, I drop the grilled cheese. "Rachel! Oh, Rachel! I was afraid I'd never see you again!"

She rushes to my bed. We cling to each other, both of us crying. I seem to lose all my strength and collapse in her arms. "You're here! I'm so happy you're here."

"I'm so happy *you're* here," Rachel says. "I don't mean here in the hospital. I mean here *safe*. I was so scared for you. From the time I left you in Boulder until the police told me you got out okay, I've been praying for you."

I pull back until we're at arm's length. "Mother died, Rachel. The baby died too."

"I know." I can hear a sob lodged in her throat. "I'm so sorry."

She sits in the chair next to my bed and leans forward as if she's about to tell me a secret. "Actually, the day before I left, I was pretty sure the baby had already died. When I brought Martha her tray, my hand touched her arm and it seemed hot. I touched her cheek and she was burning up. I knew that if she was fighting an infection, the baby was probably dead. So I point-blank asked her if the baby was still moving. She looked away and didn't answer. That's when I knew. And it's when I started to panic. She didn't dare give birth to a stillborn when Ezekiel expected a prophet. I had to get us help from the police."

"You were trying to get us help?" She nods, but it doesn't help. I'm angry. "You left me completely alone to drive the van on icy roads in the dark. And I had to face Ezekiel alone."

Rachel looks devastated. "And he did *that* to you." She covers her face with her hands and sobs, deep, loud sobs.

"Why didn't you tell me? Why didn't you take me with you?"

"Because I know you, Eva. You never would have gone with me and left your mother. You never would have believed that the police would help us."

She's right. Of course she's right. But I don't say so.

"And you're so competent, Eva. I knew you'd navigate that road just fine. I also didn't think Ezekiel would take it out on you. I knew I had to act quickly, before that baby was born."

I shiver and tuck the blanket closer around me. "I can't imagine what Ezekiel would have done if Mother delivered a dead baby at the compound," I say.

Rachel shakes her head. "One thing's for certain, he would have blamed it on us—on our sins. He would have made us pray day and night and fast until we were so hungry and weak we couldn't think straight."

"We were half-starved already." My voice is shaky. "I think that's probably why the baby didn't develop right. Mother didn't get enough nutrition."

Rachel looks as if she's someplace far away. "And why most of his wives didn't get pregnant at all or lost the baby at some point before birth. Like me."

I'm silent. When her attention returns to the room, she touches my arm. "You were so brave to rescue Mother Martha. I don't know if I'd have had your courage."

I pull away and shrug my shoulders. "What good did it do? I didn't save her."

"Nobody could have saved her by then. But you did save yourself and probably everyone else there. Is it true you put all the guns in the back of the van?"

"Yeah, except for the ones Jacob and Ezekiel were carrying. Mother actually laughed when I told her."

A little giggle escapes from my throat, and then a full-out laugh. I know it's wrong but I can't stop. "Remember his sermons?" I say when my laughter slows enough for me to speak.

Rachel nods.

I mimic him. "'The righteous shall prevail,' 'God will lead us to victory,' 'We'll take the heathens down.'"

I crack up, laughing again. "It was supposed to be a holy war. But he was the only one who got shot." Now tears of laughter are running down my cheek. "And he shot himself."

Rachel shakes her head. "It's too sad to laugh," she says.

It's true, and my tears become ones of grief. I cry because of how we lived, how we were deceived, how much time was lost following a false prophet. I cry because of the relationships I wasn't allowed with my parents and longed for desperately. I cry because I don't know how to live in the broader world.

Rachel cries right along with me, though neither of us says anything out loud.

"Do you think that Annie will get help for her asthma now, and Jacob will get his teeth replaced?"

"I don't know. It depends on what they come to believe. Right now, they're both in foster homes. I understand that they're both distressed—Jacob because he now sees Ezekiel as a fraud, and Annie because she believes she's being polluted by the heathen world."

"Did you believe in him, Rachel?"

Rachel smirks. "Completely." She sighs. "I *needed* to believe in him. I was so angry with God for taking my parents. And Ezekiel's beliefs were a great comfort to me. It was like being with my minister father again. I also liked the idea of being one of the chosen ones, safe from the fires of hell."

"I guess I liked that too," I say. "But I didn't choose him. For a long time I just wanted to go back home. I hated that he was in charge."

A nurse brings in fresh water and an ice bag for my head. I thank her and enjoy the immediate relief I get from the ice.

"So, what made you change your mind about Ezekiel, Rachel?"

"Lots of things. Everything he said and did seemed self-serving. I changed my mind ages ago. I just didn't know how to leave without money or job experience or a decent education. But the last straw for me was when Ezekiel said he was going to marry you.

"Was that when you stopped believing? Or was it when you saw that your mother's pregnancy was in trouble?" she asks.

"Remember the parable about the seeds that I had to memorize?"

"Sure, I remember."

"I really believed we were the lucky ones. We were the seeds strewn into the rich soil God gave us through Ezekiel. But then there were a hundred little things that made me wonder about Ezekiel. For a long time I was so worried about punishment that I forgot God is love. Ezekiel seemed to forget that too. Little by little, I came to realize that Ezekiel was not the good soil."

"You're right," she says.

Rachel opens the curtains and peers out my window. "You have a great view," she says.

My head isn't hurting as much now, and I'm curious. I sit up as tall as I can in my bed to see what it's like out. I gasp. My room looks over a beautiful courtyard. The snow is almost melted and the trees are beginning to bud. Little rivulets of water make their way to a stream that winds around the courtyard. But it's what I see next to the stream that takes my breath away—purple crocuses, some in full bloom, some just beginning to open.

I stifle an urge to clap. Aslan is here too. He's not just in Narnia. For the first time I feel that I'll really be okay in the bigger world.

I lie back on the bed and close my eyes, reveling in the heaven on earth I just witnessed. But then something occurs to me and I sit up again.

"Rachel, where are you hiding?"

She looks confused for a minute. "I'm in a women's shelter, Eva, but I'm not hiding. Ezekiel's in jail with no bond. With all the charges, he'll probably be locked up for a long time."

"Could I stay with you when I get out of the hospital? I won't be any trouble, and I can do chores and…"

"Hold on! You can't stay in a women's shelter. In the real world you're still a child. A social worker will help you find a relative, like they did me when my parents died, or you'll go to a foster home. But you have a father, right? Don't you want to try and find him?"

"I already know how to find him, I think."

Rachel's eyes grow large. "You do?"

I reluctantly pull the article out of the little drawer in my bedside table and hand it to her. The quizzical look on Rachel's face changes to one of amazement as she reads it. When she's done, she holds it to her chest as if it's a long-lost treasure.

"How could you be afraid to contact him? He's searched for you all this time. And how did you get this? Did a nurse pull it up on a computer?"

"No, nothing like that. It's a long story. Rachel, look at that little girl in the pictures."

"She's adorable."

"I know. That's what my father is looking for. He's not looking for a tall, spindly, almost fifteen-year-old who hasn't had a real education and who has a big bandage around her head. Now I know that he wanted me this whole time. Mother must have kept his letters and phone calls from me, though I'll never understand why."

Rachel looks at me for a long while. "You have a great opportunity here. If I could bring my parents back for one day…" She clamps her lips together and covers her mouth with a fist.

A nurse walks in with a syringe. "I can't believe you haven't asked for more pain meds," she says. "We're an hour overdue and Dr. Wilson wants us to make sure we don't let the pain get out of control."

As the nurse is putting the medicine in my IV, Rachel leans over and kisses my forehead.

"I've got to go, but I'll be back tomorrow—promise. And I'll see if I can get information about what the others are doing."

Rachel is barely out the door before I'm back to sleep.

When I wake up again, it's dark outside. The pain in my head is less intense than it was earlier, and I begin to believe that I'm actually going to get better. I pick up the cell phone on my bedside table and find the phone number printed in the article. I'm scared, but I've done other scary things. If I had the courage to rescue Mother, I certainly have the courage to make this phone call to my father.

I have to dial the number several times because I keep messing up. Finally I get it right. On the third ring a man answers the phone.

"Hello." His voice, strange and familiar, begins to fill some of the empty space inside me with warmth. It takes me a minute to swallow through the lump in my throat.

"Hello," he says again.

"Is this Charles Wells?" My voice is timid, uncertain.

"Yes, it is," he says. There is a long pause, and when he speaks again, it's his voice that's timid. "Who's calling?"

I let out a long breath, and something like relief and awe and joy fill my heart all at once. "Daddy, it's me. Lily."

August

Thirty-Two

Chicago

To: rchl@yahoo.com

Hi Rachel,

I'm glad you're still going by Rachel. It's perfect for you. I agree that since Ezekiel let you pick it yourself, it truly belongs to you, not him.

Thanks for your call. I'm so happy you'll try to come for Christmas. Dad will pay for your ticket, of course. And Trevor's too, if he can make it. I really hope you'll both come. I have so much to talk to you about. All that time when we had to be careful with our words, and now we can finally talk about anything.

At least we both have email addresses and our own computers. Dad got me a laptop right after I moved here and helped me get into a class so I could navigate better.

I have more freedom than I ever had at Righteous Path, but sometimes Dad and I argue because he wants to "be a Dad" and give me all these restrictions. But I'm done with restrictions and I just want to explore everything. I feel more like an adult than a child. So we butt heads a lot.

Still, Dad is exactly like I remember him from when I was little—warm and protective. He puts me first and spoils me with compliments and affection. Sometimes it's as if I never spent a day away from him. At those times he's my daddy and I'm his little girl.

One thing Dad is pretty open about is clothing. He doesn't mind the idea of me wearing shorts or even a bathing suit for swimming. What kind of clothes are you wearing these days? Do you ever wear shorts? I'm not ready yet. Every time I hold up a pair, my cheeks get hot and I hear Ezekiel calling me a whore.

I'd love to fit in better, but whenever I go shopping, I end up buying longish skirts and modest tops that make me look dowdy and old.

How do you like working as a receptionist? Are the doctors you're working for nice? It must be amazing to get a paycheck every week and know exactly what it will be. I hope it's enough money so you can have all the food you want and some for clothes too.

Did I tell you that our house in Hyde Park is only four blocks from the building at University of Chicago where Dad teaches? He walks or bikes to work every day. We are also only two blocks from the home we lived in before Mother and Dad got divorced. It's so easy to get around in Chicago with buses and trains and cabs. Dad only drives a couple of times a week. Can you believe that after all those trips up and down the mountain, I won't be eligible for a license for another year?

You wouldn't believe all the studying I'm doing—or maybe you would. I had to take these tests—placement tests—two weeks after I returned to Chicago. It was crushing to find out how far behind I am in every subject. But Dad and the counselor said that the tests don't show how smart I am. They only show what I've had the opportunity to learn. Which isn't much.

So I'm working with a very smart tutor to catch up. And I love every minute of the tutoring.

I want to go to a regular school and be a regular kid. But it looks like that's going to take some time.

I still haven't heard from Annie or Jacob, but I sent my address to their social workers a long time ago. Maybe they don't want to communicate.

I talked to Trevor, though. Dad thinks Trevor is wonderful because of how he helped me during my last months at Righteous Path. He's really looking forward to both of you joining us for Christmas.

Write back—and please come if you can.

Lily

August 22

Dear Lily,

Thanks for making sure my social worker had your address. I don't use computers so I'm sending this the slow way.

I'm living with Mother Helen and most of the other mothers and Annie. We rented a huge house in Boulder so we could stay together. I was in juvenile hall for the longest month of my life. It's not hard to see most of those kids as the heathens Ezekiel said they were. Anyway, I'm on probation for two years because of shooting at you. But that's better than Ezekiel. He's still in jail and his trial isn't for months. I hear he could be locked up for a long time.

It's hard to say this but I really don't want to write to you right now. I'm confused about so many things, and hearing from you is too hard. We'll probably see each other sometime—maybe at Ezekiel's trial. My social worker said we both may have to testify, so who knows?

One good thing I can tell you is that I got new teeth. I got this health card that pays for those kinds of things. It makes a huge difference in how I look and feel.

Also, Annie is getting treatment for her asthma and is doing better, but she still thinks she may be committing a sin by using modern medicine.

If I don't see you again, I hope you have a good life.

Jacob

November

Thirty-Three

To: Lily@gmail.com

Hi Lily, Trevor and I made plane reservations to visit you at Christmas. We've been hanging out sometimes and decided to travel together. That way your dad won't have to make two trips to the airport.

I'm excited about seeing you and seeing Chicago too. I've never been there. One thing I want to try is Chicago pizza. I hear it's wonderful!

To: Rchl@yahoo.com

Yes, Rachel, Chicago pizza is wonderful. If I could, I'd eat it every day. Chicago hot dogs are terrific too. When I study at the campus library, every couple of hours a hot dog truck stops outside and the owner rings a bell. The library practically empties out with people lining up to get their Chicago-style dogs.

Only three weeks till I see you. Thanks so much for coming. Think warm clothes because winter is cold here.

I grab my hat, check the pockets of my thermal jacket to make sure my mittens are inside, and grab my backpack.

"Bye, Dad," I yell up the stairs. "See you this afternoon."

"Wait a second."

I know what happens next. Sure enough, he bounds down the stairs, wraps me in a teddy-bear hug, and gives me a kiss that smells like aftershave. I roll my eyes to remind him that I'm not a little kid, but secretly I love Dad's hugs. We owe each other so many from all those lost years.

He inspects me up and down. "You look properly dressed to deal with a Windy City winter, but where's your scarf?" He reaches in the closet and pulls out my purple scarf. I wrap it around my neck. I look like a grape because my coat and gloves are purple too. I love it.

"Off to school," he says. "Don't be late." I wave and fly out the door.

I'm not really going to school. I'm going to see my tutor. Daddy's helping me get involved with other things so I'll meet other kids. So far I have gymnastics and a choir group.

On my way to Mrs. Paul's, I pass my old house. It's red brick like most of the houses in the neighborhood. If I look at it, I get a lump in my throat. If I don't look, it's like I'm not squarely facing my life, like Dr. Jack suggests. Today I don't hurry past it or pretend it's not there. I stop and look at it. I figure that if I force myself to face it, maybe it will stop hurting so much every time I pass it.

The wooden swing on the porch rocks back and forth in the wind. When I was four, I used to sit on that swing for hours and watch for Daddy to come back. Now I think of Mother. I miss her. But I'm angry too. She lied to me about Dad when she said he never wrote or called. And I still have so many questions that, now, she'll never be able to answer. Why did she want to keep me from Dad? Why did she join Righteous Path to begin with? I know she really loved Ezekiel. I could see it in her eyes and how happy she seemed when she was called to his trailer for the night. But was joining Righteous Path also a way to hide me from my dad?

Dad says she was all alone in the world except for me. Her parents died before he ever met her and the only friends she had were the friends she made through his teaching job, and they stopped being friends after the divorce. He says that she was perfect prey for someone like Ezekiel.

But I didn't choose Righteous Path. And I can't help wondering how my life would be different if none of this had happened. I imagine my family—there's been no divorce and we still live in my childhood home. But that doesn't work because even in my imagination my parents just fight.

I picture them divorced. I picture myself having regular visits with Dad. He buys me clothes and jewelry and any book I want to read. He thinks it's fine, not evil, for me to have nice things. He takes me to Disneyland and on ski trips. He doesn't go to China for a sabbatical. Instead he takes me to China for a whole month one summer.

I imagine I wear normal clothes and am popular at school. I might be involved in theater and gymnastics, and I don't know what else.

In this alternate version of my life, Mother and I are close. We talk about everything. I even tell her when a boy kisses me. She takes me to see the ocean and when she sees Dad, she's friendly.

I ask Dad to imagine it too. But mostly it makes him angry. Sometimes he slams his fist on the table and yells, "She had no right to do this to you, or to me! It will take you years to recover from all you've been through, and you'll never get your childhood back."

I try to reassure him that I'm fine. Mostly I'm just happy to have the chance to live in the world I was taught to fear. I see some of the evil Ezekiel claimed was rampant here, but I also see lots of good, loving people.

Sometimes Dad asks me questions for hours, wanting to know every detail about life in the compound. But he seems to do this to torture himself. The questioning always ends with him irate over the injustices done to both of us. The first time he did that, I started shaking.

He stopped immediately. "Are you cold?"

I shook my head. He looked concerned and calmed down right away.

But now I *am* cold. I look at my watch. I'm already ten minutes late for tutoring and have two blocks to go. It was worth it. I faced down my old house, and I hope that walking past it will be easier now.

I start to walk faster, not just because I'm late but because my feet are getting cold and I need to warm them up. In the next block a huge dog almost runs me down. An elderly man stands on his porch in pajamas and calls Buster home. Buster stops, looks at his owner, and continues running in the opposite direction. He seems to think it's a fun game.

"God damn it!" the man yells.

I instantly stiffen and the word "heathen" fills my mind.

It's happened like this before. Someone says or does something wrong according to Righteous Path, and it stops me cold. In that moment it's like I'm trapped in the midst of evil. I want to run and purify myself with a hot bath.

But I'm getting better. Before when these things happened, I thought I was wrong to be here, maybe a mistake that I left Righteous Path. At first, an incident like this could send me into a swirl of doubt for days. But now I pull out of it more and more quickly. I let go of the extremes—saved or heathen, good or evil, right or wrong—and realize that there are many different truths. The guy may not think his words are wrong. He may not even believe in God. It doesn't mean he's evil or condemned.

I follow the dog with my eyes and crouch into a near-kneeling position.

"Buster. Here, Buster." It's a trick I learned with the dogs Righteous Path had in Arizona. Buster bounces over to me and covers my face with slobbery licks. I pet him, grab his collar, and walk him back to the house. The owner is all smiles. He thanks me over and over. But I have to rush now, so I'm not much later for my appointment.

While I'm figuring out my own beliefs, Dr. Jack suggested I create a space inside my head where I can shelve things I don't understand yet. I can take the things out later, one by one, when I have more information.

Those shelves are getting pretty full.

As I hurry down the sidewalk, I think about my changing beliefs. Now I take a big breath and run to the corner. As soon as I turn right, I see the house that belongs to my tutor and bolt to the door as fast as I can. Mrs. Paul greets me with a smile and a cup of hot chocolate. I slip out of my outer clothes, pull the books and assignments from my backpack, and line them up on my desk in the order I'll need them. I relax, sitting back in my chair with my hot cocoa and purple pen.

"I'm ready, Mrs. Paul."

And I am.

ACKNOWLEDGMENTS

It takes a village to get me through writing a book…

Thanks to Pam, Jamie, Georgia, Judy and Ann, the members of my wonderful critique group. They've read a lot of versions of this and kept me going.

Thank you to Minju Chang, my agent, who patiently took on the challenge of working with me on two versions of this book, and to Kendra Marcus, who brought me on board at Book Stop Literary Agency and who always showed enthusiasm about this book.

A big thanks goes to my editor, Wendy McClure from Albert Whitman and Company, whose astute observations and clear understanding of the novel helped me elevate it to a new level. And she's a joy to work with.

I want to thank my mother. An author and columnist, she's always been my touchstone. She's nurtured my love of writing from the time I could first hold a pencil and is usually my first reader.

And I want to thank my sister, Kris. An author as well, she's unflinchingly supportive and determined.

NOTE

While Righteous Path is a fictional cult, experts estimate that as many as 5,000 cults may exist in the United States alone. Many are religious fringe groups that take issue with at least one basic tenet of organized religion. A religious cult is typically led by a single individual who sees himself (or occasionally herself) as God or as a prophet graced with an inside channel to God. He believes, therefore, that he's privy to the truth of who God is and what God wants from each of us. Salvation is often the reward for obedience to the leader.

The term "cult" is a pejorative one, based on media accounts of cults whose members have suffered major consequences— even death—by following the commands of their leaders. In *Down from the Mountain*, Ezekiel refers to one such tragedy as a cautionary tale. In 1993, during a stand-off with federal agents, eighty-three members of a group known as the Branch Dravidians burned to death in a compound near Waco, Texas. Among the dead were scores of children along with the group's leader, David Koresh. The cause of the fire remains unclear, but surviving Branch Dravidians claim it was set by government officials. This incident is Ezekiel's justification for why every member of Righteous Path must learn to shoot a gun.

People often wonder why followers don't just leave a cult when they want to get out. But there are numerous psychological barriers—mind control, attacks on self-esteem, hunger and exhaustion, fear of retribution or hell—that make it very difficult for someone to simply walk away. Additionally, cults are often geographically isolated and members may have cut off all ties to family and friends. It's not unusual for followers to feel deep loyalty to the leader and to give up their money, property and possessions as a sign of faith. There may also be rules and restrictions that followers must break in order to leave. Often, getting out of a cult requires escaping from it.

Recovery can be a long, difficult process. When I started a psychotherapy practice in Denver many years ago, I met a man who was involved in de-programming. This sometimes involved kidnapping a participant in a cult and locking them up until the de-programmer could "undo" the damage brainwashing had done to the member. That seemed counter-intuitive to me, but it jump-started my interest in religious cults and I proceeded to read whatever I could find on the subject.

My interest turned out to be helpful when a few years later I worked with a client who was actively involved in a cult and would find ways to come and see me. Soon after that I had occasion to work with other clients who had left dangerous cults and were working to recover their identities, self-esteem, and confidence in their capacity to make decisions. For some people the wounds were on all levels—emotional, social, sexual and spiritual. But they all rallied and became stronger from their experiences.

I write more about religious cults on my website: elizabethfixmer.com

DISCUSSION QUESTIONS

1. After reading *Down from the Mountain*, what do you believe characterizes a religious cult?

2. In what ways does Ezekiel exert power over his Righteous Path disciples in order to control them?

3. Discuss how Ezekiel uses knowledge, or the lack thereof, to control his disciples.

4. How are the relationships in the novel usual and normal? How are they harmful and abnormal?

5. As Eva comes of age she is exposed to the outside world, and she begins to see the holes in Ezekiel's ways. Give examples of hypocrisy in Ezekiel's teachings and behaviors.

6. Were the allusions to *The Lion, the Witch, and the Wardrobe* effective tools in helping you understand why Eva began questioning cult life? Explain.

7. What role does Eva and Rachel's contact with the "heathen" world play in how they change?

8. Imagine seeing your world through the lens of someone like Eva. How might she see your world differently from her own?

9. In what ways is Eva obtaining a library card symbolic of her freedom?

10. Do the characters in *Down from the Mountain* exhibit courage or cowardice?

ABOUT THE AUTHOR

 Elizabeth Fixmer writes novels for young adult and middle-grade readers. Her first novel, *Saint Training*, received a starred review from *Publishers Weekly*. She has an MFA in writing from Hamline University and has worked as a therapist. Elizabeth lives in southeastern Wisconsin.